KRISTIN LEVINE

THE
PAPER
COWBOY

PUFFIN BOOKS

PUFFIN BOOKS
An imprint of Penguin Random House LLC
375 Hudson Street
New York, New York 10014

First published in the United States of America by G.P. Putnam's Sons,
an imprint of Penguin Young Readers Group, 2014
Published by Puffin Books, an imprint of Penguin Random House LLC, 2016

THE LIBRARY OF CONGRESS HAS CATALOGED THE G. P. PUTNAM'S SON'S EDITION AS FOLLOWS:
Levine, Kristin (Kristin Sims), 1974–
The paper cowboy / Kristin Levine
pages cm
Summary: In a small town near Chicago in 1953, twelve-year-old Tommy faces
escalating problems at home, among his Catholic school friends, and with the
threat of a communist living nearby, but taking over his hospitalized sister's paper
route introduces him to neighbors who he comes to rely on for help.
ISBN 978-0-399-16328-9 (hc)
[1. Conduct of life—Fiction. 2. Family problems—Fiction. 3. Newspaper carriers—
Fiction. 4. Neighborliness—Fiction. 5. Communism—Fiction. 6. Illinois—History—
20th century—Fiction.] I. Title PZ7.L57842Pap 2014 [Fic]—dc23 2014004421

Puffin Books ISBN 978-0-14-242715-6

Printed in the United States of America

1 3 5 7 9 10 8 6 4 2

to my father—thanks, Dad,
for all the stories

1

THE PAPER

"Hands up!"

My best friend, Eddie Sullivan, had a newspaper rolled and pointed at me like a gun. He was only twelve, but over the summer he'd grown so much, he looked big enough to be in high school.

"No way!" I called out. I grabbed the newspaper and tried to wrench it from him. My dog, Boots, started to bark, excited. He was a small, scruffy black mutt, with paws as white as frost on the prairie.

"Surrender, you little commie," Eddie said, "and I might let you live!"

"I'm not a communist!"

Eddie pretended to shoot me with the newspaper.

I fell down, laughing. "Stalin's dead!"

"But the Soviet Union is not giving up. I'm not going to let you take over the world!"

We were standing on a mountain of newspapers. To our right, a glass-bottle hill glowed brown and green in the sunlight. A bit farther on loomed a pile of tin cans, ten feet tall, with the labels burned off so that the metal sparkled like the silver on a sheriff's star.

Eddie grabbed one of my shoes and started to pull. I was laughing so hard, I could barely swat him away. "Help, Boots!"

My dog jumped into the fray, nipping at Eddie's ankles.

It was the day of our community paper drive, when everyone placed their old papers and magazines by the side of the road. Eddie and I had spent all morning following the collection truck, watching his father swing the piles onto the truck bed. After lunch, we followed the truck on our bikes to the scrap yard. The truck would be driven onto a big scale and the homeowners' association would receive a certain amount of money for every pound of paper that had been collected. While we were waiting for our turn on the scale, Eddie and I climbed onto our truck and started poking around.

"You dirty com—" Eddie's voice cracked, so high he sounded like my little sister. He cleared his throat. "You dirty commie," he said, his voice now deep like his father's. Boots sank his teeth into Eddie's shirt and pulled him away. But Eddie didn't let go of my shoe, which came off, and I tumbled down the hill of papers.

We were both laughing so hard, it took me a moment to get my breath. Eddie was standing on top of the pile, holding the shoe over his head like a trophy. Boots was chasing him around in circles, barking. "Victory!" yelled Eddie.

I was about to scramble up the pile and join back in the fight when a headline caught my eye: THE WAR ENDS! Even though it was now September 13, 1953, finding an old

2

newspaper wasn't so unusual. No, it was the masthead that intrigued me: *The Daily Worker.*

"Eddie!" I called. "Come quick!"

Eddie slid down the hill, loose papers flying around him. "What is it, Tommy?"

I held the paper out to him. The *Daily Worker* was a communist newspaper. I knew that from the movies. And I'd found a copy, lying right beside my shoeless foot.

"A commie newspaper!" Eddie's eyes were wide, his cheeks smudged with newsprint.

"Do you know what this means?" I asked.

"What?"

"There's a communist in Downers Grove!" That was the little town where we lived, just a commuter-train ride from Chicago.

Eddie gave me a look.

"Just think about it," I said. "These papers all came from our neighborhood. That means one of our neighbors"—I paused and lowered my voice—"must be a communist."

Eddie looked around, as if he expected to see a Soviet spy parachuting down from the sky. If a Russian caught you, he'd torture you until you agreed to spy on the United States. Sure, it was bad that there was a communist in town, but it was a little bit exciting too. Like when you hear about a fire. You hope no one is hurt and you feel bad if they lost all their belongings. But there's something so thrilling about seeing that fire truck go by with all the bells ringing.

"Is this like the time you convinced everyone the old shack by the pond was haunted and it turned out there were just raccoons inside?" asked Eddie.

"No," I protested. "This is proof!" I waved the newspaper.

Eddie's dad yelled at us to get off the truck then. Mr. Sullivan had come back from the war in Korea with a bad limp, but his arms were as thick as the strong man's at the circus. He always helped with the paper drive because no one could swing the stacks of paper onto the truck quite like him.

I rolled up the paper I'd found and stuffed it into my back pocket. Eddie handed me my shoe and I put it on.

"Hey, Tommy," Mr. Sullivan said, "you want to come by and see the bomb shelter I built?"

"Love to," I said. "But I got to get home to dinner."

"It's his birthday," Eddie volunteered. "He's finally twelve like me."

"Well then, happy birthday. Tell your dad we should all go fishing again soon."

"Will do," I said as I jumped on my bike and pedaled off.

You'd think I'd be excited about my birthday. I mean, last week Dad had brought home a box that was just the right shape and size to hold a pair of genuine leather cowboy boots. Mom had promised to make pierogi and I loved the half-circle dumpling noodles filled with mashed potatoes and cheese. There'd probably be an angel food cake too, with a sweet fruit glaze on top.

But Busia, that's Polish for "grandma," wouldn't be there. She'd died a few months before, right about the same time Susie was born. And that's when Mom really started to change. I mean, she'd always been moody, but now she was like a sky full of dark clouds. Sometimes, things would clear right up without a drop of rain, and other times, there'd be lightning and hail. Never quite knowing what the weather would be like at home made my palms sweat.

And as I turned into our driveway and walked my bike to the garage, from inside the house I could already hear screaming.

2

THE BIRTHDAY DINNER

I stood outside the front door for a moment, wiping my hands on my pants, trying to decide what to do. I wanted to go back to Eddie's house, see the shelter his dad had built in case the Soviets dropped an atomic bomb on us. But if I didn't show up for dinner on my birthday, my mother would call his mother, and that would just cause more problems. So I took a deep breath and opened the front door.

My dad was sitting on the couch reading the paper, as if he couldn't hear a thing. He was a foreman at Western Electric, and usually wore a suit and tie, with a shirt starched at the dry cleaner, even on the weekends. My dad was tall and thin and looked just a bit like Gary Cooper in *High Noon*. I'd seen that movie five times when it was at the Tivoli.

The screaming was coming from the kitchen. From what I could hear, it sounded like something Mom was cooking had not turned out the way she'd expected.

"Hello, Tommy," Dad said without looking up. The dark frames of his reading glasses made his face look even thinner than normal.

"What's going on?" I asked.

"I'm not going in there to find out," Dad said, turning a page of the paper.

This was usually the best approach when Mom was in a bad mood. We all tried to stay out of her way. I was just about to sneak off to my room when Mom called, "Is that you, Tommy?"

I groaned. Ignoring Mom when she asked you a direct question only made things worse. "Yeah, it's me," I said.

Mom came to the doorway between the kitchen and the living room. She usually wore her long black hair pinned up in a neat bun. But lots of strands had escaped the bun today and the flowered apron she wore seemed too bright for her tense mood. She put her hands on her hips. "Where have you been?"

Dad rolled his eyes.

"Don't you roll your eyes at me!" Mom barked.

"It's his birthday," Dad said. "You don't need to interrogate him. He came home because it's dinnertime."

Mom's face turned red, a vein popping out on her forehead. "Dinner will be ready in a minute," she shouted. "The first set of pierogi didn't turn out right!"

Dad didn't respond, just turned another page of the newspaper.

"I'm sure they're fine," I said, trying to smooth things over. But as soon as Mom turned to look at me, I knew it was the wrong thing to say.

"You don't appreciate my effort?!" Mom snapped. Her normally hazel eyes blazed emerald green. "I was trying to make them perfect for you!"

7

"I . . ." There was nothing I could say.

Mom stomped into the kitchen and then came back carrying a pan of pierogi. "You think they're fine? Take them!" She threw a pierogi at me.

It hit me on the stomach. I stared in surprise. Mom yelled all the time, but she'd never thrown anything before.

My dad finally put the paper down. "Catherine!" A noodle hit him on the shoulder.

Mom kept throwing. Soon there were noodles all over the floor, blending in with the beige carpet.

"Stop it!" cried Dad.

I giggled uncomfortably.

"Oh, you think it's funny, do you?" Mom asked.

"No," I said.

But she was already storming back to the kitchen. She returned with the cake in her hands. "Then you might as well have the cake too!" She threw it. The delicate angel food cake crumbled against the living room wall.

"That's enough!" said Dad.

It wasn't even a little funny anymore. She was scaring me.

Mom disappeared once more and returned carrying a large shoe box. "And here's your present!"

She tossed the box onto the coffee table. It slid across the table and fell to the floor. The lid popped off and I could see the genuine leather cowboy boots I'd wanted inside.

But getting the boots didn't feel as good as I'd expected. It didn't feel good at all.

In the back room, I could hear my baby sister start to cry.

At the sound of the crying, Mom seemed to collapse, as if

she were a puppet and the string holding her up had suddenly been snipped. "I have a headache," she said. "I'm going to sleep." She stomped off and slammed her bedroom door.

I looked over at Dad, but his expression was as blank as a cowboy playing poker.

"What's wrong with Mom?" I asked. I tried to keep my voice calm.

Dad shook his head. "She's just tired. She wanted to make your birthday special."

It was a lame excuse and I think he knew it, because he wouldn't meet my eye.

The baby kept crying, but Dad just knelt down and started picking up the pierogi. So I went into the kitchen and mixed up a bottle and walked into the nursery.

If you asked me, my littlest sister, Susie, who was three months old, still looked like a wrinkled raisin, but everyone else said she was cute. Her face was bright red, her tiny fists flailing as she fought off the covers.

"Hey, Susie," I said as I picked her up. She quieted a little, and I held her to my chest. She smelled nice, like baby powder. But then she shoved a fist into her mouth, sucked it twice, and began wailing again. I gave her the bottle, and she gurgled happily. It made me feel a little better.

I carried Susie into the hall and stood still for a moment. My heart was pounding. So I hadn't gotten my birthday dinner. So what? A cowboy wouldn't be upset. Heck, I bet a cowboy didn't even celebrate his birthday. But I was disappointed, and even worse, I was mad at myself for feeling that way.

What I really wanted was to talk to Mary Lou. She always

made me feel better. I could hear water running and realized my older sister was probably hiding out in the bathroom, giving Pinky her bath. I knocked on the bathroom door. "It's me."

"Come in," called Mary Lou.

I did, and closed the door behind me, giving a little sigh as I leaned against it.

Mary Lou was sitting on a low stool next to the tub. She was thirteen, a year ahead of me in school, with brown hair she usually wore in braids. I guess she was pretty, but I could only tell because Eddie could never put two sentences together when she was around. I knew boys were supposed to think their sisters were dull and stupid, but I liked mine.

Mary Lou smiled when she saw me, a big, happy, genuine grin, but I must have looked pale or something because she asked, "You okay?"

"Fine," I lied. "But Mom started throwing things!"

"Shh!" Mary Lou whispered. "Tell me later. Not in front of Pinky."

Pinky was our other little sister, and she was four. Her real name was Barbara, but the nurse who had delivered her had remarked, "She's so pink!" and the name had stuck.

"Happy birthday!" Pinky exclaimed, splashing in the tub.

"Thanks," I said.

"Mom made a cake!" Pinky added. "She said I could have a piece."

I didn't know how to tell her that my birthday cake now lay smashed to bits on the living room floor. So instead, I changed the subject.

"Look what I found," I said brightly. I balanced Susie in

the crook of one arm and pulled the newspaper out of my back pocket. "A commie newspaper!"

"Oooh!" said Pinky. She didn't know what that meant, of course, but she'd caught my excitement. And she forgot about the cake, which, of course, was what I had intended.

"Let me see that," Mary Lou said.

"Careful!" I said. "Your hands are wet."

Mary Lou wiped them on a towel and I handed the paper over. She scanned it quickly.

"Where did you get this?" she asked.

"Found it on the paper drive."

"Tommy, you have to get rid of this!"

"Get rid of it!" I exclaimed, surprised. "But I wanted to show the boys at school."

"Why?" she asked. "Do you want them to think we're communists?"

I laughed. "No one would think that."

"You should burn it," she said, handing it back to me.

"Well, thanks for your advice," I said sarcastically. I was kind of disappointed. I'd thought she'd be excited too. Finding the paper was the best thing that had happened today.

"I mean it! You're going to get in trouble."

"Nah."

"Tommy! Remember last month when you found the BB gun in the woods and—"

"Fine," I sighed. "I'll burn the paper." But I was going to show it to the other boys at school first.

After Pinky and Susie had been put to bed, Dad and Mary Lou and I shared a tense and silent dinner of pierogi

11

sprinkled with carpet fibers. Mom had been right. They weren't very good. The filling had turned out mealy, not at all like Busia used to make them.

"Did you like the cowboy boots?" Dad asked gruffly, when we were nearly done.

"Yeah," I said. "Thanks a lot."

He nodded. I waited for him to say something about Mom throwing all the food, but he didn't. Dad took off his glasses and I could see the fine lines around his eyes. He looked tired.

After dinner, Mary Lou and I did the dishes and listened to *The Lone Ranger* on the radio. I loved how it always started the same way: "Return with us now to those thrilling days of yesteryear!" and the music and the "Hi-Yo, Silver! Away!" I loved how the Lone Ranger's best friend, Tonto, always called him ke-mo sah-bee, which means "trusted friend." I loved how in thirty minutes the bad guys were caught and all the problems solved.

When the program was over, Mary Lou shut it off. She smiled and the freckles on her nose and cheeks popped out. Sometimes, in the right light, her hair had just a tinge of red. "Hey, Tommy," she said. "I've got something for you." She pulled a small, newspaper-wrapped package out of her pocket.

I smiled. Mom might be unpredictable, but I could always count on Mary Lou.

"Take it, stupid," she said, pressing it into my hands.

I unwrapped it slowly.

It was a silver star-shaped pin, just like the ones the sheriffs wore in the movies.

"We might argue sometimes," said Mary Lou. "But you're still my favorite brother."

"I'm your only brother."

"Well, that too."

I gave her a hug. "Thanks, ke-mo sah-bee."

"Sorry you didn't get a cake," she said.

I shrugged. "It doesn't matter." But it did. Who doesn't want a cake on his birthday?

"You know Mom," she said, her voice just a little strained. "She'll probably get up in the middle of the night to make you a new one."

"Yeah," I said. "Maybe so."

Mary Lou yawned. "I better go to sleep," she said. "Got to get up early to deliver those papers."

I nodded. "See you in the morning."

Boots padded over to me then and rubbed his head against my leg. I stroked his fur absently, then went to get ready for bed myself. I was just about to climb under the covers when I heard someone moving around in the kitchen. Mary Lou was right. Mom had gotten up to bake me another cake. The smell of angel food batter and sweet orange icing lulled me to sleep.

3

BURNING THE TRASH, PART 1

The angel food cake was waiting on the counter when I woke up, looking light and fluffy, coated with an orange glaze. I wasn't sure how I felt. Glad she'd baked me a replacement, I guess. But it didn't erase the memory of her throwing the first one against the wall.

Still, cake was cake. And Dad left for work early and Mom slept late, so when Mary Lou came back from her paper route, she and Pinky and I each gobbled down a slice. With a glass of milk, it was delicious. We were almost done by the time Mom stumbled into the kitchen and Mary Lou handed her a cup of coffee.

I never knew quite how to react after one of Mom's fits. Sometimes if you looked at her funny, it would set her off again, so I kept my eyes firmly on my plate. I crushed the last bite of white cake with my fork.

"The cake was so good, Mom," Mary Lou said.

"Thanks."

Mom sounded calm. I risked a glance up.

Her eyes were clear. Her fingers didn't tremble as she

sipped her coffee. She had her pink robe wrapped around her and had even taken the time to pull her hair back into a ponytail. Maybe the throwing was a fluke. A onetime thing. The tension slowly drained out of me like a clogged sink.

"Did you like the cowboy boots?" Mom asked.

I held up one foot. I was wearing the boots.

Mom laughed. "You can't wear those to school."

"I know," I said. "I'll change into my shoes after I burn the trash."

You see, Mary Lou did the paper route because she was oldest, but my job was to burn our trash in a pit in the backyard. Newspapers were saved for the paper drive, of course, but there were always tin cans and bits of packaging and the brown paper from the dry cleaner. When the fire cooled, we'd pick out the cans and other metal. The homeowners' association got money for holding scrap metal drives as well.

I picked up the trash piled by the back door and walked out to the fire pit. There was a slight September wind, so I put a couple of soup cans on top so the paper wouldn't blow away. Then I threw in the match, just like Dad had shown me. "Always watch to make sure it lights before you turn away," he'd said. He didn't have to tell me to keep my eyes on the fire. I loved that moment when the tiny match ignited the paper and it all burst into a big yellow flame.

That morning when I got dressed, I'd rolled up the *Daily Worker* and stuck it in my back pocket again. For a moment, I thought about throwing it into the fire like Mary Lou had told me to so I could see the flames jump again. But I didn't.

"Tommy! Hurry up," called Mary Lou from the kitchen. "It's almost time for the bus."

15

I ran back to the kitchen. Mom held out the box from the cowboy boots and some more brown paper from the cleaners. "You forgot to burn these."

I didn't know what to do. I still had to change my shoes. No way the nuns would let me come to school in cowboy boots. But if I said no, it might set Mom off and she'd start yelling again. And if I said yes, I'd miss the bus. And missing the bus would . . .

"I'll do it," said Mary Lou, reading my mind and taking the paper and the box from Mom.

"Thanks," I said.

She shrugged. "Just get your shoes on."

I tucked the copy of the *Daily Worker* into my school satchel and sat down to pull off my boots. At the time the moment didn't seem so special, watching Mary Lou walk out to the fire pit, a pile of papers in her arms. But afterward, I kept picturing it again and again—the sun shining on her brown hair, which she had brushed and combed into two neat braids. Her navy-blue wool pleated skirt, white blouse and matching sweater. Her polished penny loafers leaving footprints in the wet grass. But the main thing I remember was how lightly she walked, with a little skip in her gait. I realized Mary Lou actually liked burning the trash. She'd done it until last year, when she'd gotten the paper route. She liked scrunching the paper into balls so it wouldn't blow away, lighting the match and throwing it, and the way the fire would lick across the paper, slowly at first, then bursting all at once, like a tiger lily opening in the morning sun.

She threw the match in just like Dad had shown us, and watched the flame catch to make sure no burning paper blew away.

"Mary Lou!" I called. "Thanks again!"

She turned then, suddenly, to say something mean and teasing to me. I still wonder what it was going to be. *You owe me one, cowboy!* Or *Shut up, Tommy!* Or even simply *You're welcome.* But I never found out, because as she turned, her pleated skirt flew out over the pit.

At first I thought it was just a glare—that the sun was shining on her again, making her glow orange. But then I heard the screams.

4

BRANDED

There are a lot of things I can't remember. How to spell Mississippi. Times tables. The capital of Nebraska. Then there are the things I don't want to remember—like the ride to the hospital. But that memory is seared in my head, a brand on my brain. At least, part of it is. Other parts are gone, like holes in an old coat, eaten away by moths.

Mary Lou was screaming, and then the next thing I knew, Mom was placing her in the front seat of our car, still wrapped in the blanket she'd used to smother the flames, as gentle as a mother cat licking her kitten. At some point, I'd gotten the baby and I held her squirming in my arms in the backseat of our car and though Mary Lou was screaming bloody murder, it was Susie's crying that upset me the most. "Shut up!" I snapped at her finally, and she stopped. Pinky sat still as a rock, her dress covered in oatmeal.

I remember waiting at the railroad crossing just a block from the doctor's. A train was chugging by, carrying people going to work, and it was moving so slowly, I could see the expressions on the passengers' faces. Mom alternated between curse words so bad I'd have my mouth washed out with soap if I said them, and prayers to the Virgin Mary.

Then we were double-parked in front of our doctor's office, Mom leaning on the horn. Dr. Stanton ran out to the car with a huge needle and I knew he was going to stick it into Mary Lou and for some stupid reason that scared me more than the burns did. I would have started screaming myself, but Susie had fallen asleep, a little warm ball on my chest, and I didn't want to wake her. She felt damp, like she'd soaked through her diaper. The sour smell filled the car, along with something worse, like rotten meat left on the campfire too long.

The hospital was forty-five minutes away. The shot made Mary Lou stop screaming, but every time we ran over a bump in the road, she moaned and that was even worse.

We finally got to the hospital and Mary Lou was put on a stretcher and someone picked up a corner of the blanket but her skin came off too, so they put it back down, and then she was wheeled away, my mom rushing after her.

Pinky, Susie and I were left in the reception room, alone. There was a large brown overstuffed couch and a small table in front of it. Pinky had fallen asleep, so I sat down on the couch and rocked Susie back and forth. My mind didn't seem to be working right. I'd glance at the clock and whole chunks of time would disappear. I'd look out the window, only for a minute or two, and then realize forty minutes had passed. I said so many Hail Marys, it seemed like those were the only words left in the whole world.

"Tommy?" Pinky said finally, in her tiny voice.

"I'm here."

She stared at me with her wide blue eyes. "There's oatmeal on my dress."

I looked at the clock. It was almost noon. "I don't have a change of clothes for you."

"It's sticky," Pinky whined.

"Shh!"

But the nurse at the information desk had heard her. She got up and rummaged in a closet, then brought me a plain white gown.

"Thanks," I said. "Do you have a spare diaper for the baby?"

She nodded and rummaged some more. As she handed me the cloth, she tilted her head and studied my face. "You're the brother of the burned girl," she said, as if the idea had just occurred to her.

I nodded.

Her lips made a little round O. I could see the lipstick on them. Mary Lou wanted to wear lipstick, but Mom wouldn't let her. She said it was only for loose women. I wondered what that meant, and if this woman was loose too.

"Is Mary Lou going to be okay?" The words were out of my mouth before I realized I was going to say them. If I had, I wouldn't have dared.

The nurse pushed her lips together as if she were going to answer, but then she frowned and only said, "There's a courtyard outside. You can change your little sister there."

Pinky was happy to put on a fresh dress. It was a beautiful

20

day, the leaves flecked with orange and gold and drops of purple. Pinky ran back and forth under the maple trees, like nothing was wrong, as I changed Susie's diaper. When Pinky tired of playing with the leaves, we went back inside and sat on the couch. Susie started crying and no matter how much I rocked or bounced or sang to her, she wouldn't stop.

"I think she's hungry," the nurse said finally.

"Yeah," I agreed.

"Want me to feed her for you?"

I handed Susie over to her, relieved.

While they were gone, I read to Pinky from the only book in the waiting room, a collection of Bible stories. She sat still and listened, even though usually she preferred to run around. We made it through the Garden of Eden, Daniel in the Lions' Den, David and Goliath, and were halfway done with Moses Parting the Red Sea before she fell asleep in my lap. I held her, unmoving, unthinking, exactly like Lot's wife.

I guess at some point I must have fallen asleep too, because when I finally opened my eyes, Mom was standing in the room, as still as a statue. I could tell by the light it was late in the afternoon.

"Is she . . . okay?" I asked.

"She's alive," Mom said.

Pinky woke up then, stretched and rubbed her eyes. "Mom!" she cried. She scrambled off my lap and hugged Mom's legs.

"Will she have scars?" I asked. Cowboys have scars. Bad guys have scars. Sisters aren't supposed to have scars.

Mom slapped my ear.

I gasped, not because it really hurt, but because Mom never hit us. She yelled all the time, but even if we were really bad, she'd wait for Dad to get home and have *him* spank us. Mary Lou had told me once that Busia had hit Mom all the time when she was little, and Mom had vowed never to be like her. "Ouch," I said, rubbing my cheek.

"Do you want me to slap you again?" Mom demanded.

I shut up.

The nurse brought Susie back then. She took a step toward Mom, then changed her mind and handed Susie to me. I wondered if she'd seen the slap.

As soon as we got in the car, Mom started crying. She was sobbing so hard, I wasn't sure how she could see the road.

"I didn't mean—" I started to say.

"Shut up," she screamed at me. "This is all your fault!" Most of her hair had fallen out of its bun, and it hung around her face like dark spiderwebs. "If you'd just taken the trash out like you were supposed to, this wouldn't . . . it was your job!"

The rest of the way home, none of us said a word. I held Susie in my arms and Pinky leaned against me. She kept trembling, as if she were trying not to cry. My skin itched every time we went over a bump and I remembered Mary Lou. Mom swerved all over the road and I couldn't help wondering, *If we had a car accident, whose fault would it be—Mom's or mine?*

Somehow, we made it home in one piece. Dad was in the kitchen when we walked in, wearing Mom's flowered apron over his suit and tie. "Mrs. Sullivan brought over a casserole," he said. "But I think I burned it."

The dish, black and scorched, smoldered on the stove top. Mom said nothing.

Dad cleared his throat. "How is—"

"Same as I told you on the phone," Mom said.

Dad nodded. The creases in his face seemed as deep as a desert canyon. "By the time I got the message at work, it was too late to go to the hospital."

Mom went straight into her bedroom and shut the door.

Dad and Pinky and I sat at the square kitchen table, eating peanut-butter-and-jelly sandwiches for dinner. Dad gave Susie a bottle, but awkwardly, so she kept fussing. It was like he'd never fed her before. I tried to remember if he ever had. The table suddenly seemed way too large. I longed for someone to bump into me as they reached for their water glass. The peanut butter stuck to the roof of my mouth, and I was concentrating so hard on prying it off with my tongue, I jumped when the phone rang.

Dad stood up slowly to answer it. "Hello?"

He took his glasses out of his pocket and put them on, as if they would somehow help him hear better. Dad let the person on the other end of the line go on and on before he spoke. "We'll let you know if there's any news."

More talking on the other end.

"No need. Tommy can do it."

He listened again.

"Yes. And thank you for the casserole. It was delicious." It must have been Eddie's mom. She knew everyone and liked to talk. By morning all of Downers Grove would know about my sister.

Dad hung up and walked slowly back to the table.

"Do what?" I asked.

"Mary Lou's paper route." Dad picked up another piece of sandwich and chewed seriously, as if it demanded his full attention. A blob of jelly dripped out of his mouth onto Mom's flowered apron, which he still hadn't taken off.

Me? I wanted to complain, but what could I say? It had been my job to take out the trash.

"You do know how to do the paper route, don't you?" Dad asked, suddenly worried.

"Of course," I lied.

"Good," Dad said. "And I will burn the trash from now on." He continued eating.

"Bath time!" said Pinky.

We looked over at her. Cleaning her up was Mary Lou's job.

"I'll do it," I said, getting Pinky down from her high chair.

As I gave my sister a bath, every bone in my body ached. It was like I'd been thrown by a bucking bronco, even though all I'd done was sit in a hospital chair all day. Pinky seemed just as exhausted, not even asking for a story as I tucked her into bed. I brushed my teeth, laid out my clothes for the next day and set my alarm. I knew Mary Lou got up at 4:30 a.m. each day to do the paper route. The rest I'd have to figure out as I went along.

Boots scrambled into bed with me. I put my arms around him and buried my nose deep in his dirty fur. If I imagined real hard, I could picture myself out on the prairie, ready to lay out my bedroll under the stars. Boots licked my face, and soon I was asleep.

But I awoke in the middle of the night to a whisper in my ear. *Tommy,* it said, *it was all your fault.*

No one was there.

Boots whined softly, turned over and resumed his snoring.

I closed my eyes and cried myself back to sleep.

5

THE PAPER ROUTE

At 4:30 in the morning, the alarm clock rang. It kept ringing and ringing, until I finally found the right lever to turn it off. Boots slept on.

There was a moment when I couldn't remember why I had set the alarm. A moment when I didn't feel worried or guilty, only confused and tired. And then I remembered. It was like the anvil falling on the coyote in that cartoon I'd seen at the movies.

I knew it would be dark at 4:30 in the morning, but I didn't know *how* dark. It was as dark as the time Mom made me crawl into the belly of our cold furnace to patch a hole in the firebox and my flashlight went out. And Mary Lou did this every single day.

I wanted to climb back into bed. But I couldn't let Dad down. I couldn't let Mary Lou down. I had to do this. Like it or not.

So as I got dressed, I took stock of what I knew. There were two different papers to deliver—the *Chicago Tribune* and the *Chicago Sun-Times*. Some houses got only the *Tribune,* some got only the *Sun-Times* and some got both. Mary Lou had them all memorized now, but I knew she had a huge metal ring of two-by-four-inch cards, with the names and addresses and subscription details of everyone on the route, which she'd used when she first got started. All I had to do was find that ring. Which meant I had to go into her room.

I don't know why that seemed so scary. 'Course I'd been in her room a hundred times—she was my sister—but somehow, knowing she wasn't there made it seem like I was walking into an abandoned gold mine. "Come on, Boots," I called.

My dog opened one eye and stared at me, but he obediently stretched and crept over to my side. Together, we walked across the hall and pushed Mary Lou's door open.

No one had closed the blinds, so moonlight streamed in through the uncovered window. Everything glowed silver, as if it were radioactive. The room was tidy, the desk neat, no clothes or books left on the floor. I stood there looking for a long time before I finally managed to force myself to step inside. I was careful not to look at the empty bed and went straight to the desk. I opened the top drawer. There, on a pile of papers, was the ring of cards.

Well, that was one piece of luck. I grabbed the ring and ran out of there, like the town thief running from the sheriff.

In the kitchen, I glanced at the clock. Somehow it was already almost five. How much time had I spent, standing at the edge of Mary Lou's doorway in the darkness? If I wasn't back by seven thirty, I'd miss the bus. So I grabbed a cold piece of corn bread for breakfast and wolfed it down.

Boots and I trudged out to the garage and I opened up the door. There were three or four bikes there, all in a jumble, each of them with a giant, square wire basket on the front. I pulled out mine, which was red, but the front tire was flat. A piece of glass was stuck in it, probably from the scrap yard. I didn't have the time to patch it, so I pulled out the blue bike Mary Lou used.

I felt her presence hover around me like a ghost as I walked the bike to the front of the house. There was a huge pile of papers on our front porch. I knew that Mr. Reynolds, in his old World War II jeep, dropped them off there each morning, but I'd never seen them before. The pile was as tall as I was. I tried to pull out a couple, but the papers were tied together with baling wire. So it was back to the garage to find a wire cutter. Once I had the stack open, I stuffed as many papers as I could into the basket on the front of the bike. I'd have to come back to get the rest.

I may have had another moment of despair then. I may have considered going back inside and waking Dad and telling him, *I can't do it.* I may even have dreamed of crawling back into my nice, warm bed, but if so, I'm not admitting it.

I glared at the papers.

They stared back at me.

Then I got on the bike and, with Boots trotting beside me, rode off into the dawn.

Except that it was still dark. And if I'm being truthful, what actually happened was that I only made it halfway down the driveway before I fell off the bike. It wasn't my fault. Balancing on a bike was way different with a stack of papers hanging over the front wheel. Half the newspapers fell out of the basket onto the gravel drive.

That was just the last straw. My sister was burned and it

was my fault and now I couldn't even do a stupid paper route to help my family out. Boots came over to lick the tears off my face. Did I say there were tears? Of course, cowboys don't cry. But I felt completely alone. So I may have cried for just a minute or two, till I realized no one was coming to rescue me.

I stood up, put the papers back in the basket and walked the bike down to Fairview Avenue. That was the eastern border of the route and it was paved, so I'd have smooth pedaling and wouldn't fall off. I hoped.

I'd finally gotten the hang of riding with a full basket by the time I reached the old Czech couple's house. Their real names were Mr. and Mrs. Kopecky, but everyone called them Pa and Ma. He was skinny as a broomstick and always wore a bow tie. She was round as a barrel.

Ma opened the door at the exact same time I was opening the screen to put down her paper, and scared me half to death. "You the Wilson boy?" she asked. She wore a loose flowered dress that made her look like a big bouquet.

I nodded.

"What's your name? Johnny? Walter?"

"Tommy," I admitted.

"Tommy," she repeated. "How old are you?"

"Twelve, ma'am."

"Same as my grandson, Rickie. He visits in the summer. You know him?"

I'd seen him on the ball field. I knew he was an only child, fussed over. You could tell, because his haircut was always neat, and he wore a white shirt and good leather shoes to play ball. Had a new mitt too. I'd tried to dislike him, but he let me use his glove, and if someone's willing to loan you his glove, well, then you just can't not like him. I nodded.

"Hold on a minute." She disappeared into the kitchen for a moment and reappeared with a sausage that she tossed to Boots.

"I was going to eat that!" Pa called from inside the house.

"You have enough!" Ma called back. "Dog is too skinny."

Boots gobbled up the sausage before she could change her mind.

"Thanks," I said with a smile. I could have done with a sausage myself.

Ma smiled back. "We're praying for your sister."

I nodded again, scared that if I said a word I'd burst out crying.

When I was halfway through the metal ring of address cards, I went back to the house and refilled my basket. Then I began the western part of the route. First stop was McKenzie's Grocery and Sundry Store.

Mr. McKenzie had taken over the store after old Mr. O'Malley had died two months before. Mr. McKenzie was a Gypsy, a big man, not fat, but every time I saw him, it seemed like his suit was just a little too small. He was always friendly enough, but with his dark hair and wild, bushy eyebrows, he always reminded me of a grizzly bear. I wondered if he had a crystal ball in the apartment he lived in above the store. Mr. McKenzie was outside sweeping as I rode up.

"You're Tommy, right?" he asked.

"Yes." I held out the paper.

He grasped it tightly. His hands were large and thick, his

30

fingers twice the size of mine. "I was so sorry to hear about your sister."

I nodded.

"Sam was burned when he was a baby," he said.

It took me a minute to realize he was talking about Little Skinny, the new boy at St. Joseph's, who had joined our class when school started two weeks earlier. Eddie and I had christened him Little Skinny because he was so fat. He also had a big scar across half his face. I hadn't realized that Mr. McKenzie was his father.

"A burn is a horrible injury," Mr. McKenzie continued. "I wouldn't wish it on my worst enemy."

All his talk of burns and injuries was making me uncomfortable. Mary Lou was nothing like Little Skinny. She was my beautiful, sweet sister, and she was going to be absolutely fine.

"Okay," I said finally.

I could feel him watching me as I rode off. He was just being nice, like Ma and Pa, but their sympathy made me feel like I wanted to throw up.

I was almost done with the route by the time I reached Mrs. Scully's house. She was young and pretty, with blond hair styled like Marilyn Monroe's. Her husband had died a year or so before. She lived in the big house all alone, earning her living by taking in sewing and mending. She waved from the front porch when she saw me. I was afraid she'd call out her thoughts about Mary Lou too, but she didn't say a word.

I had one final stop—our next-door neighbor's house. Actually, it was more like a shack, so run-down it looked like the Big Bad Wolf had already blown it over. An old Russian woman who played the accordion lived there, and as I threw her paper onto the front porch, I had the sudden thought that maybe the *Daily Worker* had come from her.

But the sun was fully up now, so I had no time to mull over that idea. I knew it had to be nearly seven thirty, but I was too scared to look at my watch. I was huffing and puffing as I turned into our driveway. Boots's tongue hung out as I threw the bike into the garage.

"You're late, Tommy!" Mom hollered from the kitchen.

I ran inside and yanked on my school uniform: navy pants, white shirt and a tie. Mom handed me my lunch and satchel. I took them without looking at her and dashed back outside.

The bus was waiting at the corner. The driver, an old woman with gray hair who always smelled of cigarettes, cleared her throat as I climbed on. "Heard what happened to your sister," she said in a low voice. "I'm very sorry. But I'm afraid I can't hold the bus again."

I nodded and collapsed into a seat. I'd done it. I'd delivered the papers. I should have felt proud or relieved or something. But as I watched Boots bark at the bus as it pulled away, all I felt was sick that Mary Lou wasn't there with me, and dread that I'd have to do the paper route again tomorrow.

6

THE BULLY

By the time we got to school, four different people had told me they were so sorry, Eddie had asked about Mary Lou twice and I was ready to slug anyone who mentioned her again. I practically ran to the chapel. As I slid into a pew, I could feel the weight of home falling off my shoulders, like a horse shrugging off a saddlebag.

At St. Joseph's Catholic School we had Mass every morning. That meant thirty-five minutes of peace and quiet—well, except for the standing up and kneeling, and chanting in Latin, but I could do all that in my sleep. And even if I forgot some of the words, I'd just get a real pious look on my face, lower my voice and say, *"A fiery horse with the speed of light, a cloud of dust and a hearty 'Hi-Yo, Silver!'"*

I loved school. Oh, the nuns liked to pretend they were mean, but the worst they'd do was get out the ruler and rap you on the knuckles. Not that anyone misbehaved. No, sir. St. Joe's was run like Ike's army, which was okay by me. I liked knowing what was going to happen. At home, if I accidentally dropped a plate, sometimes Mom would laugh and call me slippery fingers and help me clean it up, and sometimes she'd yell for an hour and send me to bed without dinner.

After Mass we'd say a prayer for anyone who was sick or had died or anything like that. First on our prayer list was always Cardinal József Mindszenty. He was the leader of the Catholic Church in Hungary and had spoken out against the communists who had taken over Hungary after the war. He was arrested, tortured and, at a sham trial in 1949, sentenced to life in prison. So every day we bowed our heads and prayed for his release.

I should have known what was coming next, should have expected it when Sister Ann stood up and said she had a special announcement. Like all the other nuns, Sister Ann wore a habit complete with a black-and-white wimple. She was tall and thin, except for her nose, which looked a little bit like a pickle. "Yesterday, one of our very own students, Mary Lou Wilson, was burned in a terrible accident."

There was a gasp from one of the eighth-grade girls. She must have been the only one who hadn't already heard. I longed for the earth to open up and swallow me whole.

"Please keep Mary Lou and her family in your prayers," said Sister Ann, "especially her brother, Tommy."

Everyone turned to look at me.

I slouched down lower in the pew. All I wanted was not to have to think about it for a little while. Did that make me a horrible brother? Yeah, it probably did.

I'd never been so glad to file into our classroom and start working on spelling. Lizzie Johnson was selected to hand out the composition notebooks. I groaned. Oh, she was cute enough, with curls like Little Orphan Annie in the comics and enough freckles to make it look like someone had sprinkled pepper on her face. But she always batted her eyelashes at me and spoke in this high-pitched baby voice. It was really annoying.

According to Mary Lou, I was handsome. With dark brown hair, always kept neat and trimmed, and deep brown eyes, as rich and gooey as a chocolate-covered raisin. (Her words, not mine. Who wants gooey eyes?) But I liked being good-looking. I mean, who wouldn't? When I smiled, even the nuns would soften and give me the benefit of the doubt when I was being naughty. *Tommy didn't really mean to knock over the trash can. Tommy didn't really mean to bump into you.* Even if I really did.

But sometimes, at night, I'd lie in bed and wonder, what if I hadn't been born good-looking? What if I was like Eddie, with blond hair that jutted off at odd angles and blue eyes that weren't quite the same size? When we got into scrapes together, often he'd get in trouble instead of me. I asked him about it once. "Aw, Tommy, you're just a smooth talker," he said, but I wasn't sure that was the real reason.

"Hi, Tommy," cooed Lizzie when she reached my desk, just like I knew she would.

"Hello, Lizzie," I said.

"I'm so sorry about your sister."

I frowned at her. "I don't want to talk about it." Sister Ann was writing spelling words on the board and I pretended to concentrate on that.

"Did she really burn up like a firecracker?" Lizzie asked. Her blue eyes were sparkling, but whether from concern or excitement I couldn't tell.

Eddie glared at her. "He said he doesn't want to talk about it."

"Well, I was just asking," Lizzie said.

I pulled a composition notebook from the middle of the stack, causing her to drop all the ones on top. They fell to the floor with a crash.

Sister Ann whirled around. "Lizzie Johnson, what are you doing?"

"Tommy made me—"

"Are you handing out the notebooks or is Tommy?"

"I am," Lizzie admitted.

I sat piously in my seat, my hands folded neatly on top of my desk.

"Well, if you can't do your job in an appropriate manner, I shall have to ask someone else."

"Sorry, Sister," Lizzie said, bowing her head.

Sister Ann turned back to the chalkboard. Lizzie bent down and picked up the notebooks, but before she moved on to the next desk, she stuck her tongue out at me. She kind of reminded me of Mary Lou when she did that. I swallowed, trying to force down the lump in my throat.

Eddie leaned over to me and whispered, "Did you bring the paper?"

"Which paper?" I asked blankly.

The paper.

"Oh yeah." I checked my satchel. Sure enough, there it was, right where I had put it. Right before . . . "Here it is."

"We gonna show it to the choirboys at recess?"

I nodded. "That's the plan."

The choirboys were what we called Luke and Peter. They lived in the nice part of town and Eddie and I had kind of a rivalry with them. They were always showing us the new pocket watches or army knives *they'd* gotten. Now we finally had something cool to show them. 'Cause fighting commies was one thing we all agreed on. I hated communists almost as much as I loved cowboys.

But before recess came spelling. And then reading. And after that religion. And then it was finally time to go outside.

There was no empty field or anything like that. The oldest boys in the eighth grade (that was Mary Lou's class) brought out long, wooden, black-and-white construction horses and used them to block off the cobblestone street in front of the school. They set up a couple of saw horses in the middle of the street too, creating two sections. One was for the girls to skip rope and play hopscotch. The other was for us boys. The nuns walked in circles, keeping an eye on everyone.

When the nuns were at the far end of the street, I gestured for Peter and Luke to follow Eddie and me over to a big elm tree. "Got something to show you," I whispered.

"What is it this time?" Luke asked, rolling his eyes. His mom must have made him get a haircut every two weeks, because his dark hair was always neatly trimmed. But he had a twisted arm from a bad case of polio in second grade and it just kind of hung at his side. Nobody dared say a word about it, 'cause that'd be bad luck and then maybe they'd catch polio too.

Peter snickered. He was Lizzie's twin brother, and they

looked a lot alike. He also had curly red hair, which he kept cut very short so it wouldn't curl too much, and a face full of freckles. Mention the resemblance, however, and Peter was likely to slug you. Unlike Mary Lou and me, Peter and Lizzie didn't like each other. "Probably another stupid comic book."

I grabbed Peter's tie and yanked, hard. He stumbled and almost fell on the cobblestones. "Hey," I said. "Just because *Kid Colt Outlaw* isn't as famous as *The Lone Ranger* doesn't mean it isn't a good comic too!"

"Watch it," Peter snapped, rubbing his neck. "That hurt!"

"Oh, poor baby," I teased.

"Come on, come on," said Eddie. "Just show them the paper."

I pulled out the *Daily Worker* and held it up so they could read the masthead. Their eyes went wide.

"All right," Luke said. "Now that is pretty cool!"

"A real commie newspaper!" Peter exclaimed.

"Where'd you get it?" Luke asked.

But before I could answer, Sister Ann started walking toward us. I quickly rolled up the paper and stuck it in my back pocket.

She frowned when she reached us. "What are you boys doing?"

"Nothing," said Eddie.

"Just deciding who's going to be *it*," I added.

"Then I suggest you go run and play," she said sternly. "We will be reviewing fractions this afternoon and you will need to sit very still."

I nodded.

She walked off.

"Tag again?" scoffed Luke.

"Electric-chair tag," I said.

Peter nodded in approval. "I'll be Mr. Rosenberg," he said. "Luke can be Ethel."

Mr. and Mrs. Rosenberg were convicted of spying for the Soviets. Just last June they were executed at Sing Sing prison. I'd seen pictures of them in the paper, walking to the electric chair. Mary Lou said it had given her nightmares for a week. I'd thought it was kind of exciting.

"I don't want to be Ethel again," Luke protested. "Why can't I be Julius?"

"Better run, you two," I said. "Almost time for your execution."

They ran. Luke was fast, but we finally caught up with Peter by the horses that divided the street in half. Eddie grabbed one arm and I held the other. Peter flailed wildly between us, yelling, "I don't want to go to the chair." The "chair" was over by the elm tree. We started to drag him toward it.

Tommy!

I glanced up. There was no one there, but I swore I'd heard Mary Lou, clear as day. I knew what she'd say.

You cut that out right now! Sister Ann is going to see you in a second. Didn't she say last week that the next person she caught playing electric-chair tag was going to get a call home?

She had. And the last thing I needed was a call home. So I dropped Peter's arm.

Eddie gave me a puzzled look. "What's going on?"

Peter took advantage of the moment to twist out of his grasp. "Giving up already?"

39

"No," I said. "I just decided I want to play kick ball instead."

We played kick ball a lot at school, because of Luke and his arm. But I didn't usually change my mind right in the middle of a game. I'm sure they would have protested if it hadn't been for my sister.

"Okay," Eddie said finally. "Let me go get a ball."

As he went off to find a ball, I could feel someone watching me. I turned and realized it was Little Skinny, Mr. McKenzie's son. He wore the same clothes as the rest of us—white shirt, dark pants, plain tie—but his were a size too small and he was built like his father, making him look like an overstuffed sausage. Worst of all was the scar on his face. Shaped like a saucer that has shattered, but not yet fallen apart, it was red and raised and covered his left cheek and half of his nose. It made my skin crawl.

"What are you looking at?" I asked.

"Nothing." He stared at the ground.

I'd become the freak now. The one with the burned sister. It made me angry. I knew just how to make *him* feel uncomfortable.

"Hey, Little Skinny," I called, making my voice as friendly as possible. "You're the one!"

He looked up, confused. "The one what?"

"The one who is going to come play kick ball with us."

He shook his head.

"Aw, come on," I said. "It'll be fun."

"No, thanks."

Eddie had returned with the ball. I caught his eye and he nodded, understanding my signal. We ran over to Little

Skinny and grabbed his arms, trying to pull him into the game.

Little Skinny froze like a big round turtle, as if he were trying to pull himself into his shell. Peter and Luke started laughing hysterically.

"I don't want to play," Little Skinny moaned.

Tommy!

I let go suddenly.

Little Skinny jerked away from Eddie. He looked like he was about to cry.

Sister Ann was heading toward us again. "Are you all right, Samuel?" she asked.

"Fine," he muttered, and ran off.

Sister Ann looked confused for a moment. I thought she was about to ask what had happened, so I figured I'd better cut her off. "May I help you with something, Sister?" I asked.

"Yes," said Sister Ann, turning her attention back to Eddie and me. "I thought perhaps you boys might do me a favor."

"Of course, Sister," Eddie said.

"We are almost out of chalk. I was hoping you two would run to the store and fetch me some more."

She smiled. A wide, fake smile that made her pickle nose wiggle. She was only asking me because of my sister. I hated her pity. Still, you didn't say no to a nun.

"Sure," I said. "We'd be happy to."

Sister Ann nodded and pressed a coin into Eddie's hand. And we set off to McKenzie's Grocery and Sundry Store.

7

THE YO-YOS

Main Street in Downers Grove was only a few blocks long. There was a hardware store, a drugstore, a bakery, Toon Funeral Home and Mr. McKenzie's store. A new, bigger supermarket had recently opened across town on Ogden, but Mom still preferred McKenzie's because it was so close to everything else.

Mr. McKenzie was outside opening a box when Eddie and I arrived. He was sweating and had his sleeves rolled up. I could see some sort of a tattoo on his left forearm. Even though there was a razor cut on his chin, he already looked like he needed another shave.

"Tommy!" he exclaimed, as if we were great friends.

"Hello," I said.

"Who is this?" he asked, referring to Eddie.

"I'm Eddie Sullivan, sir," Eddie said. "Nice to meet you."

Mr. McKenzie shook his hand eagerly. "You boys go to school with my Sam."

"Who?" asked Eddie.

"Sam," I said, nudging him. "You know, the new boy."

42

"Oh," Eddie said. "The one with the scar."

"Yes," Mr. McKenzie said. "It happened in the war. There was an air raid and we'd made it to the shelter. We thought we were safe." He stared off into the distance. "But a bomb caused a water heater to explode and it scalded his face."

Eddie and I looked at each other. We didn't know what to say.

"But enough talk of sad things," Mr. McKenzie said, shaking his head as if that would shake off the bad memories. "Look what I got in today!" He gestured to the box.

Eddie and I peeked inside. There were rows and rows of yo-yos. They looked like huge Life Savers, red and green, yellow and blue, pressed up in a roll together, just like the candy. They were so bright and shiny. Like happiness on a string.

I winked at Eddie. He nodded. We were going to steal them.

Don't do it, I heard Mary Lou tell me.

I ignored her.

"Only twenty-five cents each," Mr. McKenzie said.

I looked at Eddie again. We had a whole technique. One person distracts and charms. The other takes something.

No!

Shut up, Mary Lou, I said. *After all that's happened, I deserve a treat!*

And she was quiet.

"Yo-yos are great," I said. "But actually we need some chalk."

"If you have some, please," Eddie added.

Mr. McKenzie nodded. "Of course, of course. Come on in."

43

Eddie followed him. I scuffed my shoe in the dirt, like I'd just noticed there was something on it. As Eddie passed me, he whispered softly, "Hi-Yo, Silver!" That was the signal.

As soon as they were gone, I reached into the box and picked up a yo-yo. A blue one. Like a ripe plum. I stuck it in my pocket.

It was too easy.

I could hear Eddie and Mr. McKenzie talking in the shop. No one had seen me. My pulse beat faster, like it always did when we nicked something. I picked up a yellow one, slipped it into my other pocket. Just like picking a lemon. One for me and one for Eddie.

They came back then, and Mr. McKenzie gave me a funny look. For a moment, I thought he *had* seen me steal the yo-yos. They felt huge in my pockets, large as eggs and heavy as rocks. We'd always taken little things from Mr. O'Malley, the previous store owner, gum and matches and things like that. He'd never caught us, not once. 'Course he was old and half-blind, but that wasn't why. I knew the trick of stealing things. You've got to be bold.

I smiled at Mr. McKenzie and held his gaze. "Thanks for your help, sir."

Mr. McKenzie smiled back. "Nice to see you both," he said, and went back to unpacking the yo-yos. My breath caught in my throat. Would he notice that two were missing? No, he didn't say a word.

Eddie waited until we were halfway back to school before he elbowed me in the ribs. "All right, Tommy. What'd you get?"

I pulled out the blue yo-yo and handed it to him.

"Cool!" Eddie breathed. "You're the best."

I felt great that we'd pulled one over on a grown-up, and even ended up with loot. When we reached the playground, I pulled out the yellow yo-yo, and skinned the cat and rocked the baby, and the third and fourth graders gathered around, oohing and aahing like I was a hero. But the whole time, I could feel someone watching me. I looked around.

Sister Ann was walking toward me. "You're back already?"

"Yeah," I said, uncertain. Should I hide the yo-yo, or pretend like I already had it? "The new guy doesn't like to chat like old O'Malley."

Eddie handed her the chalk. She took it with a nod and walked away, then stopped and turned back.

"Nice yo-yos," she said.

"Yeah," I said. "Got them for my birthday."

"That's right. Happy birthday, Tommy." She smiled as she walked off.

I breathed a sigh of relief. I'd gotten away with it. Again.

But a few minutes later when Sister Ann rang the bell that signaled recess was over, Little Skinny caught my eye. I realized that he could tell his father that Eddie and I had come back to school with yo-yos. Of course, he probably wouldn't. Why would it even come up? But I didn't sound very convincing, even to myself.

After school, as I got off the bus and started walking toward our house, my stomach knotted up again. I thought about riding my bike over to Eddie's. Sometimes I did that. But honestly, I wanted to know if there was any news about Mary Lou. As I stood on our stoop gathering my courage, Boots ran up to me. I scratched behind his ears and tried to imagine I was as brave as Gary Cooper before he goes to face the villains in the final shoot-out. Finally, as Boots bounded off to chase a squirrel, I took a deep breath and I pulled the front door open.

"Mom," I called, "I'm home!"

There was no answer. Of course, there wasn't any crying either, so that was a good sign. I walked into the living room and took off my tie. "Have you heard anything about Mary—"

Someone cleared her throat and I looked up.

Mom stood in the kitchen doorway, wearing a navy-blue dress with white trim. She held a red yo-yo in her hands. "I stopped by Mr. McKenzie's store this afternoon," she said. The small, jeweled body rolled up and down the string like a drop of blood.

"I needed to pick up a few items for supper. He was in quite a tizzy when I arrived. Apparently someone stole two yo-yos—like this one—from his new display this morning."

"It wasn't me," I said automatically, then cursed myself for my stupidity. Nothing says *I've done it* more than denying it before Mom even asked. The yellow yo-yo felt hot as a coal in my pocket.

Mom ignored me. "Mr. McKenzie was quite sure it was one of the public high school boys who'd taken them, until his son came home from St. Joe's."

Crap. Little Skinny.

"He said you had two new yo-yos at recess today," Mom continued. "Just like this one."

She made the yo-yo fly over toward me, so that it hit me in the chest. "Do you know anything about that?"

46

I froze, knowing there was no right answer. Finally I shook my head.

It was like a dam broke in my mom then, and all her rage came pouring out.

"Why, Tommy?" she screamed. "Why would you do such a thing?"

Why? I didn't know why. They were shiny and they were there and it had never been a big deal before. Still, I knew it was wrong. Outlaws steal, not cowboys. So I just shook my head again.

"You embarrassed me!" she yelled, a vein bulging out of her forehead. "You're going to have to go back and help him on Saturday mornings to make up for it! The two you stole and this one too!"

She kept bouncing the yo-yo, up and down, frantically. My heart beat faster and faster too, in time with the toy. Finally, the string slipped off her finger and the yo-yo went sailing across the room. It hit a vase on a side table. The vase teetered, then crashed to the floor. I winced.

"Psia krew i cholera!" Mom shrieked. Busia had sometimes lapsed into Polish when she was happy or excited. But Mom only spoke Polish when she was really angry. It sent a shiver up my spine.

"Sit down on that couch and stay there until your father gets home!"

That meant a whipping. Dad always gave us one lash for each birthday. This'd be my first time getting twelve. I sat down on the couch and sighed.

"What did you say?" Mom demanded.

"Nothing."

"Tommy, I heard you!"

"I just sighed!"

The vein on her forehead pulsed. "I changed my mind," Mom fumed, eyes wild. "I'm not going to wait for Dad. Don't move!" She stormed out of the room.

I couldn't help shaking a bit as I waited for her to come back. *Stop it,* I told myself. You've gotten a spanking a million times before. But Mom had never whipped me.

Mom returned with Dad's spare belt coiled in her hand. It was dark brown leather and a little worn around the edges. "Go into the kitchen," Mom ordered.

"But—"

"Stand up!" she screamed.

So I did. I walked into the kitchen with Mom following close behind. The afternoon sun shone in through the window over the sink, bouncing off the yellow tiles on the walls.

"Your pants," Mom prompted.

This was standard procedure for a whipping. I didn't mind so much with my dad, but it was humiliating pulling down my pants and underwear in front of my mom. I put my hands on the kitchen counter.

The sun was shining in my eyes, blinding me, but I could hear the sound of the leather as it flew through the air.

One. It hurt. The first few hits were always the worst, and I hadn't braced myself for it. Two, three and four weren't as bad.

Mom started yelling again, but I didn't listen to what she was saying. Five, six and seven. The belt whipped through the air. Eight, nine. It made a whistle and then a slap as it hit me. Ten, eleven.

Twelve.

I relaxed.

Then she hit me again.

After three more, I said, "Mom, that was fifteen."

But she kept hitting me. Mom hit harder than Dad, and I had to bite my tongue not to cry. I glanced back, and for the first time, I noticed Pinky cowering under the kitchen table, watching with wide eyes.

"Mom!" I cried.

She didn't stop. Mom kept hitting me, again and again, until finally the belt snapped back and hit her on the chin. She yelped and stopped.

In the quiet, I could feel each individual welt on my buttocks. There were tears on my face, but I wiped them away.

"It's all right," I said, pulling up my pants. I had stolen the yo-yos. Mom had to punish me.

The anger ran out of Mom's face, her cheeks changing from flushed to pale. If she started crying, I didn't think I could handle it. I had to say something, anything.

"I d-d-deserved it," I sputtered.

"Yes." Mom bit her lip. "Yes, you did." She slowly rolled up the belt and left the room.

"Tommy," Pinky said, crawling out from under the table once Mom was gone. "You okay?"

"Yeah."

She touched my arm as if she was going to give me a hug. I jerked away from her.

Pinky began to cry.

I picked her up and let her sob on my shoulder. "It's okay,

Pinky," I said. "I stole the yo-yos. Mom had to punish me. It's okay."

But it wasn't. My butt hurt and I wanted to cry too. I'd never seen Mom so out of control before. But I had to hold it together for my sister.

Dad came home early, as Pinky and I were picking up the pieces of the broken vase.

"What happened?" he asked, taking off his overcoat.

I told him about stealing the yo-yos and Mom punishing me. As I talked, he sat down on the couch, as if I was sinking him with my words. "She wouldn't stop, Dad. She just wouldn't stop."

"Oh, Thomas." He sighed, shaking his head. "You shouldn't provoke your mother like that!"

"I know it was wrong to take the yo-yos, but I've never seen Mom like that."

He didn't believe me. "Tommy, she is having a hard time. With Busia dying and the new baby and now Mary Lou . . . we just need to be a little more . . . patient."

I couldn't explain it right. If only Mary Lou were here, she'd make him understand. "How is Mary Lou?" I asked.

"The same," Dad said. "The doctors don't know if—" His voice broke and he turned away so I couldn't see his face.

"Come on," he said gruffly. "Let's get this mess cleaned up."

8

DUCK AND COVER

I'd thought getting up at 4:30 a.m. was hard the day before. I'd been wrong. It was *nothing* compared to the torture of pulling myself out of bed that second day. My rear end was sore, so I rode standing up, which meant my calves hurt before I'd even gone a mile. I wasn't used to so much exercise, and with the beating on top of that, every muscle in my body ached, even my eyes from squinting against the wind. I was so tired, if Khrushchev himself had appeared on my street, I'm not sure I would have noticed. My balance was terrible and I fell off three or four times, but I kept getting back on that bike.

Ma and Pa were out in front of their house, chasing three escaped chickens that were running in circles in the street in the predawn light. Pa, tall and thin with whiskers like a broom, sighed when I handed him the paper.

"In my country, Tommy, I was a doctor. Here, I chase poultry and sell eggs to make a living." He smiled, but the wrinkled skin around his gray eyes still made him look sad.

"Got one!" Ma yelled, holding a hen high up in the air. "She's our best layer!"

Pa sighed again and went to help his wife.

At McKenzie's store, I threw the paper at the door without even stopping. The lights were already on at Mrs. Scully's and with a dress mannequin in every window it looked like she was having a breakfast party. The Russian lady was playing the accordion, a hymn we sometimes sang at school, even though I'd never seen her at our church. The only good thing about the paper route was that it meant I didn't have time to have breakfast with Mom.

School was slightly better than the day before. Instead of going to our classrooms after Mass, we all shuffled upstairs to the big assembly room and were shown a film. The movie started with a silly little cartoon turtle named Bert and a funny song that went, "Duck and cover. Duck and cover." But only the really little kids giggled, because the movie was about how to get ready for an atomic bomb.

According to the film, if there was the threat of an atomic bomb attack, a siren would sound and we should all stop what we were doing and get to a safe place. That might be a basement or a hallway. Even ducking under a desk would help, as long as you remembered to cover your head and neck.

Eddie nudged me as we watched the film. "You can come to my bomb shelter."

"Thanks," I whispered back.

But if there wasn't a warning, if the civil defense hadn't noticed the bomb in time, the first sign of an atomic bomb would be a huge, bright flash, brighter than any light you've ever seen before.

"The bomb could explode any time of the year, day or night," the narrator instructed. "We must be ready all day, every day. All the time. Even on the school bus. Or riding our bikes to Boy Scouts. Or playing ball with our friends."

This was the part of fighting commies I didn't like, worrying about how I'd protect myself and my sisters. When the movie was finally over, everyone was quiet. Sister Ann led us back to our classroom.

"We are going to do our very own air-raid drill," she informed us. "Just like you saw in the movie. I will count to three, and when I get to three, you will all get under your desks and duck and cover just like you saw in the film. You will stay in that position, absolutely quiet, until I give the all clear. Are there any questions?"

Lizzie shook her head. No one said a word.

"One. Two. Three."

Everyone leaped out of their seats and dove under their desks. I curled myself up into a ball, and pressed my hands over my head and neck, just like Mary Lou had instinctively done when she'd been burned. I could picture her, smell the fire and her burned skin.

And suddenly I couldn't stay in that position another second, not even if there was a real atomic bomb. I picked my head up and looked around the classroom.

All the students were huddled obediently under their desks, their eyes hidden. Even Sister Ann was squeezed under the big desk at the front of the room, her wimple providing extra protection for her head and neck.

It was all too much to handle. How could we worry every second of the day and night? I had to do something, anything, to break the tension. Lizzie's foot was just a few inches in front of me. I reached forward and pulled her black Mary Jane right off her lacy white sock.

"Eeeek!" Lizzie screamed.

I dropped the shoe and curled back up into my duck-and-cover position, peeking out between my fingers.

"Who said that?" Sister Ann demanded from underneath her desk. "I said absolute quiet. Lizzie Johnson, was that you?"

"Yes," she admitted. "Someone took off my shoe."

"If there were a real atomic bomb," Sister Ann reminded her, "the last thing you'd be worried about was your shoe."

I squeezed my eyes shut. I could feel Lizzie's gaze on the back of my neck, sure she was going to rat me out. But the seconds ticked by and she didn't say a word.

Finally, Sister Ann crawled out from under her desk. "It has been a minute now. You may all stand up."

At least everyone was too distracted by the drill to ask me about my sister.

Later that day, despite being more tired than an Indian pony on a buffalo hunt, I started winning the marble game at recess. I had knuckled down and captured all of Peter's marbles and was working on Eddie's last big shooter, when, wouldn't you know, Little Skinny walked by. Of course his shoe was untied. A normal person would have just stumbled or something, but oh no, he tripped and he fell right onto me, pushing me into our game and scattering the shiny glass cat's eyes I'd won all over the blacktop.

"You idiot!" I yelled at him. "Now look what you made me do!"

"I didn't do anything," he mumbled. He'd scraped his

arm and I could see a little drop of blood run down his elbow, like the red yo-yo Mom had gotten from Mr. McKenzie.

Suddenly, like a great wave was washing over me, I was furious. "You told on me!"

"What?" asked Little Skinny, confused.

"You told your dad about the yo-yos!" I screamed. "You're a rat!"

"No, I'm not," he protested. But his lip trembled and it would have been obvious even to Pinky that he was lying.

Eddie jumped up. "Tattletale!"

"I didn't say anything!" Little Skinny wailed.

I grabbed his tie, tight around his fat neck. "Admit it!"

He stood frozen, his eyes fixed on the ground.

The choirboys gathered around, watching like we were in a television show.

"You are going to be sorry you were ever born!" yelled Eddie.

"Yeah," I agreed, "now I have to go help in your stupid shop every Saturday." I bunched his collar up in my fist. The scar on his face glistened with sweat, like a stop sign in the rain. "Admit it!"

Tears leaked out of Little Skinny's eyes. "Okay, I told."

I punched him in the stomach.

He bent over double and glanced at me, bewildered. "But I admitted it!"

My heart was beating faster than ever.

"You can get expelled for fighting," Peter said.

"Shut up!" I yelled. Even though it was true. You *could* get expelled. "You gonna go tattle to Sister Ann?"

"No," Peter said, backing away, as if he were scared of me.

That made me feel even worse. I'd never actually hit any-one at school before. Mary Lou always stopped me. But she wasn't there and I hadn't heard her say anything, even in my mind. Had she died?

I ran to the bathroom and threw up. It took a long time for my heart to slow down. Finally, I washed my mouth out with water and returned to the street.

No one seemed to have noticed I'd been gone. Eddie was off tossing a ball with another guy from our class. The nuns were tut-tutting over Little Skinny's cut arm. Lizzie was jumping rope. I wanted to thank her for not telling on me about the shoe, but I didn't. The choirboys were busy gathering up all the marbles, the blue ones and the green ones, and even the big shooter with the silver and gold sparkles inside. I knew tomorrow they'd suggest we play again, and would divide them up fairly. But I still felt so angry, I wanted to cry.

9

VISITING MARY LOU

After school, before I could get on the bus, Mom met me on the front steps. At first glance, she looked okay. Her dress was neat and ironed; she'd combed her hair and put on a necklace and lipstick. But her eyes were wild, a mix of brown and green. For a moment, I thought she'd heard about the incident on the playground. But she only grabbed my arm and said, "Come on. We're going to go see Mary Lou."

I was relieved. If Mary Lou was allowed to have visitors, it must mean she was doing better! What I discovered, after forty-five minutes in the car, was that Mom and the baby were going to see Mary Lou, not me. I was so disappointed, I wanted to scream. But there was Pinky, holding my hand, looking up at me with big brown eyes.

We sat in the waiting room for two hours. I gave Pinky an old piece of paper from my school satchel and she drew big round scribbles over and over while I did my homework. After a few minutes, her paper ripped and she started to cry. Pinky climbed into my lap and I rocked her and sang "Baa, Baa, Black Sheep" about fifty-seven times.

I was so frustrated about not seeing Mary Lou, I felt like I was going to explode. Finally, Pinky fell asleep and I placed her on the couch. She rolled over, but didn't wake up. This was my chance. I ran for the stairs.

I reached the stairwell just before my mother and a doctor walked into the lobby. I could hear Mom wailing, "Morphine? But she'll become an addict!"

"We know what we're doing," said the doctor, his voice low and soothing. "There's nothing else to control the pain. We can wean her off it slowly and . . ."

I didn't wait to hear the rest. I ran up the stairs two at a time and poked my head out into the hall. No one was there. I was pretty sure Mary Lou's room number was 320, so I ducked into that room and pulled the curtain.

The figure in the bed didn't move. It was wrapped up in bandages, lots of them, like a mummy I'd seen in the encyclopedia Mom had at home. The person was turned away, facing the wall, so all I could see was long brown hair. There was a brush on the bedside table, and the hair was smooth, as if someone had just finished combing it.

I crept over to look at the person in the bed.

It was Mary Lou. I couldn't speak. She looked both better and worse than I had expected. Her legs were covered with bandages so thick, they resembled sausages. Her face was puffy but unmarked, except for a scar on her forehead that her hair would cover. As I stared at the freckles on her nose— just the same as they'd always been—her eyelashes fluttered, like spiders dancing on her eyelids.

"Mary Lou," I whispered. "It's me."

Her eyes opened for a moment, looking big and unfocused. "Tommy?" she mumbled.

I waited a long time, but she didn't open her eyes again. Her breathing was slow and steady, as if she were asleep. But she was breathing. She was alive.

Finally, I turned to go. I hurried down the hall, then sat in the stairwell for a minute, just to catch my breath. That's when I started crying. Really sobbing. My sister was alive and I knew I should be happy and thanking God, but I couldn't stop crying. It was embarrassing. All I could think was, cowboys do not sob like babies. But then I remembered that Mary Lou might end up looking like Little Skinny, and the thought only made me sob harder.

Suddenly, I heard a door open on a floor above me. I held my breath. Someone else was in the stairwell with me. I jumped up and started down the stairs, wanting to avoid whoever it was.

But the door hadn't been on the floor above me, it had been on the floor below, which meant I ran smack into a boy standing in the stairwell.

It was Little Skinny.

Even though I'd just been thinking about him, he was the last person I expected to see. For a moment, I was so embarrassed, I couldn't breathe. There I was, my eyes all red, my face smudged and dirty. That was when I realized he was crying too, great big silent tears that fell down his red scar onto the white, starched collar of his shirt.

"Are you going to hit me again?" he asked.

I didn't answer, just pushed past him and ran back to the

lobby. Mom, Susie and Pinky were sitting on the couch, waiting for me.

"Where have you been?" Mom snapped.

"I had to go to the bathroom," I said.

"Well, come on," she said. "It's time to go home."

Mom didn't cry or yell as we got in the car, but she started driving way too fast. I didn't dare ask her to slow down.

WORKING FOR MR. McKENZIE

Little Skinny stayed out of my way all that week at school. I was glad. Every time I saw him, I wondered why he'd been at the hospital, and if Mary Lou's scars were going to end up looking like his.

I didn't want to spend my Saturday helping in Mr. McKenzie's store, so I decided to give back the yo-yos. Then my debt would be repaid and I'd never have to set foot in his store again. I still had the yellow yo-yo and the red one too. Eddie gave me the blue one back and I promised not to rat him out. "I know," he said. "We keep each other's secrets."

Saturday, September 19, was raining and miserable. It took me a long time to do the paper route. I kept imagining what I'd do if I saw that bright flash that meant an atomic bomb, kept looking for places where I could duck and cover. A wall. An embankment. Something like that. I saw no one. Everyone else was safe and snug in their beds, even the chickens. But Boots loyally came along, his black-and-white fur sticking to his sides, making him look like an oversized rat in the rain. By the time I was done, I was soaked through. I put the yo-yos, wrapped in brown paper, into my school satchel and walked slowly to the store.

When I arrived, there were a couple of customers walking up and down the aisles. Little Skinny sat at the front counter working the cash register. He flinched when he saw me and had to count out change for the little old lady buying eggs three times before he got it right. I'd decided to leave the yo-yos on the counter and get out of there, when Mr. McKenzie hurried out of the back room.

"Tommy!" His voice was a big, booming growl. "You're late."

I shrugged.

He put his hands on his hips, looking like a huge, angry bear. "Why did you do this to me? I would have given you a yo-yo had you asked!"

I didn't answer.

He sighed and held out a broom and dustpan. "Sweep out the store. Front to back."

"Actually . . ." I let the words trail off.

"Actually, what?" His bushy eyebrows huddled together, like a caterpillar on his face.

I gave him my sweetest, most innocent smile. "I decided to just return them," I said, handing over the small package.

His face froze, as if an ice storm had suddenly blown into town. Stiffly, he unwrapped the paper.

"See," I said, grinning even broader. "Good as new."

Mr. McKenzie did not reply.

"Well," I said. "See you around!" I turned to go.

He grabbed my shirt. "No."

I jerked away. "What do you mean, no?"

"How long do you think I would stay in business if I allowed boys to 'borrow' items whenever they wanted?" Now he spoke so softly, I had to strain to hear him. "No, the deal with your mother was you'd work for me on Saturday mornings, from nine until twelve."

"Fine," I said, crossing my arms. "Then give me back the yo-yos."

"Oh, Tommy." He laughed. "You are a funny boy!" He held out the broom again.

I glared at him.

"Sweep," Mr. McKenzie said. "Front to back."

I took the broom. "Yes, sir," I said, sarcastic as can be. He didn't even look at me as he walked off.

So I started sweeping. Every time I thought I was done, he pointed out another spot I'd missed. Five times. Even Mom wasn't that picky.

When I was finished with the floors, I had to wash the windows. And dry them, even though it was still raining. Then it was carry boxes from here to there and there to here. While all Little Skinny did was wrap up the items people bought in old newspapers and work the register, pecking at the keys like a hungry bird.

My anger grew with each new task. Sure, I'd known it was wrong to take the yo-yos, but to make me work when I'd returned them? That was ridiculous!

It was almost noon, almost time for me to go, and the store was crowded. Little Skinny complained that he was hungry.

"You go on back and make yourself a sandwich," Mr. McKenzie said. "I'll take over at the register for a while."

I was hungry too. And my feet hurt. But no one offered *me*

a break. No, I just had to keep on restocking canning jars on a shelf. I was paying attention, I really was, but one of the jars was wet, which was probably why I dropped it.

The jar bounced and then shattered loudly into a million pieces.

Everyone came scurrying over to my aisle to see what had happened. Mr. McKenzie walked up and inspected the broken glass on the floor, like he'd never seen a broken jar before.

"Clumsy," he said finally.

All the customers were looking at me. It was embarrassing. *I've been up since 4:30,* I wanted to yell at them. *I'm tired!*

Mr. McKenzie clucked his tongue. "Tommy, that was careless."

I was so furious, I wanted to slug him. Deal or no deal, I wasn't going to take that. I turned on my heel and walked off.

I was almost to the front door when I came up with a great idea. If I left now, Mom would find out and beat me again for sure. But if I found another way to get back at him . . .

Everyone else, even Mr. McKenzie, was still gathered in the back of the store where I'd broken the jar. I quickly searched through my satchel. Yes, I still had that commie newspaper. It was a little wrinkled and wet, but that didn't matter. I slipped my copy of the *Daily Worker* under the counter, onto the pile of papers they used to wrap the purchases. The next time someone bought a salad dish or a gravy bowl, they'd get quite a surprise. Mr. McKenzie would be humiliated and then he'd see how it felt.

I picked up the broom and dustpan and sauntered down the aisle.

Mr. McKenzie looked at me.

The clock struck twelve.

"I'll clean it up," I said, bending over with the dustpan.

"You certainly will." Mr. McKenzie huffed. He marched off and the rest of the customers followed him.

I quickly swept up the glass and walked back to the front of the store to throw it out.

Mr. McKenzie was wrapping a purchase for Eddie's dad, Mr. Sullivan. "Hi, Tommy," he called out to me. He wore overalls and a white T-shirt, revealing his muscular arms. "Eddie and I were thinking about heading over to Mud Lake one of these weekends before it gets too cold. You and your dad interested in coming?"

"Yes, sir!" I replied. Fishing was one of the only things my dad ever did with me. I never missed a trip.

"There you go," Mr. McKenzie said, handing Mr. Sullivan the newspaper-wrapped package.

The masthead was clearly visible on the front. Eddie's dad noticed it immediately. "What's this?" he asked, without touching the paper. "Some sort of joke?"

"What are you talking about?" said Mr. McKenzie. "It's the lightbulbs, like you asked for. Sixty watts."

Mr. Sullivan took the package and unwrapped it, as if it were a baby blanket containing a dead fish. He pulled the paper off and smoothed out the crinkled pages. "Since when do you get the *Daily Worker*?" he asked, his voice cold.

Mr. McKenzie laughed. "The *Daily Worker*? That's a good one."

But Mr. Sullivan's face was deadly serious. A muscle in his arm twitched.

Mr. McKenzie stopped laughing and looked down at the paper. His face blanched when he saw the masthead. "I don't know where that came from," he said. He looked over at me. I held his gaze, defiantly. I wanted him to know it was me. Finally, he turned away. "I just used the first newspaper on top of the pile."

He reached for the paper to crumple it up, but Eddie's dad snatched it back from him. "I'm going to have to show that to Officer Russo," he said.

Mr. McKenzie laughed again, but it sounded forced. "I'm no communist!"

"So you say," said Mr. Sullivan. "It's just a precaution. I'm sure you understand."

Mr. McKenzie rolled his eyes. "What do you think? That I'm holding secret communist meetings in my stockroom at night?"

"It's a possibility," Mr. Sullivan said. "All I know is what I read in the papers. And if Senator McCarthy is finding them in the State Department, we can't be sure they aren't here too."

"Mr. Sullivan," Mr. McKenzie growled. "I am not a communist, but I've known some. They were locked up with me in a German work camp."

"The commies aren't our allies anymore," Eddie's dad retorted.

"No," Mr. McKenzie said. "Not anymore." He pulled out a new sheet of newspaper, glanced at the front page (it was the *Chicago Tribune*) and wrapped up the lightbulbs. "Got an article about your friend McCarthy right here!" He jabbed a finger at the paper. "Now take your lightbulbs and get out of my store."

Mr. Sullivan held the package with one hand and slammed the door with the other as he stormed out. The little bell above the threshold rang wildly.

Everyone in the store was staring at Mr. McKenzie. Including me. They'd all heard Mr. Sullivan accuse him of being a communist. Mr. McKenzie took one deep breath, then another. "Store's closing for lunch," he said finally. "You'll have to finish your purchases this afternoon."

Without a word, the other customers left one by one. I started to join them.

"Tommy," Mr. McKenzie called after me.

I froze, but turned to face him anyway.

He knew. I could tell by the look in his eyes that he knew, 100 percent for sure, that I'd put that paper there. But could he prove it? Had Little Skinny seen me with the paper at school? I didn't think so, but I wasn't sure.

"I'll see you next week," Mr. McKenzie said finally.

I nodded and hurried off. Suddenly, planting the paper in the store didn't seem like it had been such a good idea.

11

GUILTY OF TREASON

The knot in my stomach only tightened as I walked home. Mr. McKenzie was probably calling Mom right now. I could barely breathe as I opened the front door and stepped in.

Dad was sitting at the kitchen table and Mom was at the stove cooking lunch. Her long black hair was braided and pinned up on her head, as if she were going to a party. Her cheeks were flushed with excitement. "Oh, Tommy," she cried when she saw me. "The doctor called. Mary Lou woke up!"

A wide grin crept across my face. "She's going to be okay?"

"Yes," said Mom, tossing the spaghetti into a colander with such enthusiasm that a few strands of pasta wriggled over the edge and fell to the floor. Mom giggled.

"They *think* she's going to be okay," my dad added in a serious tone.

I turned to look at him. He was unshaven and had a bunch of papers spread out before him. "The burns on her legs were severe. She's going to need extensive skin grafts."

"What's that?" I asked.

"When they take skin from her stomach or her back and put it on her legs."

It sounded like something from a monster movie at the Tivoli.

"There's a risk of infection," Dad went on. "And, of course, even when the grafts are healed, she'll have to learn to walk again."

"Learn to walk again?" Thinking about skin grafts and infection made me feel kind of sick, like the time I ate a hot dog and a bag of popcorn before getting on a roller coaster. Suddenly, I could smell the wet grass of that morning, see Mary Lou's penny loafers as she skipped across the lawn. Maybe she would never walk like that again. Maybe it was all my fault.

"Oh, you two worry too much!" exclaimed Mom. She went to the record player and put on Dick Contino playing the accordion. She turned the volume up loud and danced around the kitchen.

I walked over to the table and picked up one of the papers, just to clear a spot to eat. It was a bill from the hospital. *Payment due. $300. Please pay promptly*.

Dad snatched the paper out of my hand. "I'll put these away," he said without looking at me.

Three hundred dollars was a lot of money. But if I asked Dad about it, I knew he wouldn't answer. "When can I see Mary Lou?" I asked instead.

"A week or two," he said. "She's not allowed to have visitors just yet."

After lunch, we all went out into the yard to hang the laundry and work in the garden. Pinky kept running back and forth under the sheets, Boots chasing her like she was a squirrel. Mom laughed so hard, she almost started to cry. She wasn't even upset when Boots got mud on a pillowcase, just told me to take it down and throw it in the laundry again.

Every time the phone rang, I flinched, but Mr. McKenzie never called. Dad picked corn from our garden for dinner, and Mom's Polish plum cake browned perfectly. But a bit of the gooey plum filling oozed over the side of the pan and burned in the oven. The smell reminded me of that awful car ride, and I spent the rest of the evening trying not to remember, so I couldn't even enjoy the cake.

The next day I kept worrying about running into Mr. McKenzie and Little Skinny at church, but we didn't see them. Afterward, Eddie and I went off to the double feature at the Tivoli. The movie theater was just across from the station where my dad caught the train to go to work. The Tivoli could hold almost 1,400 people and had ushers in little caps and jackets to show you to your seat. There were chandeliers overhead, and even an organ that a little old lady played before the show. When the lights dimmed, I let out a deep breath. Here, at least, I could relax.

The first movie was *Guilty of Treason*, about that Hungarian cardinal József Mindszenty. We prayed for him every day after Mass. I'd seen the film at least twice before (once at school when the nuns had shown it to us) but I liked it. There was this tough American newspaper reporter who went to visit Mindszenty when he was hiding out in the hills around Budapest. The cardinal had all these great lines. He sounded kind of like a cowboy defending his homestead. "One must take a stand somewhere. One must draw a line past which one will not retreat." And "We shall teach there the gospel according to Jesus Christ, not according to Karl Marx."

Karl Marx, of course, was the father of communism. The guy who'd written *Das Kapital* and *The Communist Manifesto* and those other books commies liked to read.

But there was another line in *Guilty of Treason* that I hadn't remembered from before. The characters were talking about how the communists would try to discredit Mindszenty and spread ugly rumors about him in an attempt to reduce his influence. Then the cardinal's mother says, "It only takes a little poison to ruin a well on a farm, or to spoil a reputation in a big city."

Well, I started squirming in my seat when she said that. I mean, Downers Grove wasn't exactly a big city, but planting a commie newspaper . . . wasn't that a little like what she was talking about?

I shook off the thought. It was just a silly joke and I wasn't going to worry about it. I was relieved when *Guilty of Treason* was over and the next movie came on. *Big Jim McLain* starred John Wayne as a congressional investigator fighting commies in Hawaii. That was more like it!

When the movies were over, we walked back to Eddie's. Main Street went past Mr. McKenzie's store and I stopped short when I saw it.

The large front window was shattered and pieces of glass glittered all over the floor, as if someone had spilled a bag of ice. A brick lay among the shards. Mr. McKenzie stood outside, waving his hands in distress and talking loudly to the man who owned the hardware store. I could only catch part of what he was saying. "New glass . . . immediately . . . lose business . . ."

I felt kind of dizzy as I remembered the words from the movie, *It only takes a little poison* . . .

"Come on, Eddie," I said. "Let's go home down Odgen." That was in the opposite direction.

"Takes longer," he said.

"It's a nice day," I said. "I wanted to walk."

Eddie shrugged and we turned around. He didn't seem to notice I was distracted, and I guess he didn't see (or didn't care) about Mr. McKenzie because he didn't mention the broken glass either. Once we got to his house, we went straight to the bomb shelter his dad had built. It was in their basement. The walls were made of concrete blocks, creating a space just big enough for three bunk beds hung on the wall, a small table and a pantry full of canned goods, water and other supplies.

"You see," Eddie explained, "if the Soviets drop an atomic bomb on Chicago, those people are all dead. But my dad says Downers Grove is far enough away, so we stand a good chance of surviving. And look!" He pulled back a small curtain in the corner. "There's even a toilet!"

They also had a radio, a record player and a pile of books. "How long would you have to stay here?" I asked.

"Depends," he said. "Maybe two weeks after the blast. Then you could go out during the day, but you're supposed to sleep inside the shelter for the next couple of months. Limit your radiation exposure."

He sounded so matter-of-fact. But it kind of scared me.

My family didn't have a shelter. What would happen to us if the Soviets dropped an atomic bomb on Chicago?

Eddie knelt down and pulled out a box from under one of the beds. "We've got a gun in here too, to ward off any intruders, and Dad even bought a Geiger counter."

"What's that?" I asked.

"Measures the radiation, so you know if it's safe to go outside."

Upstairs, a door slammed and we could hear Eddie's dad start yelling. His words were slurred as if he'd been drinking.

Eddie shoved the box back under the bed. "It did cost a lot of money, building a place like this," he admitted. "Mom was kind of upset about it."

There was more screaming from upstairs. I wanted to say something to Eddie, wanted to say I understood. "Wish I had a Geiger counter that told me when my parents were in a bad mood," I joked.

"Yeah," Eddie said, but he didn't laugh. "Me too."

I went to bed early that night and fell asleep quickly. But I dreamed of Mr. McKenzie and Cardinal Mindszenty in Eddie's bomb shelter and they were reading the *Daily Worker*.

12

PAINT ON THE WINDOW

When Saturday rolled around again, it was almost a relief. I'd face Mr. McKenzie, see that everyone had understood it was just a joke and life would go on.

I got up extra-early and finished the paper route in plenty of time. I even had some breakfast and put on a clean white shirt before I went to the store. When I arrived, Mr. McKenzie was outside, washing his front window. Phew. He'd gotten it replaced. The brick probably had nothing to do with me planting the paper in his store. I wasn't sure why the replacement glass was so dirty, but at least it was there.

Mr. McKenzie grunted when he saw me. "So you showed up again."

"Yeah."

"Wasn't sure you would."

I shrugged.

"How's your sister?" he asked in a kinder tone.

"Better. I guess." I'd gone with Mom to the hospital twice that week, but hadn't been able to sneak off to see Mary Lou.

He gave me a grimace that was almost a smile. "Grab a sponge," he said. "Help me get this off."

That was when I realized it wasn't dirt on the front window. It was paint. Someone had painted a hammer and sickle on the new glass. The symbol of communism. I picked up the sponge and scrubbed and scrubbed. It came off slowly. My insides felt rubbed raw too, guilt and regret peeling the lining of my stomach like old wallpaper.

"Is this . . . because of me?" I asked finally.

"Why would it be your fault, Tommy?" His tone was even, but there was an edge to his voice.

He knew. I knew he knew. And I was just so tired. I wanted to stop hearing Mindszenty's mother say, "It only takes a little poison" over and over in my head. Even so, I was a little bit surprised when I heard myself admit, "Because I was the one who planted that paper."

"Oh," he said quietly, not looking at me, not stopping his scrubbing. "Then I imagine it is."

That wasn't what I'd expected. "I didn't mean—"

"It doesn't matter what you intended," he said. "The damage has been done. It's easy to start a rumor. Much harder to stop it."

I scrubbed harder. The paint chips stuck under my fingernails like bits of dried blood.

We finally got the last of the paint off and went inside. I was glad to sweep out the store and to move boxes. Little Skinny worked the register, but there were few customers that day. He was careful never to catch my eye.

"Slow day," Mr. McKenzie said once.

I had a horrible feeling in the pit of my stomach. Mr. McKenzie having no customers, my sister needing to learn to walk again, my mom's moods, it was all my fault. But thinking about it made me feel even worse, so I focused on mopping the store's floor like my life depended on it, noticing nothing but the stuck-on dirt.

At noon, Mr. McKenzie put up the CLOSED FOR LUNCH sign. I took off my apron and hung it up. "I'll see you next week," I said.

"No," said Mr. McKenzie. "Come on back and have a sandwich, Tommy. I want to talk to you."

Now, I'll admit it. I was scared. I'd heard that some shop owners kept a shotgun in the back room. He was probably really mad at me, and rightly so. Maybe he thought I'd thrown the brick too!

"Tommy," he repeated. "The back room."

As I followed him, I felt just like Gary Cooper in *High Noon*, walking down the street to confront the bad guys all alone.

In the back room were a table and four chairs. Little Skinny was sitting at the table. Mr. McKenzie gestured for me to sit too, then pulled three root beers out of a cooler and sat down at the table.

"Tommy, do you know about Senator McCarthy?" Mr. McKenzie asked.

That puzzled me. I expected him to yell at me, not chat with me about politics. "'Course I know about him," I said. "He's rooting out all the communists in the government."

"That's what he says he's doing. Others think he's just spreading fear and terror. Conducting a witch hunt, accusing

76

innocent people and destroying their reputations for his own reasons."

I thought about *Guilty of Treason* again and how the communists had made up false charges against Mindszenty. Surely our own government wasn't doing the same.

Mr. McKenzie went on. "By planting that paper in my store, you were playing into that hysteria. Now, I hope this will all blow over. Just another mean rumor. We're already known to be Gypsies, even if we did change our name to McKenzie. But if it doesn't blow over, if the rumor keeps people out of the store . . . well, I don't want to think about what would happen then."

"What would happen then?" I asked.

"We might not be able to pay my wife's medical bills. We might lose the store."

Little Skinny stared at the floor, his face so pale, it made his scar look even redder.

"Your wife . . . ," I said slowly, putting all the pieces together, "is in the hospital."

Mr. McKenzie nodded. "Shortly after Sam was injured, I was sent to a work camp." He pulled back his left sleeve. Z8914 was tattooed on his forearm.

I'd heard of the prisoners in German concentration camps with numbers tattooed on their bodies. But I'd never met one.

"The *Z*," he said quietly, "is for *Zigeuner*. That's German for 'Gypsy.'"

He pulled his sleeve back down. "I should have died there, but my wife managed to bribe a guard and get me out. We had to go into hiding. There wasn't enough food and my wife got very sick. She's never been the same since."

"She caught tuberculosis," said Little Skinny. "TB. It's why she's going to die."

We both turned to look at him.

Little Skinny's face was still pale, but I noticed his eyes were brown with yellow flecks, like the muddy water of a stream where a cowboy pans for gold. His hair was the same shade of brown as mine, and he looked angry.

"She's not going to die," said Mr. McKenzie in a voice that was just a bit too bright and cheerful. It was the voice grown-ups always use when they're telling a lie. "They have drugs to treat it now."

Little Skinny said nothing.

Sometimes I didn't like my mom, but I didn't want her to die. I wondered if that was what happened when you spent a lot of time in the hospital. Was Mary Lou going to die too? Medicines didn't always work. I wanted to say I was sorry. I wanted to tell Little Skinny I hoped his mom really would get better. But before I could find the words, Mr. McKenzie went on.

"Tommy, I may need you to speak to Officer Russo, to tell him you were the one who placed the newspaper here in the store."

"Fine," I said. "But please don't tell my mom."

He thought about that for a long moment, long enough that I wondered what her reaction had been when she'd re-alized I was the one who had stolen the yo-yos. "It's a deal," he said finally.

I let out a long breath, one I hadn't even known I was holding.

Mr. McKenzie told me not to move and went to make a phone call. He was only gone a minute, and when he came back, he made us sandwiches on heavy dark bread, with thick slabs of roast beef and rich spicy mustard. They were delicious. We ate the sandwiches in silence. I was just finishing the root beer he'd given me when there was a knock at the front door. Mr. McKenzie stood up to answer it.

That had to be Officer Russo. I didn't realize I'd have to confess today! The sandwich sat in my stomach like a stone. Mr. McKenzie returned a moment later with Officer Russo. He was the only police officer in Downers Grove and a friend of my father's. His brown hair was just turning gray, and he'd gained some weight since I'd seen him last. He didn't have his uniform on, but he still came in and sat down as if this were his interrogation room. Mr. McKenzie handed him a beer.

"Hear you've got a story to tell me, Tommy," Officer Russo said.

Believe you me, the last thing I wanted was to rehash what I'd done, but when a cowboy has a nasty horse to shoe, he just tries to get it over with as quickly as possible. So I started talking and when I was done telling him about finding and planting the paper, Officer Russo shook his head.

"Tommy, Tommy, Tommy. Where did you find this paper?" he asked.

"On the paper drive."

"So we don't know where it came from?"

"No," I admitted. "But I didn't throw the brick. Or paint the window. Really I didn't!"

"I believe you, Tommy," said Mr. McKenzie.

Officer Russo clucked his tongue. "This kind of nonsense takes time away from us pursuing real criminals, like the Rosenbergs. Or Alger Hiss." He shook his head. "Your dad would be most disappointed if he found out."

"Please don't tell him," I said. "I mean with my sister, he . . ."

Officer Russo glanced at Mr. McKenzie.

Mr. McKenzie stared at me a long time. Then he turned to look at Officer Russo. "As long as you pay no more heed to Mr. Sullivan's story," he said finally, "let's just keep this between the four of us."

"No," said Officer Russo. "We need to let people know who put that paper there. Might help clear your name."

"Do you really think that'll help?" Mr. McKenzie asked.

Officer Russo took another long sip of his beer. "You know," he said, "you're right. It probably won't. Once a rumor gets started . . ."

"Then if anyone asks, let's just say one of the schoolboys did it. Doesn't matter who," Mr. McKenzie said firmly.

"Fine with me," Officer Russo agreed.

Relief washed over me like rain after a storm in a dry canyon. "Thank you, Mr. McKenzie." I wasn't quite sure why he was helping me. Probably because he felt sorry for my sister. But in any case, I was grateful.

Mr. McKenzie nodded. "Go on, Sam. Walk Tommy out."

Little Skinny made a face, but he stood up and walked me to the front. With one hand on the door, I turned to Little

80

Skinny. I'd dodged all sorts of bullets that day, but there was one more thing I was wondering. "Why didn't you tell your dad I hit you?"

Little Skinny snorted.

"But you could have gotten me expelled."

"You think that would make a difference?" he snapped. "You think the others would have been nicer to me?" He looked down again. "It's the same everywhere. I've changed schools a bunch of times. I've told my dad. He doesn't do anything. He just tells me to toughen up." The spark went out of his eyes and the scar seemed to overwhelm his face.

I didn't know what to say. "It's too bad about your mom," I muttered finally.

"Yeah, well." He paused. "Your sister said hello and smiled at me on the first day of school. She was the only one who did that. She seemed nice."

"Yeah," I agreed. "She's pretty special."

"Is her face burned?" he asked suddenly.

"No," I said. "Just a little mark on her forehead. Her legs are the worst."

"Good," he said. "Legs can be covered. Not faces."

For the first time, I really looked at his scar. It was just red, puckered skin. Nothing really scary at all. Kind of like when you pick a scab off your elbow and it's not quite healed yet. Were Mary Lou's legs like that too? One huge big scab that would be picked off?

"Any idea who the communist really is?" Little Skinny wondered aloud.

"What?" I asked.

"I mean, you said you found it on the paper drive."

He had been listening.

"That means it had to belong to someone in our neighborhood."

"Yeah!" I agreed.

"Maybe if you could find out who the real communist is, people might believe it's not my dad."

I thought about what Little Skinny had said as I walked home. I owed Mr. McKenzie now. For stealing the yo-yos. And getting his window broken. And most of all, for not telling my dad about the paper. A cowboy always paid his debts. Maybe I *should* try to figure out who the communist was. Gary Cooper followed his gut. And if I had to place a bet, I'd put my money on the Russian lady who lived next door.

13

THE DEAL

The question was, how could I get into the Russian lady's house and find something, a membership card or another newspaper, that would prove she was the communist? Even though she lived next door—and had for years—we weren't exactly friendly. I needed a reason to go and talk to her.

On the first of October, Sister Ann provided me with the perfect excuse. Every year St. Joe's raised money to send to Catholic missions around the world by having a magazine sale. The Russians were our allies during the war, you know. They helped our boys liberate Poland and Hungary and Czechoslovakia from the Nazis. But once the war was over, the Soviets stayed and took over the local governments in those countries. As Sister Ann put it, "It is a race to save the souls of all those poor people in Eastern Europe from the Red Menace, those godless communists in the Soviet Union." That was why we needed to support the missions—to fight the spread of communism, to help stop its slow creep across Europe.

In any case, we were supposed to go door-to-door to all our friends and neighbors to see how many magazine subscriptions we could sell. So that night after dinner, I set out. My plan was to visit everyone on Mary Lou's paper route, saving the Russian lady for last. The truth was, now that I was actually going to do it, I was a little scared. I mean, I'd never spoken to a real live communist before. It was like I was in the movies and I was on a secret mission.

The first few families each purchased several magazines. Ma and Pa bought *Woman's Day, American Rifleman* and *Boys' Life* (for their grandson, of course). I felt a little envious. He only visited them on holidays and in the summer, and yet they were willing to pay for the magazine for the whole year. I imagined them saving the extra issues in a closet and presenting them to him when he arrived.

I moved on to the next house, but the old lady I visited there refused to buy a thing—not even *Look* or *Life,* and everybody bought those. I couldn't get her to budge, not until I mentioned my poor sister Mary Lou, and how she was still in the hospital. Then she couldn't pull out her wallet fast enough. I felt a little guilty about that, but I shook it off.

The seamstress, Mrs. Scully, bought three subscriptions: *Life, House & Garden* and *Model Railroader.*

"Who's that one for?" I asked.

"Oh," said Mrs. Scully, blushing a little. "*Model Railroader* is for me."

"Really?" I asked.

She nodded. "My husband"—she crossed herself—"God bless his rotten soul. When he wasn't spending all his money on booze, he bought model train cars. Hundreds of them. He had a whole basement full of them." She shrugged. "Funny, it bugged me no end when he was alive. But now, I kind of like them."

It was fully dark by the time I walked up the path at the Russian lady's house. Except it wasn't really a path. There were no paving stones, just a piece of plywood thrown over a big muddy patch in the front yard. There was accordion music coming from inside, a lively polka. She sounded as good as Dick Contino. If I could sell her a magazine, it would give me an excuse to come to her house again. And if I could search her house and find another newspaper, or a communist party membership card or a telegram from Moscow, maybe I could use that evidence to clear Mr. McKenzie's name.

I had to knock on her door three times before she answered it, wearing a shapeless dress so faded, I couldn't tell what color it might have once been. "Why should I buy?" she asked when I finished my pitch. Her wispy white hair swayed in the evening breeze like cobwebs.

I lowered my eyes and put a pious yet tearful look on my face. "You know, my sister Mary Lou is still in the hospital."

"I know," she said. "Does her no good if I buy copy."

That may have been true, but no one else had dared to say it. "Well, then, uh . . . *Life* tells you what's going on in the world."

"In English. I no read good."

"What?" I asked. "You get the paper."

"To learn!" she said. "To see pictures. Read headlines."

"Well, that's fine, then. *Life* has lots of great pictures!"

She gave me a funny look.

"You don't have to read it," I insisted.

"No," she said firmly. "Why I buy magazine I no read? Stupid." She crossed her arms in front of her huge bosom.

"Maybe you should learn to read English."

"Of course I should learn." She sighed. "Why you think I get paper for five years!"

"Can I come in and show you—"

"No!"

"Well," I said slowly, coming up with an even better idea, one that would definitely get me in her house. "I could teach you to read English."

"You?"

"Sure."

"I no take charity," she said.

"Oh, it wouldn't be charity," I said. "We'd trade."

"Trade what?"

I thought fast. I couldn't exactly ask her to teach me all about communism. But I did remember the music I always heard coming from her house. "I'll teach you to read English," I said. "And you can teach me to play the accordion."

I grinned.

She gave me another funny look. "You want learn accordion?"

"Of course!" Actually, I'd never considered it before. But I remembered Mom playing the Dick Contino records around the house. I was pretty sure she'd love the idea.

"Okay," she said finally. "I buy the *Saturday Evening Post*." She grinned back at me, her mouth full of rotten teeth. "Such pretty pictures. You come by Sunday afternoon, we start our lessons."

86

It wasn't until I was walking in my front door that I realized I'd committed to going into a communist's house. To spend time with her. She might corrupt me. Brainwash me into becoming a supporter of the Soviet Union. It felt dangerous—and a little bit exciting too.

I was right. Mom loved the idea when I told her about it the next evening after dinner.

"Yes, yes," she exclaimed, "then you can play carols at Christmas. And 'Auld Lang Syne' on New Year's Eve! Just like Busia used to do." Her eyes brightened at that. "Come with me."

I followed Mom into the hall and up the little pull-down ladder that led into the attic. We rarely went up there. There were just a bunch of boxes, including one of Dad's old papers from his semester at college. Every time the paper drive rolled around, Mom begged him to get rid of it. But he never did. I think having it there made him feel smart.

We climbed past the boxes. You had to be careful in the attic. There wasn't really a floor, only boards laid across the rafters. If you accidentally stepped off the wooden planks, you'd go straight through the ceiling.

"There!" Mom pointed to a large, squat suitcase in the corner.

It took a bit of careful shoving and pushing, but finally I managed to get the suitcase down the ladder.

"What is it?" I asked Mom, whose eyes were gleaming like Pinky's when she's given a lollipop.

"Open it and see," she said.

I carefully undid the three rusted clasps.

It was an accordion. A big, shiny one. The bellows flashed red, gold and green as I pushed the air in and out.

"It was your grandfather's," Mom said, giving me a rare hug. "You never got to meet him, because he died before you were born. But he'd be so happy if he could see you with his accordion today."

And here's the worst thing about my mom's moods: there she was, acting completely nice and normal. And instead of enjoying it, all I could think was, great, how long is it going to last this time?

14

TEA FOR TWO

Sunday after church, I found myself lugging the accordion on my old red wagon next door to the Russian lady's house. According to the paper route cards, her name was Mrs. Anastasia Glazov. The pumpkins in her vegetable garden were enormous. Carefully, I rolled the wagon over the plank that led to the front door. The plank rattled loudly and suddenly the door opened.

"What you doing here?" Mrs. Glazov asked, hands on her hips. She was wearing either the same dress as before or another one that was equally faded.

"I promised to teach you to read."

She scowled. "That lie you told to get me buy magazine."

"No," I protested. "I'm here, aren't I?"

She gestured to the suitcase. "What this?"

"An accordion." I grinned. "You're still going to teach me to play, right?"

Finally, she threw her head back and laughed. "Fine. Come in. I make you tea."

So with a touch of fear and a touch of excitement (I was going to root out a real live communist!), I ducked into her little wooden shack, lifting the accordion off the wagon and placing it just inside the door.

The only light came from the window and one kerosene lamp. The walls were the same rough-hewn wood that could be seen outside. The room was neat and tidy enough, but there wasn't much furniture, just a small wooden table and three plain, hard chairs. Everywhere there were piles of magazines and newspapers. I didn't see any copies of the *Daily Worker,* but surely she wouldn't leave them out in plain view. A large wood-burning stove sat in one corner. It heated the room, and I guess she also cooked on it.

On the stove was a fat, barrel-shaped pot. But it was too pretty to be a normal kettle. It looked like copper, shiny, with little carvings all over it. On top of the barrel sat a teapot. Mrs. Glazov caught me looking at it.

"My samovar," she announced proudly. "Nazis take my old one, send me work camp. Me! Old woman. But I survive. And when I arrive in America, first thing I do, I buy new samovar."

Mr. McKenzie had said he was in a camp with communists. She had to be the one! But I needed proof.

"Sit!" she told me.

So I did. Mrs. Glazov brought over a plate of tiny sandwiches, open-faced, with pats of butter. Some had ham or green vegetables that looked like cucumbers on top. On the table there was also a sugar bowl and a plate of lemons, sliced so thin, you could practically see right through them.

"Didn't think you come," she said, blushing. "But hoped."

I didn't know what to say.

"How you like your tea?" she asked.

"Uhhh," I said. I didn't usually drink tea.

"Not too strong for growing boy," she said. She picked up a cup, or actually it was a half cup made of metal, and inserted a plain glass inside. Then she took the teapot from the top of the samovar and poured a thick black liquid into the glass. Only a little, just so it barely covered the bottom. Then she replaced the teapot and added some hot water to the glass from a little spout near the bottom of the samovar.

"Now you drink," she said.

Drink? I didn't want to drink. But if a cowboy was trying to make friends with a tribe of Indians, he had to smoke the peace pipe when it was offered. My heart was beating fast, faster than I expected. She was just a little old lady. But Soviet spies were devious. They could look like anyone.

"Drink!" she ordered again.

Automatically, I took a sip. It scalded my tongue and though I tried not to, I guess I made a face.

"You add sugar and lemon." She laughed. "Soon, you love it!"

I waited a moment to see if I would suddenly collapse in searing pain. I mean, I didn't really think she was trying to poison me, but imagining that she might be made the whole situation more exciting.

When she started to pour herself a glass (she put a whole lot of the black stuff and only a little water in her cup), I figured I was probably okay. So I added about half the bowl of sugar and a bunch of lemon slices. When I took another sip, it tasted like hot lemonade.

"Now," she said, sitting down at the table, "you teach me read."

Oh yeah. I guess I'd kind of thought I'd find proof immediately and wouldn't need to hold up my side of the bargain. But I'd been in her house a whole ten minutes and I hadn't found a thing. "What do you want to read?"

"You bring comic book?" she asked.

"No."

"Boys always read comic book."

"Yeah, I like to read them, but . . . I don't have one with me today."

She sighed. "Bring next time. Today we start with paper."

"Which one?"

She gestured at the piles on the table. "Take your pick."

I jumped up. This was my chance. I thumbed through every pile, but I didn't find anything. Only the *Chicago Tribune* and some magazine in Russian that seemed to be devoted entirely to tea, cooking and flowers.

"Tommy, I not know how read any of them. Pick one!"

I finally grabbed a *Tribune* at random and pointed to a headline. "Uhhh. Sound this out."

What came out of her mouth made absolutely no sense. She sounded like Pinky trying to talk with a mouthful of marbles.

"No," I said. "It says, New Restaurant Opens."

"*Restaurant* same word in Russian," she said sadly. "But spelled all different."

"How do you write it in Russian?"

She picked up a pencil and wrote in the margin of the paper: *pectopah.*

92

"*Pectopah*?" I said.

"No," she insisted. "Restaurant."

"But it starts with a *p*," I said.

"Start with *r-r-r-r* sound."

"*P* makes an *r-r-r-r* sound in Russian?" I asked.

"Yes, of course!" she said. "Not in English?"

"No," I said.

"Ahh," she cried, resting her forehead on the table. "English too hard. By time I learn to read, I too old to see."

"No," I scoffed. "You just need to start with the alphabet."

I wrote out the alphabet on the back of the paper and told her all the sounds. I had to admit, Mrs. Glazov learned fast. I went over the alphabet three times, all the English letters and the sounds they made, and by then she knew them pretty well. It was kind of fun. I was about to teach her a couple of words when she pushed the paper aside and said, "Now your turn."

"To do what?" I asked.

"Learn from me," she said.

She stood up and pulled a huge accordion out from under the table. It was almost as big as she was, with black and white keys like on a piano running down one side and tiny buttons on the other.

"No, no," I insisted. "You don't have to—"

"I no take charity!" She hefted the accordion up like it weighed nothing at all and put the straps around her arms. Then she came back to sit on the chair.

"First, you listen."

She started playing a song. A happy song, like the polkas Mom sometimes played on the record player. Mom and Dad used to push the coffee table aside and start dancing, right in the living room. Once when I was six years old, my father asked Mary Lou to dance. As they polkaed across the floor, my mom picked me up and spun me around. We all laughed and laughed, flying across the carpet in time with the music.

When Mrs. Glazov finally stopped, she asked, "You like, Tommy?"

"Yes," I admitted.

"You get yours out now," she said.

So I did. And she showed me how to hold it and pull the bellows out nice and smooth, and even play a chord or two. And the best thing was that while I was playing the accordion, I didn't think about Mary Lou or Mr. McKenzie or my mom or anything else. I just focused on the music.

When I was done with my lesson, Mrs. Glazov gave me a pumpkin to take home, twice as big as my head. Mom broke out in a huge grin when she saw it. "Get out the flour, Tommy. We're going to make a pie."

As we mixed and baked, my thoughts were mixed up too. I knew communists were bad and evil. I knew they wanted to deny us, and even their own people, freedom of speech. Commies didn't believe in freedom of religion either. Heck, they didn't believe in religion at all. The Reds wanted to take all the businesses away from their owners and give them to the government. According to Mr. Sullivan, they might even be planning to drop an atomic bomb on Chicago! So why did I kind of like Mrs. Glazov? What was wrong with me?

15

TALKING TO MARY LOU

The next day, Monday, October 5, I was finally going to be allowed to visit Mary Lou. The first skin-graft operation had gone well and she was feeling a little better. It had been exactly three weeks since she'd gotten burned. Pinky and I had spent nearly every afternoon after school sitting in the hospital lobby. Mom wrapped up a couple of slices of pumpkin pie for me to eat with Mary Lou. I carried them carefully up the stairs and paused for a moment outside her door. The sun was shining in a hallway window, making the floor glow orange, just like Mary Lou had, just before she started shrieking.

"Who's there?" Mary Lou's voice called out. "Is someone lurking outside my door?"

She sounded like her old self. I shook off the memory of her screams and stepped inside her room.

"Tommy!"

Mary Lou was propped up on a bunch of pillows so she was half sitting, half lying on the bed. Her brown eyes were bright and clear this time. The scar on her forehead looked like a smudge of pink paint. I didn't dare look at her legs.

"It's so good to see you!" she exclaimed, a smile creeping over her face.

Until that moment, I hadn't realized how worried I'd been. "You're awake," I said.

"Of course I'm awake," she said. "I couldn't be talking to you otherwise."

I smiled.

"Is everything okay?" she asked. "I mean, are you managing okay at home with—"

"It's fine," I said. Of course that would be Mary Lou's first question.

"Who's giving Pinky her bath?" she demanded.

"Me."

"And are you really doing the paper route?"

"Yep."

"Be careful. At first it's kind of hard to balance with all those papers."

"Yeah," I said. "I learned that one the hard way."

We both giggled. She was the same old bossy Mary Lou. "Hey," I said, "Mom made pie. Want some?"

"Sure." She struggled to sit up a little straighter and winced in pain.

I put the pie down on a side table. "Let me help you with—"

"I got it," she snapped. She struggled a bit more and the blanket over her legs fell off the bed.

I couldn't help staring. Her legs were covered in enough bandages for an elephant. Each one was almost as thick as her torso.

Mary Lou noticed. "They look bad, don't they?"

"No," I lied.

"Tommy," she sighed.

I avoided her gaze and didn't answer. They looked about fifty times worse than I'd imagined. How would she ever walk again if her legs were so swollen and . . .

"Hand me that pillow?" Mary Lou pointed to a pillow on a nearby chair.

I grabbed it and helped prop her up, grateful to have something to do.

Mary Lou resettled the blanket over her legs. I felt awful that *she* was trying to make *me* feel better. "Want some pie?"

"Sure," she said.

I handed her a piece. We ate quietly for a minute.

"It's good, isn't it?" I said, just to break the silence.

"Mom's pies always are." Mary Lou took another bite. "Did you know that wool doesn't burn easily?"

"No."

"Yeah. The doctor said my wool sweater probably saved my life. It was why I didn't have more burns on my stomach and my back." Her voice was calm and conversational, as if we were discussing the Lone Ranger, but there were tears on her cheeks, magnifying each of her freckles as they rolled by. "They took skin from my back for the grafts. I'm going to have a big scar there too. And on my stomach when they take the skin for the second graft. Sometimes, it hurts so bad I . . ."

She stopped talking.

I reached over and took her hand.

"I'm scared, Tommy," she said finally. "I'm so scared. I can't even walk!"

97

"I know."

The sun was still shining orange through the window. She turned her head to look at it.

All I could think of was the orange blooming of the paper as it caught fire. "If I'd just taken out the trash . . ."

"It's not your fault," she said, wiping her eyes.

"Mom said it was." I kind of thought it was too.

Mary Lou snorted, then winced in pain. "Mom always looks to find someone else to blame."

That was true.

Mary Lou forced a smile and took a couple more bites of pie. "And what about school?" she said. "Are you behaving?"

I'd planned to tell her all about stealing the yo-yos and hitting Little Skinny as soon as she woke up. I wanted to get it off my chest. But now it didn't seem right to put any extra burden on her.

"Yeah," I lied. "I've been an angel."

16

HALLOWEEN, PART 1

Halloween was approaching and I was going trick-or-treating as a cowboy, of course. Eddie was planning on being a cowboy too, but I had the better costume: chaps, a vest, a hat, even spurs I could attach to my new genuine leather cowboy boots. I was just showing him the star Mary Lou had given me when Peter and Luke rushed over.

"Tommy, Tommy," Luke cried. "Did you see the note in yesterday's *Downers Grove Reporter*?"

Of course I'd seen it. The local paper was published once a week, which meant on Thursdays I had three papers to deliver, not two. But I took the clipping from him and glanced at it.

𝕯𝖔𝖜𝖓𝖊𝖗𝖘 𝕲𝖗𝖔𝖛𝖊 𝕽𝖊𝖕𝖔𝖗𝖙𝖊𝖗

Thursday, October 15, 1953

Mary Lou Wilson suffered severe second-degree burns when her skirt caught fire last month. She is a patient

at St. Charles Hospital. According to the latest reports, she is progressing satisfactorily and is expected home this weekend.

She wasn't coming home this weekend. I knew that. The day after I'd visited Mary Lou last week, she'd had the second skin-graft operation. It hadn't gone well. She'd developed an infection and had been put in isolation. Mom had kind of fallen apart, her optimism collapsing like a bubble in a cake. I wanted to cry too, but someone had to give Pinky her bath and feed Boots and deliver the papers. Mom had spent most of the past week in bed, complaining of back pain or headaches. Twice I came home from school to find Pinky still in her pajamas. I always got her dressed before Dad came home.

Mom and Dad had gotten in a huge fight over the newspaper article last night. "Why did you talk to that stupid columnist?" Dad had exclaimed. "Why did you say such a thing? Now everyone will be asking us when she's coming home!"

Mom only cried.

I thought it was pretty dumb of Dad to go on and on about it. I knew why Mom had said it. She wanted it to be true.

Luke's clipping had been cut out with pinking shears. The edges curled up as I held it.

"Wow," Eddie said as he read over my shoulder.

"Pretty cool," Peter said enviously. "I've never been in the paper."

I wanted to yell at him. *She almost died. It's not cool at all!* But I didn't say a word.

The article was passed around the circle. Even Little Skinny took a look at it. "She's not coming home this weekend," he said.

"That's what it says, stupid. It's in the paper," Eddie said.

He shook his head. "Not if she was burned as bad as they said she was. Those things take a long time to heal. I know." The scars on his face seemed to burn extra-red for a moment as he handed the slip of paper back to Luke.

"You don't know nothing," I said, even though I knew he was right. Somehow, his being right made me even angrier, and I gave him a shove. He lost his balance and fell into the dirt. It had rained the night before, and when he stood up, one side of his body was covered with mud.

When Sister Ann punished Little Skinny for getting dirty on the playground, I laughed like everyone else. But I kept seeing the scar on his face, glowing like a hot coal as he flushed red with embarrassment.

The rest of October flew by. Doing the paper route wasn't as bad as it had seemed at first. I liked being alone in the quiet of the morning, and Ma and Pa often gave me a cup of hot chocolate or a fresh hard-boiled egg. Mrs. Scully liked to get up and work early in the morning. As a joke, she'd started asking me my opinion of different fabric choices. I laughed the first time I saw one of the ladies at church wearing the style I'd picked out. Working at McKenzie's was more of a mixed bag. I liked restocking the shelves and scrubbing the floor, because when I was there, I didn't have to think about Mary Lou or my mother or anything else. I just completed the tasks I was given. And Mr. McKenzie always made me a sandwich when I was done. But there were fewer customers each week, and try as I could, that fact got harder and harder to ignore.

The best part of October were my Sunday afternoons with Mrs. Glazov. She was getting so she could read all of *Kid Colt Outlaw,* and even most of an article in the paper, if it didn't have too many big words. And I was getting really good at the accordion. Apparently, I had a hidden talent for it. Mrs. Glazov only had to show me a chord fingering once and somehow my hands knew what to do. It was really nice to be good at something.

I made no progress in proving that she was a communist. Sometimes, when I lay in bed at night, I wondered if I really wanted to. I liked her. If I did find evidence of a communist connection, maybe Officer Russo would arrest her and cart her off to jail. Surely that would bring the customers back to Mr. McKenzie. But sending an old woman to jail didn't sit quite right with me either. And if Mrs. Glazov were gone, who would teach me the accordion?

All month my thoughts went round in circles, like Boots chasing his tail. October 31 fell on a Saturday, so I spent Halloween day working at Mr. McKenzie's store. His shop was still full of candy. And costumes. But no customers. And while the hardware store and the drugstore and all the other shops on Main Street had Halloween displays in their windows, Mr. McKenzie's front display case was bare.

He caught me looking at it. "Usually the shop owners get the schoolkids to create a Halloween display for their windows," I told him.

"I know," said Mr. McKenzie. "I called St. Joe's, but no one ever got back to me." He was trying hard to sound like he didn't mind, but I knew he did.

Little Skinny was sitting bored behind the cash register. It *was* Halloween. Kind of felt like we should do something special.

"We'll do it," I said.

"Do what?" asked Little Skinny warily.

I made him go upstairs and find some old clothes. We stuffed them with a bale of hay. Little Skinny opened a can of paint and drew bats and skeletons on the front window.

"You can paint!" I marveled.

He shrugged. "Yeah, I guess I can."

I hadn't known that about him. It made me think of the accordion. I wondered if there were other hidden talents Little Skinny—or I—might have.

"All we need now is a pumpkin," said Mr. McKenzie, smiling a little.

"Give me twenty minutes," I said.

I rode my bike to Mrs. Glazov's house and banged on her door. The pumpkin she gave me barely fit in my basket, but somehow I managed to ride back to McKenzie's.

Little Skinny was excited. He studied the pumpkin from every angle before announcing, "That bump there. That'll be the wart on her nose." On the leathery orange skin he drew an elaborate witch with big, sharp teeth. He carved, I scooped out the goop and Mr. McKenzie baked the seeds in the oven.

When we were done, the three of us stood there admiring the pumpkin, crunching the hot, oily seeds between our teeth, grinning like the jack-o'-lantern. "It looks a little bit like Sister Ann," Little Skinny said.

I laughed. It did. It even had her pickle nose.

"But don't tell her I said that!" Little Skinny said nervously.

"Your secret's safe with me," I said, and pounded him on the back, just like I would have done with Eddie. It was only when he gave me a surprised look that I remembered that Little Skinny and I didn't like each other.

"It's a great window display," Mr. McKenzie said.

But though passersby stopped and looked and many of them smiled, very few of them opened the door and came inside.

When it was time to go, Mr. McKenzie shook my hand. "Thank you, Tommy," he said. "Sam and I haven't had that much fun in a long time."

"The display will be sure to bring the customers in!" I said.

His smile faded a little. "Yeah, maybe."

"Did you need me to speak to Officer Russo again?"

"No," he said quietly. "I don't think that did much good."

I'd had fun, but I felt awful as I walked home. Nothing I did seemed to make a difference. And I didn't know much about running a store, but I was pretty sure about one thing: you needed customers.

17

HALLOWEEN, PART 2

So I was already in a bad mood when I got home only to discover Dr. Stanton leaving our house, his white coat draped over one arm, his black bag in the other. I suddenly felt weak, as if I'd roped a runaway calf and it was taking all my strength just to hold on. "What's wrong?" I asked. "Is Mary Lou okay?"

"She's fine, as far as I know," Dr. Stanton said. "I was here checking on your mother."

Mom?

He tipped his hat at me. "Happy Halloween, Tommy." He got into his car and drove off.

Inside, Dad was sitting on the couch, a pile of papers spread out on the coffee table in front of him.

"What's wrong with Mom?" I asked.

Dad sighed. "According to Dr. Stanton, nothing. He can't find a reason for all her back pain and headaches. She needs to relax. Calm her nerves. He suggested we invite some of her friends over."

Did Mom have any friends? Sure, there were women she talked to at church, but . . .

"I thought we might have a card party next weekend," Dad continued.

Mom did like cards. Back before Busia had died, Eddie's parents, the Sullivans, had come over now and then to play bridge. But a party? With Mary Lou in the hospital? It seemed kind of wrong. I said as much to Dad.

He shook his head. "If Dr. Stanton thinks it's a good idea, it's worth a try."

I didn't agree, but I wasn't going to argue. I sat down next to Dad on the couch and picked up one of the papers. It was a bill from the hospital for $700. *Second notice,* it said. *Please pay promptly.* I wasn't that good at math, but I knew my dad made about $9000 in a year. "What's this, Dad?" I mean, I knew what it was, but . . .

Dad plucked the paper from my hand. "You don't need to worry about that."

So of course I started worrying. Seven hundred dollars was a lot of money!

"I'm afraid I need to go to the hospital tonight," Dad said as he started gathering up the papers. "Just need to talk to the doctors about . . ." He pasted on a grin so big, I knew it was fake. "I need you to stay home and watch Pinky and Susie."

"But Mom's here," I said. "And it's Halloween!"

"I know," Dad replied. "But Dr. Stanton gave her a pill and she probably won't wake up until tomorrow."

I nodded. What else could I do?

It was an awful evening. I gave Susie a bottle, made bologna sandwiches for dinner for Pinky and me and got ready to hand out candy to the trick-or-treaters who came to the front door. I dreaded seeing Eddie, but it was Little Skinny who showed up first.

He was dressed as a pirate with a black hat and an eye patch. His scar only added to the costume, almost making me believe he'd really been in a fight at sea. "Tommy," he said. "I thought you were going to be a cowboy."

"Mom got sick and Dad's at the hospital," I said. "I had to stay home and take care of my sisters."

"Oh," he said. "My dad's at the hospital too. Visiting Mother."

I knew I should ask how his mom was doing, but I was too upset about being forced to stay home. Instead, I gave Little Skinny a big handful of candy corn. I suddenly realized he was out trick-or-treating by himself. I wasn't sure I would have had the guts to go without my friends. I kind of admired him for it.

As soon as Little Skinny was gone, I turned off the porch light and didn't answer the door again.

"Sorry, Tommy," Pinky whispered as we sat in her bed eating the leftover candy corn. "I know you wanted to go get candy."

"It's not your fault," I said. But part of me wanted to yell at her anyway, just because she was there.

I checked on Mom after my sisters were in bed. She slept quietly, her black hair spread out peacefully on her pillow. Dad got home late. He smelled like whiskey. "Grabbed a drink with Mr. Sullivan," he said guiltily.

I shrugged and went to bed.

• • •

At school on Monday, Eddie, Luke and Peter were talking about all the fun they'd had, the treats they'd gotten and the tricks they'd played.

"Too bad you had to stay home," said Peter.

But I could tell by his tone that he didn't really mean it. I watched as Little Skinny showed up on the playground with a big bag of Halloween candy, and suddenly I had an idea.

"That's all right," I told Peter. "I'll just get some now."

I sauntered over to Little Skinny.

"Little Skinny," I said, "you're the one!"

"The one what?" he asked, confused. I didn't usually speak to him at school. Then again, we had had a nice time carving that pumpkin.

"The one who is going to give me his Halloween candy!" I snatched the bag from him.

"Hey!" he protested.

"You don't need this, fatty," I said, taking out a piece of chocolate and popping it into my mouth. "I'm doing you a favor."

Peter, Luke and Eddie laughed.

"It's mine!" Little Skinny tried to grab it back, but I jumped aside. He was heavier, of course, but I was nimbler and stronger.

"Guys," I called to Eddie and the choirboys. "Want some candy?"

I tossed candy to all of them.

"Give it back," cried Little Skinny. "It's mine!"

"Oh, you don't mind sharing, do you, Little Skinny?" I asked.

Tears started to run down his face, but still he stood there, watching us eat his candy.

Pretty soon, there was only the rotten stuff left, the jawbreakers and mints nobody wanted.

"Here you go," I said, handing the bag back to Little Skinny. "Thanks for the treats."

Little Skinny took the bag and dumped what was left onto the ground. "I was going to share it with you!" he yelled. His whole face was as red as his scar.

The candy sat like a stone in my stomach.

"I thought I was wrong about you," he spat. "But no. You really are a jerk."

He stormed off and all the boys laughed. Including me.

Eddie walked over and punched me on the shoulder. "Did you hear that? He was going to share it with you!"

I laughed again. A weird, hollow laugh, but no one seemed to notice.

18

THE PARTY

The party to improve my mother's nerves was scheduled for the first Saturday in November. Three couples had been invited for dinner and cards: the Colvins from church, the Starrs from my dad's work and Mr. and Mrs. Sullivan.

Dad set up two card tables in the living room, one for the men and one for the women. I helped Mom peel potatoes and carrots for the pot roast. Once it was in the oven, Mom went back to bed, complaining of a headache. Dad ironed the tablecloths and I filled little bowls with peanuts. Pinky and Susie entertained themselves on the living room floor, playing with a bowl and a spoon, while Boots kept an eye on everyone from under a chair.

In the late afternoon Dad went to wake Mom. Behind the closed door I could hear yelling. But by six o'clock, it seemed like Mom had pulled things together. She was dressed, the table was set and the food was ready. Everything went smoothly at first. When the grown-ups were finished eating, they all went into the living room to play cards.

Once I put Pinky and Susie to bed, I had to do the dishes. From the kitchen, I could hear the conversation.

"My compliments on your dinner," Mrs. Starr said. Her dark hair was short and she wore a pearl necklace over her black dress.

"Thank you," said Mom. "McKenzie's had a good cut of meat and I just—"

"McKenzie's?" interrupted Mrs. Sullivan. Eddie's mom was a small woman, with shoulder-length brown hair, cat's-eye glasses and a thin, raspy voice. "Why did you go there?"

"He's the closest grocer," said Mom.

"Oh," whispered Mrs. Colvin, a plump blond woman in an ugly lace dress. "I stopped going there."

"McKenzie?" Mr. Sullivan, at the other table, sniffed. He was already on his third beer. "He's lucky they didn't arrest him and send him to Sing Sing like the Rosenbergs."

The Rosenbergs were the spies who'd inspired our game of electric-chair tag.

"You know, Catherine," Mrs. Sullivan whispered, "my husband was the one who found the copy of the *Daily Worker* in his store."

"Come now," said my dad. "I heard that was a prank. One of the schoolboys."

I suddenly felt short of breath, as if a hammer and sickle were tattooed on my forehead.

"Isn't that exactly what he'd say if he really *were* a commie?" asked Mr. Starr.

"Please," my dad said. "An old newspaper is no evidence. Don't be a McCarthy."

"I like McCarthy," said Mr. Sullivan. "He cleaned up the State Department."

"McCarthy is a cowboy," said my father. He spat the word "cowboy" as if it were another term for criminal.

"Well," Mr. Colvin said, "his numbers do keep changing. First it was 205 communists in the State Department, then 57, then 81."

"McCarthy is a hero," Mrs. Sullivan added, peering over the tops of her glasses. "If you ask me, even one communist in the State Department is one too many."

"He's been investigating for years and they've never found a single one," my father replied.

"They just don't want publicity is all," said Mr. Sullivan. "I bet they've found plenty."

"Oh my," said my mom loudly. "I didn't mean to start such a fuss. I only went to McKenzie's because the meat was on *sale*."

Everyone laughed.

"I hope it was a going-out-of-business sale," Mr. Sullivan muttered.

I walked into the living room to refill the nut bowls.

"How is Mary Lou doing?" asked Mrs. Colvin.

I froze. Just mentioning Mary Lou was often enough to set Mom off. But she stayed calm. "Fine, thank you. We had a minor setback last month, but she's doing well now."

Mrs. Colvin nodded. "We're praying for her. Be sure to let us know if there's anything we can do."

Mom bit her lip so hard, a drop of blood welled up. "Please excuse me," she said. "I need to whip the cream for the pie."

I followed Mom back into the kitchen. She whipped the

cream so hard and long, her arm turned red. "I think it's done, Mom," I said quietly.

She didn't respond.

"Mom." I touched her arm gently.

She jumped as if she hadn't even known I was there. The bowl fell to the floor. "Now look at what you've done!" she yelled.

I knelt down and started mopping up the mess.

Mrs. Starr wandered into the kitchen. "Is everything okay?"

"Yes," Mom said. "Tommy just made me drop the whipped cream."

"Let me help clean—"

"No," Mom snapped. "Tommy can do it."

"But it's really no bother."

Mrs. Sullivan and Mrs. Colvin poked their heads into the kitchen. "What's all the fuss?" joked Mrs. Sullivan.

"Nothing!" The vein popped out on Mom's forehead. She was embarrassed, and when she was embarrassed, the best thing was to leave her alone. But I realized these ladies were just acquaintances, not real friends, and they didn't know that.

"Oh dear, you had a little spill," said Mrs. Colvin. "Let me just help—"

"I said, everything's fine!" Mom roared.

I stared at the floor and scrubbed a spot that was already clean just so I wouldn't have to stand up. Out of the corner of my eye, I saw the three women glance at one another as if they were trying to figure out what to do.

"We were just trying to help," Mrs. Starr said.

"Help?" Mom sneered. "By sashaying in here with your fancy pearls!"

Mrs. Starr's hand automatically went to her necklace.

"You think you're so much better than us because you have a little money," Mom taunted.

Mrs. Starr turned pale. "They are fake," she said finally. "I just thought they were pretty." She turned on her heel and walked out.

"Catherine," Mrs. Colvin chided gently, "that wasn't very polite."

"Oh yeah?" Mom said. "And what do you know about good manners? Mrs. Starr might be a snob, but at least she didn't show up to my dinner party in a dress that looks like it was made from a tablecloth!"

I've got to hand it to my mom. She does know how to insult people.

Anyway, Mrs. Colvin turned as red as Little Skinny's scar. She gave a little gasp and marched into the living room. "It's time to go," I heard her tell her husband.

Mrs. Sullivan, still in the kitchen, sighed. "Catherine, Catherine. You're having a bad evening."

"I'm not!"

"I hope you feel better soon," Mrs. Sullivan told my mother.

"And your glasses are ugly too!" Mom called out.

Mrs. Sullivan laughed nervously in the living room.

I was horribly embarrassed. I picked up the bowl and went over to the sink to wash it. The front door squeaked open and closed a couple of times, and I could hear good-byes being said. Mom sat down at the kitchen table and began to cry, but I didn't look at her.

After a minute, Dad came into the kitchen. "What happened?" he demanded. "We were having such a nice evening."

Mom only cried harder.

"Tommy?" Dad asked.

I shrugged.

"Tommy made me drop the whipped cream!" Mom announced.

As if that were the real problem. As if she hadn't just insulted all our guests for offering to help.

"You're crying over whipped cream?" Dad asked.

Mom was hysterical now, sobs breaking in between each syllable. "You . . . don't . . . understand!"

"No, I don't," said Dad.

Mom gave a cry of frustration and ran off. I heard her door slam.

"Party didn't work out so well, did it?" I asked.

"Shut up, Tommy." Dad looked old and tired. "Just do the dishes."

He walked off after Mom. I gathered up the plates and glasses from the living room and cursed Dr. Stanton and his stupid idea.

Sunday afternoon, I was playing the accordion at Mrs. Glazov's again, but I kept missing notes. "We stop now," she said finally.

"No, I want to get it," I said.

Mrs. Glazov shook her head. "You no play good today. We sit and drink tea and talk."

I put the accordion away, and poured myself a glass of tea with sugar and lemon. As I stirred, the tea splashed over the edge of the cup, running down like the tears on Little Skinny's face when I'd taken his candy.

"Talk!" Mrs. Glazov demanded.

I wanted to talk to someone. That's what I missed most about Mary Lou. She was always there to listen to me and cheer me up. And the reason she wasn't there, the reason she was in the hospital, well, that was because I had been too lazy to take out the trash.

I couldn't tell Mrs. Glazov about the dinner party. Or planting the paper. But maybe I could tell her about taking the candy. Maybe that would help. "There's this boy at school," I said slowly. "Little Skinny."

"Little Skinny?"

"His real name's Sam," I said.

"He too thin?"

"No, actually he's fat."

"Why you call him skinny?"

"It's a joke."

"Ahh. Joke," she said dryly. "Go on, go on."

"I didn't like him. I don't like him. Sometimes, Eddie and I and the choirboys, we tease him."

"Ahh," she said again. "He laugh too?"

I shook my head. I knew what Mary Lou would say. *Shame on you, Tommy! Picking on that poor boy.* And now she would have scars just like him. How would I feel if someone picked on her?

"What did you do?" Mrs. Glazov asked, her voice soft, like a priest at confession. It surprised me. I'd never heard her sound so gentle.

"I took some candy from him," I admitted.

"You stole it."

I shrugged.

"Ahh."

"It's not my fault! If Mary Lou had been there, I never would have done it!"

Mrs. Glazov laughed. "You don't need sister. You need conscience."

I had the horrible feeling that she was right. I wasn't a cowboy at all. I was an outlaw.

19

SPEEDING TICKET

The second Tuesday in November, I was finally able to see Mary Lou again after the skin-graft infection. This time, she did not look like herself at all. Her face was thin, her eyes hollow, and even her freckles seemed faded to only specks of dust.

"Hey, Tommy," she said. Her eyes welled up with tears.

I couldn't look at her. The sky was overcast. It looked like it might rain, or if it was cold enough, maybe even snow.

"Say something," Mary Lou ordered.

What should I say? *Mom fell apart at the card party in front of all our neighbors? I stole Little Skinny's candy when he was trying to be nice? I planted a commie newspaper at McKenzie's and now he has no customers? I still feel awful that you got hurt trying to help me?* "I'm learning to play the accordion," I said finally.

"Really?" said Mary Lou. She sat up a little straighter.

"Yeah," I said. "Mrs. Glazov, that's the Russian lady who lives next door, she's teaching me. She says I'm good at it."

Mary Lou smiled and looked more like herself again.

118

"Will you bring it to the hospital sometime? Maybe play a few songs for me?"

"Sure."

She bit her lip, just like Mom had done at the party. Her skin looked so thin, I was afraid her lip might start bleeding too. "Every day here is the same. There's nothing to do." She pressed her palms to her eyes, as if she were trying to force the tears back inside. "This is so embarrassing! I promised myself I wouldn't start crying."

"Hey," I said, sitting down on the edge of the bed. "It's just me."

"I know." She picked at a stray thread on the edge of the white pillowcase. "I just wanted to finish eighth grade with my friends," she whispered.

I thought about Eddie and Peter and Luke moving on a grade, leaving me behind.

"Mom dropped out, you know," Mary Lou continued. "She never finished eighth grade."

And I could hear what my sister didn't say: *I'm afraid I'm going to end up just like her.*

"No matter what," I said, "you'll never be like Mom. You're too nice."

Mary Lou sighed, and laid her head on my shoulder. "But she must have been nice too, once. I mean, why else did Dad marry her?"

I thought about that for a minute. "She makes good pies."

Mary Lou giggled. "Yeah. And she likes to dance."

"Sometimes." I took a deep breath. "Is Mom acting strange?" I asked. "I mean, when she's here with you."

"Yeah," said Mary Lou. "She's acting nice. Braiding my hair. Reading me books. Like I'm a baby."

"Oh." I wanted to tell her how Mom was changing at home. But if she started acting nicer to me, would she be meaner to Mary Lou?

Mary Lou sighed again. "Thanks for coming, Tommy. You always cheer me up."

I didn't want to make my sister worry. So I didn't say a word.

That night, Mom made an unusual turn on the way home from the hospital. "Where are we going?" I asked.

"I have an errand to run," Mom said, in a tone that clearly meant, *Don't you dare ask me any more questions.*

But we didn't stop at the dry cleaner or the market. Instead, Mom turned into a parking lot in front of a small gray building. It wasn't until we walked inside and through the door labeled TRAFFIC COURT that I realized where we were. We sat down on a row of pew-like benches and waited.

"Catherine Wilson?" called the judge, after what seemed like hours.

"Yes, sir," said my mother, handing Susie to me and standing up.

"He's wearing a black bathrobe!" Pinky exclaimed.

I shushed her, but apparently not fast enough, because the policeman at the end of the row glared at us.

"You received a speeding ticket on the morning of Tuesday, October 6, 1953?" the judge asked.

"Yes, sir." My mother walked forward and smoothed her hair back, although as far as I could see, it was already arranged perfectly. "I need to explain. You see, I was going to visit my daughter in the hospital and—"

"Were you speeding?" he asked.

"Maybe," she said. "But—"

"The ticket stands." He stamped the folder and passed it to his assistant.

The officer came over to lead Mom back to her seat, but when he touched her arm, she jerked away. "But my daughter was going to have surgery!"

"Next time, I suggest you leave home earlier," said the judge evenly.

"Listen here, you *pieprzony dupku!*"

I sank down in my seat. Once Mom started swearing in Polish, all you could do was stay out of her way.

"Madam, watch your—"

Mom stood up even taller, her eyes blazing. "My daughter was burned over forty percent of her body! You can't tell me—"

The judge banged his gavel twice on his desk. "Calm down or I will have you removed."

"I'll not let a *dupku* like you tell me to calm down!"

I watched as the judge, who was nearly bald, turned a bright shade of red, from his neck to his ears to the very crown of his head. "Unfortunately for you, madam," he said, "I speak Polish as well. And you will not disrespect this court's authority with your cursing!" He turned to the policeman. "Take her away."

The policeman took her arm and didn't let go this time. He dragged her off, and as he did, I noticed a vein bulging on her forehead, just like it had when she beat me for stealing the yo-yos and at the dinner party too. It was like a little warning sign that Mom was about to lose her temper, except it always came a couple of moments too late. Mom was still yelling curse words in Polish as the officer pushed her through a side door and she disappeared.

The room was quiet.

The judge sighed. "Next case."

Pinky and I sat there frozen and listened to the next case: a man who had had too much to drink had backed his car into his neighbor's bed of prize-winning roses. Susie slept on.

"Where's Mommy?" Pinky asked finally, in a voice so low, I could barely hear her.

I shook my head. I didn't know what to do. We listened to two more cases, before I realized no one was coming to get us. I didn't have any money to take the bus home. I didn't even have a dime to call my dad. It was up to me to get us home, so when the next case was over, I stood up. "Sir," I called out.

The judge glanced around the room, before letting his eyes rest on me. "What is it, boy?"

"My mother—"

"Speak up, boy!"

"You took my mom somewhere, sir. I'm not sure how my sisters and I are going to get home."

"And I need to go potty!" added Pinky, standing on the bench next to me.

Everyone laughed. Even the policeman cracked a smile. But the judge remained stern. "Your mom is the Polish-cursing speeder?"

"Yes, sir."

He turned toward the policeman. "How long has she been in there?"

"'Bout an hour, Your Honor."

He sighed. "I'm sure she's calmed down by now. Let her out, have her pay her fine and take these kids home."

I thought we were doomed for sure, like soldiers at the Alamo, but Mom seemed okay when they brought us to her. The lady at reception where she was paying her bill was young with dark hair and bright green eyes. Her name tag read *O'Brien*. "You Irish?" Mom asked.

"Yes." The woman sighed.

"I'll bet you hear a lot of jokes about the Irish temper," said Mom as she wrote a check, "but we Poles are the ones who really know how to get mad."

The woman laughed. She had a pretty giggle and an even prettier smile. "You must be the one who cursed out His Honor."

"Yes, I am," Mom said proudly.

"Wish I'd been there to see it," she said enviously. "The whole building's been talking about it." She suddenly looked pale. "Not that he's a bad boss or anything. I love my job and—"

"Don't worry, sweetie," said my mother kindly. "Your secret is safe with me."

20

TALKING BACK

On the way home, Pinky and I huddled tensely in the back-seat. Frankie Laine was on the radio, singing the ballad from *High Noon*. Mom sang along.

"Do not forsake me, oh my darlin'
On this our wedding day."

I couldn't figure out what was going on. Mom seemed absolutely fine. Wasn't she embarrassed about being in jail?

Boots was waiting for us on the front stoop. I threw my arms around him and he licked my face. He followed us into the house.

Dad was sitting on the couch in the living room. His tie was loose around his neck, the furrow deep between his eyes. "Where have you been?" he fumed. "I've been worried sick."

Mom ignored him and breezed past him. "Have to put the baby to bed," she said, holding a sleeping Susie in her arms.

Dad grabbed my shoulder, so hard it kind of hurt. "Where were you?"

"Nowhere."

"Tommy, did you get in trouble again?" Dad asked.

"No," I said. "Mom went to pay her speeding ticket."

"Speeding ticket?" asked Dad.

Oh crap. She hadn't told him.

"Never mind," I said.

"Thomas, tell me what is going on." His voice was calm, but behind his smudged glasses his eyes blazed with anger.

I shook my head.

"Thomas John Wilson, I—"

Pinky piped up. "Mom got thrown in jail for saying bad words to the judge."

Mom picked that moment to come back into the living room. "What did you say?" she hissed.

I pushed my sister aside and stood in front of her. "Pinky was just telling Dad why we were late."

"Are you making fun of me, Tommy?"

"No!"

"I think you are." Mom pulled her hair out of its neat bun, put her hands on her hips and flounced around the living room, throwing her hair from side to side. "Look, how amusing! Mother was thrown in the slammer."

"Of course not, Mom," I said.

"It was humiliating!" she screamed. "And now you're humiliating me again!" The vein popped out in her forehead.

Boots walked over and sat down next to me, his warm body leaning against my leg.

"Now, Catherine," said Dad. "Maybe we should just calm down and—"

"Don't you tell me to calm down! Why don't you ever go to the hospital? Why don't you ever go sit there with her?"

In the bedroom, Susie started crying.

"I'll get her," said Dad quietly.

"Don't walk out on me when I'm speaking to you!"

"I'm not talking to you when you're so upset," said Dad. He picked up Pinky and left the room. Unfortunately, he didn't take me too.

"What are you looking at, Tommy?" she fumed.

"Nothing," I said.

"You think I deserved it, huh? I deserved to be thrown in jail like a common criminal. Because I lost my temper and—"

"Well, cursing out the judge wasn't exactly a good move!"

I froze. One thing you never did to my mom was talk back. I knew what was coming next.

"In the kitchen," Mom commanded. "Now!"

She went off to get the belt. Boots looked at me with wide eyes. "Stay here," I told him. I went into the kitchen and pulled down my pants.

When Mom started whipping me, I tried to make myself concentrate on normal things. The dirty dishes in the sink. The sound of water running in the bathroom. Pinky fussing as Dad rinsed her hair. But Mom just didn't stop. I could feel welts forming on welts on my butt. And when a lash went wild and hit my back, I couldn't help crying out.

I heard a growl. I glanced over and saw Boots standing in the doorway. The belt hit my back again, at an odd angle, so that the leather cut the skin. Pain exploded across my backside.

"Ow!" I cried.

Boots started to bark.

"Shut up!" Mom yelled.

Boots crept closer and kept barking.

126

"I said, shut up!" Mom kicked Boots aside. My poor dog slid across the kitchen floor and slammed into a cabinet. He whimpered once, but stopped barking. Mom kept hitting me. It felt like a thousand bees, stinging me all at once.

I hated her then. Maybe I had been rude, but Boots hadn't done a thing. He was just trying to protect me. I gritted my teeth. No matter how much it hurt, I would not cry out again.

Mom kept on. And Dad never came in to see if I was okay.

When she was done, Boots and I went out. Nowhere in particular. Just to walk. I couldn't be in that house any longer. Somehow, I found myself outside Mrs. Glazov's shack. I waited. Just standing there. It would have made more sense if she'd been playing the accordion, then I could at least have told myself I was listening to the music. But I wasn't.

After a few minutes, or maybe an hour, the front door opened.

I jumped.

"Who there?" she called.

I didn't answer.

"I taking trash out to fire pit. I got no money."

She was afraid of me. She thought I was a hoodlum. Or a robber. Or worse. "It's me," I said.

"Tommy?" she asked.

"Yeah."

"What you doing in cold? Come on in."

So we did. We went into the communist's house. Boots curled up by the wood-burning stove while Mrs. Glazov made me a cup of the bitter tea. It tasted good. I guess I had learned to like it, just as she had predicted I would.

"Need more lemon," she said.

"I'll get it." I jumped up, and my whole backside ached. I tried not to wince as I found a lemon and the cutting board and knife and started slicing.

Mrs. Glazov cleared her throat. "You got blood on shirt."

I didn't answer. Just concentrated on cutting those lemons as thin as she did.

"Get in fight?" she asked.

"Not exactly." I brought the lemons back to the table.

"Show me."

"No!" I protested. It was bad enough pulling down my pants for Mom. I wasn't going to do that in front of Mrs. Glazov!

"I help," she said. She walked over to a shelf near the stove and came back with a bottle of iodine and a box of bandages.

There was that cut on my back, next to my spine. It hurt. I lifted my shirt and showed her that.

She didn't say anything, just got to work patching me up. The iodine stung a bit, but she put the bandage on so gently, I didn't mind.

"Aren't you going to ask what I did to deserve a beating?"

"No," she said. "You good boy, Tommy."

That was when I started to cry. "No, I'm not."

"You good boy," she repeated. "Who else give old Russian lady English lessons just to sell stupid magazine I buy anyway?"

"You said you wouldn't."

"I lie." She smiled. "I know about problems, Tommy. The Nazis not just throw me in camp. They kill my boys and my

128

husband too. Now I never have no grandchildren. No family at all."

Mrs. Glazov had had a family? Sons? A husband? I'd never thought of that before. I'd pictured her always being dumpy and faded and old and alone.

She shook her head. "No. You good boy. And good friend. The others, they call me communist."

It seemed so ridiculous then. Of course she wasn't the communist. She was way too nice. And patient. In fact, her bossy kindness reminded me of Mary Lou.

"I show you something," she said.

She stood up heavily and plodded over to a box in the corner. "Before I leave Russia, I save one box." She rummaged through it, pulling books out and laying them anywhere. "Need to unpack, but . . ." She shrugged. "Too many memories. Aha!"

Mrs. Glazov held up a small silver frame. "Many books, and one picture." She brought it over for me to look at.

It was a picture of a young, pretty woman with four boys gathered around her. The eldest looked about twelve, just like me.

I glanced up at Mrs. Glazov. She had tears in her eyes, but under the wrinkles and white hair I could see she had once been the pretty woman in the picture.

"Been long time," she said quietly. "Thank you, Tommy. Good to see photo again."

Embarrassed, I went to put the books back in the box. They were nice ones, bound in real leather. "You need a bookshelf," I said.

"Can't afford."

I picked up a small red book and started to look through it. It was in some foreign language; I thought it might be German. I flipped back to the front page. "I could build—"

Suddenly, I froze. The title page read: *Das Kapital* by Karl Marx.

This was a communist book. It was *the* communist book by *the* Karl Marx. The father of communism. The man mentioned in *Guilty of Treason*. This was proof!

My hands began to shake. There, on the first page, was a name: *Anastasia Glazov.* I slammed it shut.

"You okay, Tommy?" Mrs. Glazov said gently. "Need another bandage?"

"No," I managed to choke out. I put the book back in the box. I hoped she didn't notice how my hands were shaking. "Just tired. I better go."

Boots jumped up and followed me out. My house was dark and I made it to my bedroom without seeing anyone. But as I slipped into bed, I started to cry again. She couldn't be the communist. She just couldn't.

FISHING

I didn't know what to do. I barely managed to pull myself out of bed the next morning. On the paper route, Ma and Pa told me I looked pale and Mrs. Scully invited me in for a dough-nut and a cup of hot chocolate. Even though it wasn't that cold, I couldn't stop shivering. If I turned in Mrs. Glazov, she might go to jail, or even the electric chair like the Rosen-bergs! But if I didn't report her, Mr. McKenzie might lose his store.

I didn't know what to do. I picked arguments with the choirboys twice on the playground, though when Eddie asked me what it had been about afterward, I couldn't re-member. I yelled at Pinky in the bath and fussed at Susie when she wouldn't nap. She was five months old now and kept sitting up when she was supposed to be sleeping in her crib. I even snapped at Mary Lou when she reminded me to put a small plastic tarp over the basket for the papers when it rained.

Boots was the only one I could tolerate. In the mornings, his nose was always warm against my cheek as he woke me up, usually just before my alarm. His quiet presence kept me company, even if it was cold or rainy, as I pedaled through the darkness, delivering the papers.

The next Saturday at McKenzie's was tense. Ever since the Halloween candy incident at school, Little Skinny wouldn't speak to me. Mr. McKenzie must have noticed, but he didn't say anything, just gave us jobs that kept us apart. I thought about how much fun we'd had carving the pumpkin and wished it could be like that again.

Only three people came in all morning. One of them was Mrs. Glazov. "Hello, Tommy," she said, friendly as ever.

"Morning," I managed to choke out, unable to look her in the eye. It was her fault Mr. McKenzie had no customers. Except it wasn't. Not really. Mrs. Glazov might be the communist, but I was the one who'd put the newspaper in the store. I was the one who'd started the rumor.

When Mrs. Glazov left, Mr. McKenzie, Little Skinny and I looked at one another. The floors were clean, the windows sparkling. Mr. McKenzie put up the CLOSED FOR LUNCH sign and made us sandwiches early that day.

"I still have some time," I said as I chewed my ham-and-cheese. "Got any boxes to unload?"

Mr. McKenzie shook his head. "No point in ordering any more supplies if I can't unload the stock I already have."

"Oh."

When I finished my sandwich, Mr. McKenzie sighed. "Might as well go on home, Tommy."

"See you next week," I said as I left.

"Yeah," said Mr. McKenzie flatly. "See you next week."

His tone felt like a knife at my back, urging me to make a

decision. But I couldn't figure out which friend to save and which to sacrifice.

At home, Dad suggested we skip church the next day and go fishing. "Eddie and his dad are busy," said Dad, "so it'd just be the two of us."

I knew this was an apology of sorts, for going off with Pinky and not helping me when Mom lost her temper five days before. I was still angry with him for that. But a fishing trip wasn't offered often, so of course I said yes.

The next day we were out of the house by seven. We didn't talk at all in the car. When we got to Mud Lake, we parked the car at the side of the road and walked down a narrow, shaded path to the water. Dad carried the tackle box and I took the poles. He had a varnished-cane casting rod with a cigar grip and a Zebco spinning reel, and a whole collection of lures. I only had a simple bamboo pole with a fishing line and hook, but it worked all right.

Mud Lake was really just a big pond, surrounded by reeds and bushes. But it was quiet and usually deserted. Only the serious fishermen came out in mid-November. We sat down on the old wooden dock and started fishing.

Dad and I didn't talk much, just "Pass the worms," and "Do you have some more line?" and stuff like that. But it was a good quiet, calm and peaceful. I'd almost managed to stop thinking about Mrs. Glazov when Dad cleared his throat and asked, "How's it going with Mr. McKenzie?"

"Fine," I said.

"I talked to him yesterday," he said. "You can stop going after next week."

"Great." But it didn't feel great. I liked helping Mr. McKenzie. "No one goes there anymore anyway," I said. "He doesn't need the help."

"Yes," said Dad. "It's unfortunate. I had hoped no one would believe those rumors."

A duck quacked in the distance. No one else was there. The sun shone on our faces. The wind whispered of winter, but it wasn't quite cold yet. I believed, just for a moment, that I could get the guilt off my chest. "It's my fault."

Dad laughed. "Tommy, stealing is bad, but a few yo-yos won't make or break a business. Officer Russo said some public school boy was playing a joke and—"

"No," I said. "It was me." And then I told him.

Dad's hands gripped his fishing pole tighter and tighter, till his knuckles turned white. "Thomas John Wilson." He shook his head.

"I didn't mean—"

"You've destroyed a man's reputation!"

"I know. I feel terrible about it."

"Terrible!" Dad ran his hands through his hair. "Tommy, have you ever heard of Milo Radulovich?"

"Radulo-who?" I asked.

"Milo Radulovich," Dad continued, "was a lieutenant in the United States Air Force. He recently lost his job over communist allegations."

"Well, he must have done something to make them suspect him," I said, trying not to remember that Mr. McKenzie hadn't done a thing. It had all been me.

Dad shook his head. "He did nothing. His sister and father might have—*might have*—attended some sort of a communist meeting. Or read a communist newspaper. No one really knows because he was not allowed to see the evidence against him. Basically, he was found guilty by association. You've done the same thing to Mr. McKenzie."

If I felt bad before, I felt even worse now. But cowboys don't admit they've made a mistake. They just press on. "I'm trying to make it better," I argued. "I've found the real communist!"

"What?" Dad turned to look at me and, if anything, he looked even more surprised than before.

"Yeah," I said. "It's Mrs. Glazov."

"The Russian lady who lives next door?"

And then it all came tumbling out. "I started giving her reading lessons so I could get inside her house and investigate and I found this book, *Das Kapital*, and now I don't know what to do because she's so nice and I don't want to turn her in, but I don't want Mr. McKenzie to lose his store either."

"Tommy," Dad said sternly, "Mrs. Glazov is not a Soviet spy."

"How do you know?"

"You're being ridiculous!"

"That newspaper had to come from somewhere!"

"Tommy!" Dad roared, as angry as I'd ever seen him. "No more of this investigating or pretending you are some sort of avenging cowboy who can just swoop in and make everything okay!"

Dad never yelled. Never. His tone hurt more than his words. Thank goodness I pulled in a fish then, and another one, in quick succession. I didn't want to talk to him, or even look at him. Then I volunteered to gut the fish, even though I usually hate that part.

While I cut up the fish, Dad prepared the fire, building a ring of stones and pulling out his cast iron frying pan. He hesitated a moment before he threw the match in. As the flames licked the dry leaves and sprang to life, I wondered if he was thinking about Mary Lou. It was chilly and the fire felt nice, but it seemed wrong to enjoy something that had hurt my sister so much.

Later, after we had eaten the hot fried fish, Dad finally spoke again. "Tommy. We've all been under a lot of stress. The hospital bills for Mary Lou . . ." He trailed off.

She'd been in the hospital for two months now. I knew Dad was worried about how we were going to pay for that. I was worried about it too. But I didn't think that was why he had barked at me. "What about Mom?"

"What about her?"

"She's always yelling and crying."

"Mom's always been like that."

"No. She's worse. She threw those pierogi. And broke a vase. She even kicked Boots when she was mad at me!"

"Tommy, you provoke her."

"Dad, some days she forgets to do the dishes. Or get Pinky dressed!"

He said nothing.

"Something's wrong with her. She insulted our guests at the party. She cursed out the judge!"

"I already called the doctor," Dad said quietly. "He couldn't find anything wrong. We just need to give it time and . . . ignore her outbursts as much as possible."

How was I supposed to ignore getting beaten? "But—"

"I mean it, Tommy. You need to let it go. It's not your problem. I don't want you to worry about Mom. And I don't want you to investigate this communist thing anymore."

"Fine."

We didn't speak the rest of the way home.

22

SEE IT NOW

On Monday, I was still feeling out of sorts. I slept through my alarm and was late for my paper route. I barely got it done in time, and I didn't even have a second to grab a banana as I ran for the bus.

"Late again, Tommy," Lizzie teased as I climbed onto the bus, my heart pounding like a galloping horse.

"Shut up, Lizard-Face," I said.

Lizzie pouted. "Don't call me Lizard-Face," she said. "My name is Elizabeth."

"No one has called you that since you were two, *Lizzie*," I said, sliding into the seat next to Eddie. "Besides, I wasn't referring to your name."

She turned back in her seat to face us. "Then why—"

"Well, if you took a pen and connected all the dots . . ." I pantomimed drawing a line from one freckle to another, all over Lizzie's face.

Eddie laughed. "Yeah, exactly like a lizard!"

Lizzie gasped in indignation and turned as red as her hair.

Behind Eddie and me, Peter laughed. It irked me. He

should be defending his sister. That's what I'd do if someone were teasing Mary Lou.

"You think it's funny, Peter?" I asked, twisting around to face him.

"Yeah." He chuckled.

"I wouldn't laugh if I had so much pepper on my face," I said. "Ah-choo!"

"Stop it," Peter said, turning as red as his short curly hair.

"Or . . ." I picked up my imaginary pen and started drawing again. I nudged Eddie. "What do you think, Eddie? Monkey-Head?"

"Oh yeah," Eddie agreed. "I can see the big ears and the tail right there." He pointed.

"Your freckles do kind of look like a monkey," Luke said.

"Luke!" Peter fumed.

"I'm just saying . . ."

"Luke doesn't have any freckles," I pointed out. "Maybe Peter'll give you a few."

"Nah," Luke said. "I like my face how it is."

I don't know what made me say it, but I added, "And you like your arm too?"

Luke turned as pale as a polar bear. His bad arm from the polio hung at his side. He looked out the window, pretending his eyes weren't filling with tears.

"You're an idiot," Peter said, and turned his body in the seat so he couldn't see me anymore.

I sat back down. My heart was beating quickly again, even though I'd recovered from the bike ride. I wiped my palms on my pant legs and they left two little stains of sweat.

"What's got into you?" asked Eddie.

"I don't know," I said. We didn't tease people about polio. That was off-limits. I wasn't sure why I had crossed that line.

Eddie sighed. "Didn't see you at the Tivoli this weekend."

"Went fishing with my dad," I said. Then, grateful to change the subject, I added, "Why didn't you come?"

Eddie looked sick, kind of green, like he'd swallowed a rotten sardine. "Don't tell anyone."

"'Course not!"

"My dad lost his job."

"What? Why?"

Eddie shook his head. "Dad said the boss had it in for him. But Mom said he was drinking at work."

"Sorry."

Eddie shrugged. "Next-door neighbor needed his basement painted. So I spent all Sunday doing that. Earned a few extra dollars for my mom." He looked at me. "Think I could get a paper route like you?"

"Huh." I snorted. "You don't want one."

But as we filed off the bus and into Mass, I remembered how good it felt to hand over my wages every other week to Mom. For a minute or two, when I gave her the money, she looked at me like she actually liked me. Maybe the paper route wasn't such a bad thing after all.

At recess, Peter and Luke asked Eddie to play marbles with them. They didn't say a word to me, and after how I'd acted on the bus, I didn't think I should join them. So I walked around like I didn't care, from one end of the school yard to the other. Little Skinny was sitting under the elm tree, doing his homework or something. He was concentrating really hard, I guess, so I snuck up on him and announced, "You're the one!"

Little Skinny jumped and his papers flew everywhere.

I leaned over and picked one up.

"Don't touch that!" he snapped.

I'd never heard him speak so forcefully. So of course that made me want to look at the paper instead of just handing it back to him. It wasn't a school assignment. The paper was different and it was mimeographed, just like the weekly church bulletin my mother received.

"Give it back!" he screamed, and then he started crying and wailing, like I was hitting him.

The Adventures of Cowboy Sam was written across the top, as if it were the first page of a story. "Did you write this?" I asked. I was trying to make it sound like I thought it was really stupid, but I couldn't hide my admiration. I struggled to write a paragraph in school—and he'd practically written a whole book. Not that it mattered how I said it. Little Skinny was screaming so loud, you'd have thought he was being scalped. He couldn't hear a thing.

Sister Ann came running toward us. Little Skinny was practically hysterical now, tears running down his face, yelling "Give it back!" over and over again. He was crying so hard, you could barely understand the words.

"Tommy, what's going on?" asked Sister Ann.

"I don't know," I said. "There was a big gust of wind and his papers blew away. And I came to help him pick them up and he just started . . ." I waved my hand at him.

Sister Ann looked at me, uncertain what to do.

Suddenly Little Skinny grabbed the paper from my hands.

"Samuel!" said Sister Ann sternly, in her no-nonsense voice, the one she used with the first graders. "That's not how we treat our friends. Apologize."

Little Skinny sniffled.

"Oh, that's okay—" I started.

"Tommy was trying to help you clean up," Sister Ann said to Little Skinny. "You grabbed the paper from him. You need to apologize."

"Sorry," whispered Little Skinny. His whole face was red and flushed, the same color as his scar.

Me too, I wanted to say. It didn't seem fair that Sister Ann was scolding him, when he hadn't done a thing. But I couldn't get the words out.

That Friday, Dad and I were watching TV in the living room. Mom had gone to bed early, and we'd just had sandwiches for dinner, so there weren't many dishes. I was sewing a button back on one of my school shirts, badly, but I'd rather do it myself than risk Mom asking me why I'd been so careless.

Douglas Edwards with the News came on. We watched the show most nights at 6:30. "Good evening, everyone, coast to coast," Mr. Edwards intoned seriously.

I didn't pay much attention. At least not until I heard a name I recognized: Radulovich. I looked up at Mr. Edwards.

"U.S. Air Force Lieutenant Milo Radulovich was reinstated today, as a direct result of the program done by our very own Edward R. Murrow on October 20, just one month ago." Murrow was a TV newsman, so famous even I had heard of him.

Dad sat rigid next to me. I could tell he was paying attention because he didn't move a muscle.

142

Apparently, Radulovich had been featured on this show called *See It Now*. They played a clip from it. Radulovich was a young man with dark hair. "If I am being judged by my relatives," he said, "are my children going to be asked to denounce me?"

"He got his job back?" I asked Dad.

"Shhh," he hissed, his eyes fixed on the program.

A clip of Edward R. Murrow came on again. His voice was deep and gravelly. He was talking about how no one had seen the evidence against Radulovich. "Was it hearsay, rumor, gossip, slander, or hard, ascertainable facts that could be backed by credible witnesses? We do not know."

"Murrow investigated," I said to my dad. "And he got Radulovich his job back!"

Dad got up and turned off the TV. He walked out of the room without saying another word.

For a moment, I felt strangely happy. Someone had looked for the truth and it had made a difference. My dad was wrong. And if Dad was wrong about Radulovich, maybe he was wrong about Mrs. Glazov too. Maybe she really was the communist.

And then I started worrying again. Because even if I could get my hands on that book, I wasn't sure what I should do with it. All that night, as I tried to fall asleep, I kept hearing Mr. Murrow's voice repeating: "We do not know. We do not know."

23

THE BOOKSHELVES

November 21 was my last Saturday at McKenzie's. It was another quiet day at the store. After I'd done everything Mr. McKenzie had asked me to do, and even organized all his tin cans too, Little Skinny and I ate stale Halloween candy and read the papers.

I kept thinking about Murrow and how he was trying to make things right. Maybe I didn't know how to save the store or fix my mom, but I guessed I could try to apologize to Little Skinny. He was sitting a few feet away from me, the comics held up in front of his face like a shield.

I cleared my throat. "So, uh, Little Skinny. I wanted to ask you something."

He grunted. He sounded just like his dad.

"What's *The Adventures of Cowboy Sam*?"

"Nothing," he answered, still hiding behind the comics.

"Is it a story?" I asked. "A western?"

"Maybe," said Little Skinny.

"Like *The Lone Ranger*? Or *Kid Colt Outlaw*?"

"Yeah. Kind of like that."

"Cool." I'd never thought about someone writing those stories. They just appeared in comic books at the drugstore. "Can I read it?"

"No," Little Skinny said, finally putting down the comics. "And why are you asking me all these questions?"

I was trying to apologize. But somehow the simple words *I'm sorry* just didn't want to come out.

"You might as well go home, Tommy," Mr. McKenzie said, walking over to us. "Don't think I need you anymore."

I knew this was going to be my last week. But I felt kind of sad. "Can I have a sandwich before I go?" I asked. "They're really good."

Mr. McKenzie looked surprised. "Okay."

Little Skinny shrugged. "I'm hungry."

So we sat in the back room, with the root beers and the sandwiches. I chewed the thick bread carefully, savoring each bite. And I realized, if I wanted to be a cowboy, I had to do what I knew was right. I had to turn in the communist. Even if I liked her. Even if she went to jail. I had to come up with a plan to get Mrs. Glazov's copy of *Das Kapital* and save Mr. McKenzie's store.

So the next day, Sunday, after I had given Mrs. Glazov her reading lesson and we had practiced the accordion for a while, I stopped playing and said, "I'm going to build you some bookshelves." I said it real casual, like I had just come up with the idea.

"You?" asked Mrs. Glazov doubtfully.

"Sure," I said. I couldn't think too much about how I was going to trick her or I'd lose my nerve. "Bookshelves are easy.

145

Mount some brackets on the wall, paint a few boards, you're done."

Mrs. Glazov shook her head.

"Come on," I coaxed. "Don't you have a few extra old planks out back?"

She shrugged, so we trekked out to look. Sure enough, there were three or four long boards there. "These'll do," I said.

I worked all afternoon in our garage, cutting and sanding the boards with my father's tools. Dad and Mom knew their way around tools, so I'd never thought knowing how to cut and saw was anything special. But Mrs. Glazov watched, fascinated, as if I were performing a magical feat.

And the whole time, I felt awful. Because I was deceiving her, pretending to be helpful, pretending to be nice, when the whole point of the bookshelves was to give me a reason to get my hands on that book. I was going to steal it from her and turn her in to the police. I was going to send an old woman to jail!

At least she'd get a fair trial by a jury of her peers. Unlike when the Soviets arrested someone. They tortured them. Manufactured evidence. Just look what had happened to Cardinal Mindszenty! But had the United States done that too? Radulovich had lost his job because of rumors. And Mr. McKenzie—he had no customers because I'd played a stupid joke. Here I was, about to destroy Mrs. Glazov's whole life, and she'd only ever been kind to me. But the difference between Mrs. Glazov and Radulovich was that I knew she was a communist. I knew it was the right thing to do. Even if it felt so wrong.

．．．

The next day after school, Mrs. Glazov gave me a quarter and I rode my bike over to the army-surplus store. They only had one color of paint—olive green—so that was what I bought. Mrs. Glazov helped me paint the boards, putting on each coat carefully, and grinning like Eddie did when he was winning at marbles. "How I doing?" she asked.

"It's just paint," I said, "you can't really do it wrong."

"Your dad teach you all this?" she asked.

"Yeah," I said.

"He handy."

"Yeah, I guess he is."

By the time the paint was dry, Mrs. Glazov was tired. I suggested she go take a nap while I finished things up. Her eyes drooped and she must not have been feeling well, because I hadn't really expected her to agree, but she went to the other room to lie down.

So it was almost too easy. I put up the brackets and boards on the long wall while she slept. Then I opened the box and arranged all the old books on the new shelves. They fit perfectly, with just enough room at one end to display the framed photo. The small red book, *Das Kapital*, I slipped under my shirt.

It burned like a hot coal against my chest.

Mrs. Glazov walked back into the room then, her white hair wild about her head. "Still here?" She paused and glanced at the wall. Then she smiled and sat down heavily on one of the chairs at the table. "Thank you, Tommy," she said finally, wiping her eyes with a corner of the tablecloth. "It looks wonderful."

147

It did. The light of her kerosene lamp glinted off the silver frame.

"The paint is kind of an ugly color of green," I mumbled.

"It beautiful," she said. "Color of grass along river at home."

Before I left, she gave me a big bear hug. I was terrified she was going to feel the book under my shirt.

I walked down the street as slowly as possible. I had to turn her in. I knew that. I had to save Mr. McKenzie's store. But in the movies they never told you how awful it felt to betray someone who had trusted you. Even if they had done something wrong.

Officer Russo's house was two blocks away. I knocked on his door and waited, my heart beating like I was the one who had committed a crime.

"You need something?" The old lady next door poked her head out the window. "Officer Russo and his family went away for Thanksgiving."

Truthfully, I was relieved to put it off a little longer. "No," I said. "That's fine. I'll wait till they get back."

At home, I hid the book in my closet and threw myself onto my bed. Boots snuck his head in under my arm. The whole situation made me feel sick. I wished Mary Lou were around. She'd know what to do. She'd been right after all. I should have burned the paper when I'd first brought it home.

24

THANKSGIVING

This was the first Thanksgiving since Busia's death. She and Mom used to argue a lot, always in Polish, so I didn't really know what they were saying, but I'd liked her. Busia used to carve birds out of bits of wood with an old penknife and give them to Mary Lou and me when she visited. She'd been doing it for years and her hands were scarred with fine cuts from when the knife slipped.

When I heard from Dad that Mary Lou would not be allowed to come home for Thanksgiving, I tiptoed into her room and picked out one of the wooden birds to bring her. Mary Lou cradled the tiny sparrow in her hands when I gave it to her at the hospital.

"Thanks, Tommy," she murmured.

I shrugged, embarrassed, and we both stared at the bird as if we were waiting for it to take flight.

At home, Mom went into a frenzy of activity, washing all the curtains in the house. When she was done with that, she moved on to the tablecloths, spending hours ironing them until there wasn't a wrinkle to be seen. Pinky and I scrubbed the floor, vacuumed and dusted until the house gleamed. After the disaster of the card party, Mom was determined to make Thanksgiving perfect. I was just glad she wasn't lying around in bed anymore.

I put on a polka record, thinking it would make the housework more fun. Pinky and I started to dance around, laughing as we dusted.

"Shut it off," Mom said. "It's giving me a headache."

"But it's your favorite," I said.

"Please. Turn it off."

So I did.

The night before Thanksgiving, Mom started polishing the only silver we had—forks and knives and spoons in a mahogany box—just as I was going to bed. When I woke up in the morning to do the paper route, she was still at the dining room table, fast asleep. I tiptoed out, careful not to wake her. Two hours later, when I returned, I could hear the yelling as I walked my bike back into the garage. I stood still for a moment, but there was nowhere else to go.

I poked my head into the kitchen.

The turkey was in the sink, thawing. Pinky was at the table, a bowl of oatmeal in front of her, but she wasn't eating. Her eyes were wide. And Mom was crying and screaming at the same time. Something about potatoes.

"But I got them!" Dad pleaded desperately, holding up the bag.

"Those are the wrong kind!" Mom whined. "Busia always used the red ones. Red mashed potatoes are Mary Lou's favorite!" She'd slept in her clothes and her navy dress was wrinkled now, like an old lady's face.

"But the rest of us don't care," exclaimed Dad. "And Mary Lou's not here!" The lines around his eyes looked deeper this morning.

"I just wanted one thing to work out!" Mom wailed. Her long black hair hung loose around her head, wild as if she were in a windstorm. She picked up a small pumpkin pie and threw it across the room. It smashed against the wall. Orange guts dripped down onto the floor.

The kitchen was suddenly silent.

"I have a migraine," Mom said. "I'm going to bed." She walked out of the room, as if she hadn't been screaming a moment before.

I could hear the ticking of the clock in the silence. Pinky picked up her spoon and took another bite of oatmeal. The scrape of the spoon against the bowl sounded abnormally loud. Dad took a sip of coffee and swallowed heavily. The cup clanked as he set it down on the counter.

"Tommy." His voice cracked. He cleared his throat. "Tommy, would you . . ." He gestured to the pumpkin mess in the corner.

I nodded.

"Good," he said. "Because I need to go out for a little while."

"But—"

Dad stopped. "What is it, Tommy?"

"Who's going to cook Thanksgiving dinner?"

"I'm sure your mother will calm down eventually." Then he walked out the door.

Pinky and I looked at each other. She finished her oatmeal as I picked up the pieces of smushed pumpkin pie.

Boots walked over and licked up the crumbs. Mom did not come out of her room. Susie started crying, so I got her up and changed her and gave her a bottle. The minutes ticked by. Dad did not come back. And I got more and more furious. How dare Dad run away and leave me with the problem of Thanksgiving!

"What are we going to eat, Tommy?" Pinky asked.

"There's plenty of bread and bologna," I said.

"I want turkey," Pinky whined.

Yeah. I did too.

"Come on," I said. "We'll figure this out."

I placed Susie's playpen in the living room and set it up where I could see her from the kitchen. Then I dragged a step stool over to the sink and Pinky climbed up to help me, scrubbing the dirt off the big white potatoes with her tiny hands. I filled a pot with water and put the potatoes on the stove to boil. There was a pile of green beans on the counter. "Snap off the ends," I told Pinky. "I'll be right back."

I went out the back door and looked at Mrs. Glazov's house. Before I could think about it too much, I walked over to her front door and knocked.

"Tommy!" she said, surprised. It was only then, seeing her face, that I realized how upset I must have looked. "What wrong?"

I shook my head. "Could you just come over for a minute?"

She nodded and pulled on a faded coat. It had finally gotten cold and together we walked the few steps across the frozen mud to our house.

Mrs. Glazov stepped into our kitchen and looked around. Pinky was struggling to snap the end off a rubbery green

152

bean. Susie was chewing on a toy in her playpen. Boots was pacing the room like a guard. The turkey still sat in the sink. "Ahh," she said. "Cooking emergency." She smiled, taking off her coat and rolling up the sleeves on her shapeless flowered dress. "I help."

So all afternoon, Mrs. Glazov, Pinky and I chopped and boiled and simmered and roasted. I think Mom had taken another one of those pills from Dr. Stanton, because she was passed out on the bed, snoring softly, when I went to check on her.

When Susie started fussing, Mrs. Glazov cooed, "Pretty baby!" at her and insisted that she be the one to give her the bottle. Susie gurgled happily.

By the time my dad walked back into the house, it was late in the afternoon. He smelled like alcohol again. "I stopped by the Sullivans'," he said. "Eddie says hi." He paused in the dining room. Pinky and I had set the table with the polished silver.

Mrs. Glazov walked in, carrying the turkey. "Ahh, good. Mr. Wilson. You home."

"Wh-wh-what's all this?" my dad sputtered.

"Turkey," Mrs. Glazov said. "Time to eat."

A slow grin spread across Dad's face, erasing the lines on his forehead.

Pinky and I went to wake Mom. I shook her shoulder gently. "Turkey's ready," I said.

"What?" she mumbled.

"Mrs. Glazov helped Tommy and me make dinner!" Pinky exclaimed.

As I watched, I could see the emotions shift across Mom's

face, like tumbleweed blowing across the desert, uncertain where it would land. For a moment, I thought she was going to start yelling again, but then she smiled. "Give me a minute to get dressed," she said.

When Mom walked into the dining room five minutes later, she wore a clean, freshly ironed pink dress. Her hair was pulled back in a simple ponytail and her cheeks were rosy, as if she'd splashed them with cold water. Pinky and I sat in our places, Boots at my feet, waiting patiently for me to slip him a bite or two. Susie was in her highchair, Dad sat at the head of the table, and Mrs. Glazov took Mary Lou's seat.

I thought that would make me feel funny, but it was sort of comforting not to have to see the empty spot. Mom sat down in the chair at the foot of the table and folded her hands in her lap. Dad said grace and we started passing the food around.

Mrs. Glazov piled her plate high with turkey and mashed potatoes and green beans, then covered them all with gravy. She dug in like a cowboy who hadn't seen a chuck wagon in a week.

Pinky stared at her.

"What?" asked Mrs. Glazov.

"Mom says it's rude to chew with your mouth open," Pinky said seriously.

I glanced at Mom, worried. Her face was screwed up liked she'd bitten into something sour. If Pinky started crying, it would ruin the mood and . . .

But before Mom could say a word, Mrs. Glazov laughed, her mouth still wide open. She covered her face with her hands and finished chewing. "Your mother's right," she said finally. "It's just . . . I not see point in cooking for one. Usually eat tea and sandwiches. This good, so good!"

Everyone smiled then, even Mom, and the moment passed. Dad told a funny story about how when he was a boy he'd switched the jars of salt and sugar one Thanksgiving and the cherry pie had turned out as salty as a pretzel. "The look on my mom's face when she took the first bite was worth the spanking!"

Pinky laughed so hard, milk came out her nose. For a moment, she looked as scared as a jackrabbit that's spotted a coyote, but Mom just mopped her up with a napkin and poured her some more milk.

After dinner, we were all too full for pie, so Mom put Dick Contino's "Lady of Spain" on the record player and we pushed back the couch and danced. Mom and Dad polkaed smoothly together. I grabbed Pinky's hand and swung her in circles until she squealed. Mrs. Glazov watched and smiled. When the song was done, Mom put it on again, and Dad walked over to Mrs. Glazov and asked her to dance.

They made a funny pair, my tall, thin dad and the short, squat Russian lady, but they whirled across the floor just fine. Mrs. Glazov looked so happy, she reminded me of Mary Lou when the boy she liked had asked her to the fall social. That was back before, of course. She hadn't gotten to go.

I was still thinking about Mary Lou when Mom walked over to me. "Want to dance, Tommy?" she asked.

Maybe it was all the turkey, but for once I didn't feel angry at her. "Sure."

We spun around in circles. The dizzier I got, the more I could make myself believe that we were just a normal family like everyone else.

When the pie was finally eaten and all the dishes were done, I walked Mrs. Glazov back to her house. "Thanks," I said, "you really helped—"

Mrs. Glazov clasped my hand and held it between her two fleshy palms. "No, Tommy," she said. "Thank you. I never celebrate this American Thanksgiving before. What I, lonely old woman, no more family, what I have to be thankful for?" She smiled. "But it pretty nice holiday after all." She put her hand on her front door. "See you Sunday."

As I watched her open the door, I got a lump in my throat. After saving Thanksgiving, I didn't think there was any way I could turn her in. Even if it meant letting a communist go free.

"Mrs. Glazov?"

"Yes?"

It was now or never. "Are you a communist?"

She didn't smile or frown as she tilted her head to look at me. "Why you ask that?"

"Because I found this," I said, pulling out the small red book. "I took it when we were building the bookshelves."

She held the book in her big hands, glancing once at the spine. "Ahh," she said, "*Das Kapital.*"

"Are you a Soviet spy?" I blurted.

"No. I raised communist. That true. But I believe that no more."

"Then why do you have that book?"

"Book was gift from favorite teacher. It reminds me of him."

"Was he a communist?"

"Yes."

"Then you should get rid of it!"

"Why? Because he thinks differently?"

I didn't know what to say.

"Tommy, this book only full of ideas. Some good. Some bad."

"But isn't it in German?" An even worse thought occurred to me. "Are you a Nazi?"

Mrs. Glazov laughed now. "No, Tommy. In Russia, I educated woman. Music teacher. Taught at the university." She shrugged. "Here, I poor old woman who sells vegetables."

"But why here?" I asked.

"Lived in Chicago first. But it so crowded. And St. Joseph's bought this land. Gave mortgage to immigrant like me at good price. That why I come here."

"American dream," I said.

"It good dream, Tommy. All men equal."

"But I found a copy of the *Daily Worker* in the truck after the paper drive."

She laughed again. "The *Daily Worker* is communist paper in English, right?"

"Yeah."

"How I read it? You still teaching me English."

That was a good point.

"Tommy," she said. "I no communist."

"I know." And I did. I stared at my feet, embarrassed and relieved. I didn't want her to go to jail. But what was I going to do about Mr. McKenzie?

"Tommy," she repeated. "Why you asking about communist?"

And there, in the dark and the cold of Thanksgiving evening, I told her about planting the paper in Mr. McKenzie's store. When I was done, she was quiet.

"Say something," I said.

"What you want me to say?"

"That you know who the communist is. That it's not my fault if Mr. McKenzie loses his store." And in my head I went on: *That it's not my fault Mary Lou got burned.*

"It is your fault," she said.

It was weird, because I'd thought hearing someone else say the words that had been rattling around in my head would make me feel worse. But it didn't. In some strange way, it actually made me feel better, because she was taking me seriously.

Then she smiled. "But I know you, Tommy. You will find way to make it better."

She went inside and closed her door. As I walked back home, for the first time all day, I felt okay. She had faith in me. I would find a way to make it better. Even if I had no idea how.

25

'TIS THE SEASON

But despite my dizzy dreams on the dance floor, after Thanksgiving things didn't get better, at least not with Mom. She seemed worse. Some days at dinnertime, I'd find the breakfast dishes still piled in the sink. Susie got a horrible diaper rash. I started changing her when I got home from school and giving her a bottle in case she was hungry because Mom had forgotten to feed her. When I asked Pinky what she did all day, she shrugged. "Played with my dolls. Mom slept a lot."

The weird thing was, Mary Lou was doing better. She was finally learning to walk again. But Mom's moods no longer seemed to have anything to do with Mary Lou's progress. They were as random as a roll of the dice in a saloon. Pinky got a wide-eyed look about her, like a rabbit startled by a rattlesnake. She never cried, though, unlike Susie, who got colic so bad, I thought she was never going to stop crying. Dad got more and more quiet, as if not mentioning Mom's behavior meant it wasn't happening. He started working later too.

And I had to hold it all together. It didn't seem fair. I was the kid. Sometimes, at night, I wished more than anything that Mom or Dad would take care of me.

One day in early December, after school, I was waiting for Mom to pick me up when I saw Mr. McKenzie come out of the school building. Little Skinny was trailing behind him. They didn't see me, but I wondered, were they going to the hospital too? Was his mother getting worse?

The sun was shining, glaring off the snow, and Mr. McKenzie's car was dirty. As they approached it, I could just make out a word someone had traced in the dirt on the grimy hood.

Commie.

Mr. McKenzie noticed it at the same time. I could tell, because he froze, like a bird on a branch when there is a cat in the yard. Little Skinny blushed, red as any Soviet.

Mr. McKenzie picked up a handful of snow and scrubbed the words off the car. His fingers must have been freezing, because there were holes in his old brown gloves. Then he ushered Little Skinny into the car and drove off. My hands burned with cold, as if I were the one with the old gloves.

Later that afternoon, I lugged my accordion up the steps to Mary Lou's room. My arms started to ache, but the smile on my sister's face when I finally got there made it all worthwhile.

"You're going to play!" Mary Lou squealed.

I grinned. "What do you want to hear?"

"'Hark! The Herald Angels Sing.' It's my favorite."

"I knew it," I said, and began to play. My fingers trembled at first, but after a moment, Mary Lou started to sing. Her voice was soft, but sweet as a lollipop, and it gave me confidence. I played better, my fingers finding the right keys without me thinking about it. By the end of the song, three nurses had gathered in the hallway.

As I played "Joy to the World," "Angels We Have Heard on High," and even "Rudolph the Red-Nosed Reindeer," more nurses and a few other patients gathered outside Mary Lou's door. When I was done, everyone applauded. I caught sight of Little Skinny in the hallway, standing next to a pale woman in a wheelchair.

"Oh, Tommy," Mary Lou said, her eyes shining. "That was wonderful!"

"Play another," called out a nurse. "'Jingle Bells'?"

Everyone started calling out suggestions, but I went up to the woman in the wheelchair. She was so thin, I could see all the bones around her neck, and the shape of her skull. Her limp dark hair had faded to gray. She wore a yellow dressing gown with pink roses embroidered around the collar. "What would you like to hear?" I asked her.

"'Silent Night,'" she whispered.

So I played it, and the whole time I was thinking, this is Little Skinny's mother, the one who is so sick. And yet her eyes still blinked and her lips still moved as she sang along in a voice so quiet, I couldn't hear a word. When I was done, I put the accordion away and went back into the hall, but Little Skinny and his mother were already gone.

• • •

The next day at school, Eddie spent recess imitating his mother. "There won't be any Christmas presents this year!" he yelled in an angry falsetto. "Your father doesn't have a job and he spent all our savings on the bomb shelter!"

"At least it makes a good hideout," I said.

"Yeah," said Eddie, "but it still means no presents."

"I can't steal anymore," I said.

"What if we didn't steal them?" Eddie said. "What if we got him"—he gestured to Little Skinny—"to give them to us?"

"How?" I asked.

So he told me. It was a good plan, the kind of idea I might have come up with myself. But after seeing Little Skinny's mom in the hospital, just like Mary Lou, well, I kind of felt differently about him now. I shook my head. "No, I don't think so."

"Oh, come on, Tommy," Eddie said. "It's Little Skinny. You don't even like him."

No, I didn't. Not really. But he seemed like more of a person now and I didn't know how to explain that to Eddie. So I just shrugged and followed Eddie across the cobblestones.

"Little Skinny," Eddie called out, "you're the one."

"The one what?" Little Skinny asked hesitantly. Two buttons had popped off his too-small shirt, revealing a bit of white belly under his thick wool jacket.

"The one we wanted to talk to," I said.

"Why?" asked Little Skinny.

"Well, since it is Christmastime," said Eddie, just as we had rehearsed, "we figured we should be a little nicer to you."

162

"Yeah," I added. "'Cause we feel bad about the Halloween candy." I really did feel bad about that.

"Good," said Little Skinny. "It was mean."

"So we had an idea," Eddie continued smoothly, holding up an old sock. "We'll each fill a stocking full of treats for you, and you do the same for us."

"Why?" asked Little Skinny.

"So we all get some treats!" Eddie replied.

"No," said Little Skinny. "Even if I wanted to buy you guys presents, which I don't, I don't have any money."

"It doesn't have to be anything expensive," Eddie explained. "Maybe just bake some cookies or skip buying milk one day and put in some penny candy."

Little Skinny shook his head. "No."

"It's okay, Little Skinny," I said. I was glad he didn't like the idea. That meant I didn't have to decide if I was going to follow through on Eddie's idea. "If you don't want—"

"My name is Sam," he interrupted.

"What?" Eddie asked.

"My name is *Sam*," he repeated. "You start calling me that, I'll do it."

"Sure," I said. *"Sam."* Maybe he really was stupid. Why would anyone agree to this plan?

Little Skinny nodded. "All right. When should I have the stockings ready?"

Didn't he know we were going to cheat him? Couldn't he tell? Or maybe he was like a cowboy riding bravely into an ambush he knew he couldn't win.

"The last day of school before the Christmas holiday?" Eddie suggested.

"Fine," said Little Skinny.

"Do you need a stocking?" I asked.

"I got old socks," Little Skinny joked.

"Wonderful," Eddie said in his sweetest voice. "Then I'll just use this sock for you."

Little Skinny gave a hesitant smile and walked away. As he left, I realized Peter and Luke were standing around watching us. "Why didn't you ask us to join in your little stocking exchange?" Peter asked.

I couldn't quite tell if he was angry or jealous.

"Because they are going to trick him," said Luke, his bad arm hanging at his side.

"And what if we are?" I snapped. "You gonna tell him?"

Luke stared me straight in the eyes. I'd never noticed, but his eyes were hazel, just like my mother's, and his nose was as pert as Mary Lou's. All I'd ever seen before was his arm.

"No," Luke said finally. "We mind our own business. Come on, Peter." They walked away.

Eddie chattered on, thrilled that his plan had worked, but I felt awful. Little Skinny was the brave one. I was the coward. The one who didn't dare tell his best friend what he really thought—that his plan was a terrible idea.

26

GIFTS

I couldn't make up my mind. When I was with Eddie, I laughed about his plan to put coal in Little Skinny's stocking. But when I was alone, I felt so guilty. I kept seeing his mom, picturing her chapped lips mouthing the words as I played the accordion. Maybe there was a compromise. Maybe I could put an orange or some penny candy in Little Skinny's stocking instead. Maybe I could keep the bargain after all.

I was still mulling it over one night while doing the dishes when my dad came in to speak to me. "Tommy," he said quietly. "Do me a favor?"

"What is it?" I asked.

"I had an idea about your mother."

Finally. Finally, we were going to talk about Mom.

"I know we have the bills for Mary Lou, but I managed to save a little extra." He showed me a five-dollar bill. "What if tomorrow, on your paper route, you stopped by Mrs. Scully's and asked her to make Mom a new dress for Christmas?"

That was it? That was his big plan? A new dress? "Does she need a new dress?"

"Well, she keeps complaining she has nothing to wear," Dad said. "I thought it might cheer her up." He handed me a bundle wrapped in brown paper. "Here's one of her old dresses to use as a pattern."

I took the bundle from him.

"Put it back in her closet when you're done," Dad instructed.

I nodded. It was worth a try.

The next morning when I arrived at Mrs. Scully's house, I got off my bike and knocked on her front door. "Hello, Tommy," she said sweetly. She was wearing a dress that looked like one of the fancy cakes in the bakery downtown, pink with white icing flowers. "Do you want some hot chocolate?"

"No. I'd like to order a new dress for my mom for Christmas."

"Sure," said Mrs. Scully. "Come inside."

The house was a mess. There were bolts of cloth everywhere and a dress pattern on the table flew up like a paper ghost as I walked by. "Wait here," she said. "I'll get some fabric for you to look at."

Her dining room table was covered with newspapers, mail and patterns. There were a couple of dishes mixed in with all the papers. I automatically started to gather them up, accidentally knocking a pile of paper onto the floor as I did so. After placing the cups and saucers into the sink in the kitchen, I scurried back to the dining room to clean up the papers.

On top of the pile was a pamphlet titled *League of Women Voters*. I wasn't exactly sure what that was, so I opened the pamphlet. It contained a calendar of events. A list of members.

Dates. The addresses of houses where they were meeting. My heart started beating faster. A series of discussion topics was listed: congressional investigations, subversive activity. In that John Wayne movie I'd seen, he'd broken up a secret communist cell in Hawaii. Was it possible that we really had a commie cell in Downers Grove? After all this time, had I stumbled onto the communist?

"Now, I've got a couple of choices for you," Mrs. Scully called from the hallway.

I slipped the pamphlet into my pocket just as she came back into the room.

She laid three bolts of cloth on the already crowded table. The pile of papers I'd knocked over fell off again. Mrs. Scully sighed. "Sorry, I'm a little disorganized."

"Don't worry about it," I said.

Mrs. Scully smiled and I turned my attention to the cloth. The first was brown, very practical, but it reminded me of the couch at the hospital. The second was yellow and way too bright. But the third one was green, and not green like the bookshelves, but green like an apple before it turns red. "That one," I said. "It'll match Mom's eyes."

"Nice choice," she said, putting the other bolts onto the floor.

"Is five dollars enough?" I asked.

"Exactly right," she said.

I reached into my pocket to pull out the money, but she waved me away. "Pay me when it's done. Now, just tell me your mother's measurements and I'll get started on—"

"I brought an old dress," I said.

Mrs. Scully pulled out her tape measure and got right to work, measuring and making notes in a little book. "Got it," she said when she had finished.

"Thank you," I said. "I really appreciate it."

"I know you do, Tommy."

I snuck the dress back into the closet that night while my mom was doing the dishes. She never even noticed it was gone.

I'd decided I was going to buy Little Skinny something for his stocking after all, maybe some penny candy or a deck of cards. I still had a couple of dimes left over from my birthday. Little Skinny always worked the cash register on Saturdays, so I snuck off one day at recess. When I walked into the store, I found Mr. McKenzie was slumped on the floor, an open letter in his hands.

He scrambled to his feet as I entered, and wiped his face with the white apron. His eyes were red, almost as if he had been crying. It had only been a couple of weeks since I'd seen him, but he looked thinner too, like a bear at the end of a long winter's hibernation.

"Tommy," he asked, sounding surprised. "What are you doing here?"

"What's wrong?" I asked.

He shook his head and held out the letter to me. "Another bill I can't pay."

The letter was from the hospital, just like the one my dad had. *Third notice,* it read. *Please pay immediately.* I couldn't bear to look at the amount. After a moment, I folded the letter and placed it on the counter. "What are you going to do?"

Mr. McKenzie shrugged and slumped to the floor again. "I don't know. Don't tell Sam. We'll stay open at least till Christmas. Maybe I can hang on a bit after that. But if things aren't better by Valentine's Day . . ." He shrugged again. "I don't know. I guess we'll go back to Chicago. I've got a cousin there and . . ."

He started to cry. I felt so awkward, like I should go, but I couldn't just leave him there.

"His mother is going to die. I keep telling him she's going to get better, but it's a lie."

Finally, I sat down next to him. I didn't say a word, but we sat like that for a long, long time.

27

DECK THE HALLS

Every year in December, Mary Lou and I linked together colorful rings of paper to hang on the tree. Since we couldn't do it at home this year, I gathered an armful of paper and glue and took them to the hospital. Mary Lou was thrilled. "It's so boring here, with nothing to do," she complained. We spent the afternoon linking the rings together. The next week when I visited, she'd made a chain so long, it went all the way down the hall.

I missed Mary Lou something terrible, especially in the evenings. There were carols on the radio, and Dad made hot chocolate, but it just didn't seem like Christmastime. Mom usually went to her room right after dinner now, and was often asleep before we put Pinky to bed. In the morning Mom still seemed tired, and sometimes, if she'd taken one of Dr. Stanton's sleeping pills, she woke with red-rimmed eyes.

Even though Mary Lou and I always made the paper chains, we weren't allowed to decorate the tree. Oh no. That was my mom's job, because it had to be absolutely perfect. We might put the ornaments too close together or, God forbid, drop and break one. Mom decorated the tree alone on Christmas Eve, after we'd gone to bed, so that when we woke up the next morning, it would appear like magic, fully trimmed.

But I was allowed to pick out the tree with my father. So one cold night, while my mom was doing the dishes from dinner, my dad and Boots and I went to find a tree.

The Christmas tree lot was in a wooded area near the edge of town, and was run by an old man. He'd brought in a bunch of new trees that morning. A light snow was falling and the moon was bright, so all the trees glowed like they were covered with tinsel. While my dad talked to the old man about the price, I chose a tree. It was a huge Douglas fir, with branches as thick and strong as the tail of a horse. Boots ran in circles, snapping at the snowflakes, until he lay down dizzy in the snow.

We carried the tree home on our shoulders, Dad and me. Even though my arms were aching, I didn't complain.

"Dad," I asked, "what's the League of Women Voters?"

Dad turned to look at me. "Why do you want to know about them?"

I shrugged. "Just heard about them somewhere."

"It's a civic organization for women who are interested in politics and democracy."

Oh.

"I've been trying to get your mom to join. Thought it might do her good to get out of the house."

"But they discuss 'subversive activity.' And 'congressional investigations.'"

Dad gave me a funny look. "How do you know that?"

"I . . . saw a note about it in the paper."

I guess he believed me, because he nodded. "They are discussing Senator McCarthy and his congressional investigations to root out suspected communists in the government. The League has been quite critical of him."

"Oh," I said. I remembered what Mr. McKenzie had called those investigations. *A witch hunt.*

Dad dropped his end of the tree as we stopped to rest for a moment. "Tommy, are you still trying to find this supposed communist?"

"No," I lied.

"I think you are."

"But Mr. McKenzie is going under. I saw him last week and—"

"Tommy," Dad said slowly, "some problems we just can't fix."

We picked up the tree again and kept walking. Maybe my father was right. But I kept thinking about Gary Cooper in *High Noon.* Even when he couldn't find anyone else willing to face the bad guys with him, he never stopped trying.

Mom, wearing her bathrobe and slippers, met us in the garage with a bucket of water. We placed the tree in the bucket and held it upright as Mom walked around inspecting it. "Pretty good," she said. "Except for that bald spot."

Dad waved a hand in the air. "It looks fine."

"It looks like a big gaping hole," said Mom.

"Put it toward the back," Dad suggested.

"I'll still know it's there."

"Catherine." My dad was exasperated. "It's a tree, not a precisely engineered statue."

"I didn't say it was a big deal," she replied. "I'll just drill a few holes and put in a couple of extra branches."

"Fine," Dad said. The phone started ringing and he walked off into the house.

I stood there stupidly, still holding the tree.

"You did a good job this year, Tommy," said Mom. "I think it'll make a lovely tree. With a little work."

I wasn't sure if I should feel complimented or offended.

Dad came back into the garage a moment later. "That was the doctor," he said, his voice serious.

No one spoke, but my breath caught in my throat.

"He said"—Dad broke into a huge grin—"that he thinks Mary Lou will be well enough to come home for a few days this Christmas!"

"Mary Lou—home?" Mom asked quietly.

"It's just for a few days," said Dad. "Christmas Eve to New Year's. She'll have to go back for more therapy once the holidays are over but . . ."

I couldn't think of a better present.

This news, welcome as it was, sent my mother into a cleaning frenzy. Every spare minute she had us bleaching sheets, washing curtains, rugs, pillows, until our house was as sterile as the hospital. Suddenly, Mom was hardly sleeping at all. Once when I woke up at 4:30 to do the paper route, I found her on her knees in the hall, scrubbing the floorboards with a toothbrush.

There was a lot of snow that December, which meant there was salt and sand all over the roads. I kept skidding and falling off my bike. Finally, I said something to Mary Lou on one of our visits and she said, "Tommy, once there's snow on the ground, it's easier just to take the sled." The next morning, I loaded the papers into our homemade paperboy sled. It had a long wooden box bolted to a super-long sled. Mary Lou was right: even with having to pull the load up and down hills, the route was easier with the sled. Boots got salt and sand stuck in his paws. I had to wash them with a rag every morning when we got back, but still he gamely came along.

On the last day of school before Christmas break, Little Skinny walked in smiling. "I got the stockings," he said. "You're going to love them!"

"You too!" I said.

Eddie grinned at me and I tried to force myself to laugh. The night before, Eddie had come over and we'd filled the socks with coal from our basement. But when Eddie had gone, I'd dumped one of them out again and placed a few real gifts inside. An orange. A nickel. An old tin soldier. Then I placed a couple of pieces of coal back on top, so it'd look to Eddie like I was sticking to the plan.

And I'd come up with an idea, something I could do for Mary Lou. When it was time for recess, I walked over to Sister Ann. "What is it, Tommy?" she asked.

I told her Mary Lou's fears about not finishing the eighth grade. "I thought maybe someone could go and tutor her? Help her keep up with her class?"

"Tommy." Sister Ann smiled. "That's very sweet of you.

But your sister needs to focus on physically getting better. There will be time to—"

"But her mind's okay, even if she can't walk too well yet. And sometimes . . . sometimes I think it would help if she had something to do."

Sister Ann studied my face for a long time. "You're a good brother, Tommy, to notice that about her."

"Does that mean you'll—"

"I'll speak to Father Miskel about it. But yes, I think you might be right. Perhaps a distraction is just what Mary Lou needs." She smiled again, and when she did, I realized her nose didn't really look like a pickle anymore. Sure, it was big, but it kind of suited her.

"Run along now and play with your friends."

I couldn't put the stocking exchange off any longer. Eddie and Little Skinny were already waiting for me under the big elm tree. "Here!" said Little Skinny, bursting with excitement. He thrust a sock into each of our hands.

We opened them immediately. There were tiny cookies filled with jam and dusted with powered sugar, wrapped in wax paper. There was a brand-new pencil and an eraser and, best of all, a tiny compass from McKenzie's store.

I glanced at Eddie. He looked thrilled. Eddie already had one of the cookies in his mouth.

"My dad helped me with them," Little Skinny said. There was a strange expression on his face. I realized that it might just be a real smile.

"Here's your stocking," Eddie said, handing it over.

Little Skinny reached right inside the stocking and pulled out a lump of coal. It was horrible, watching his face change from eager excitement to embarrassed disgust.

"I knew it," Little Skinny yelled. "I knew I shouldn't trust you!" He held the stocking by the toe and shook the coal onto the ground.

Eddie started laughing.

"Here," I said, thrusting the stocking I had filled at him. "Open this one."

Little Skinny took it from me and threw it aside. "Eddie, I understand. But I thought you were . . . I don't know, maybe my friend."

He stormed off then, not even bothering to peek inside the stocking I'd given him. Eddie laughed harder.

Peter was laughing too. "Why in the world," Peter asked, "would he think you might be his friend?"

I didn't answer.

"Share your cookies with us?" Luke asked.

"Didn't you think it was a mean trick?" I asked.

"Sure it was mean," he said. "But you did it, not me. I can eat the cookies with a clean conscience." He grinned.

I handed him a cookie.

Lizzie came storming past the barrier then, even though girls weren't allowed on the boys' side. Her curly hair frizzed around her head and her cheeks were rosy with anger. "Tommy Wilson!" she fumed. "I saw what you did. You are a mean jerk!"

Her eyes sparkled like the blue yo-yo had in the sun.

"Hey, Lizzie," I said. "Want a cookie?"

"No, I don't want a cookie! I used to think you were

handsome. But you're always picking on people. You have a rotten soul and now I don't even think you're cute at all!"

I laughed. What else could I do? Eddie and Peter and Luke were standing there, watching her yell at me. So I laughed like I didn't care. But I did. For the first time, I realized I actually liked Lizzie. Admired her sass. She reminded me a bit of Mary Lou with her freckles and her temper, but not in a sisterly way. And here she was, telling me that I was a rotten person. The worst part was, I kind of agreed with her.

"Miss Elizabeth Johnson!" Sister Ann called out. "What are you doing on that side of the barrier?"

"Lost a jack!" Lizzie called out, holding up a handful of jacks. "Coming back right now."

She stomped off. Yeah, I liked her. Not that she'd ever speak to me again.

"Give me another cookie," Peter demanded. "You rotten soul!"

The boys all burst out laughing.

I handed over the cookies. They seemed to enjoy them, but I didn't eat a single one.

The next afternoon, Boots and I went over to Mrs. Scully's house to pick up the present for Mom.

"I've got it all ready for you," she said as she pulled a sheet of brown paper off a hanger.

Mrs. Scully held up the dress. It was green like my mother's eyes, and had a wide skirt that would fly out when she vacuumed.

"Thank you," I breathed. "It's perfect." I pulled the five-dollar bill out of my pocket and handed it to her. Then

I pulled out the League of Women Voters pamphlet and placed it on the table too. "And I, um, accidentally picked this up last time I was here."

"Thank goodness you found it," she said. "I'm supposed to bring the snacks next month and I couldn't remember when we were meeting." She sighed. "I like to sew, not cook."

"Merry Christmas," I said.

"Merry Christmas, Tommy."

I clutched the hanger tightly to my chest as Boots and I walked home. Maybe it would be a merry Christmas after all.

28

CHRISTMAS

On Christmas Eve, we got a ride to church with Eddie and his parents. Mr. and Mrs. Sullivan kept snipping at each other in the car, but we all pretended not to notice. Mom wasn't with us because she'd gone to pick up Mary Lou from the hospital and it had taken longer than she'd expected. She'd called and told us to go on without her. I held Susie and Pinky sat in Dad's lap.

When we stepped inside the church, the first thing I saw was the huge Christmas tree, twice as big as the one we'd picked out, and dozens of red poinsettias. There were also two smaller trees. They were decorated with nothing more than blue lights that shone like moonlight on water in the dim church.

The second thing I noticed was Lizzie Johnson in a green-and-red-plaid dress that clashed with her hair. She looked so pretty. I walked over and said hi. She crossed her arms, muttered an insincere "Merry Christmas" and turned her back on me. But at least she was speaking to me.

We sat down in our pew and the service started. After a while, Pinky slumped against me, half asleep. Little Skinny and Mr. McKenzie were there too. I cringed as I looked at Little Skinny, sinking down lower in my pew, hoping he hadn't told his dad about the stockings. Pinky woke up for the Christmas carols at the end—and the very last one was "Hark! The Herald Angels Sing." That was a good sign. I wondered if Mary Lou would really be there when we got home.

It was snowing as we all filed outside, solemn yet joyous. Clanking chains on the car tires rang through the night. If I'd been a little younger, I might have believed Mr. Sullivan's story that they were the bells on Santa's sleigh. I was pretty sure that Pinky did.

When we pulled up to our house, I could see our car in the driveway. I ran inside, and there, in the living room, sitting in an armchair, was my sister.

Mary Lou was talking to my mother, who was sitting next to her on the couch. There were no lights on, only a few candles on the mantel. The tree was still in the garage, waiting to be decorated by my mother. When Mary Lou turned to me, she seemed to glow, like the trees at church, her long brown hair falling loose about her head, the candlelight making her brown eyes shine. She didn't really look like my sister. She looked like an angel.

"Tommy," she said, and smiled.

Pinky beat me to her. She threw her arms around her, and though she winced, Mary Lou hugged her back. I could just see her bandaged legs peeking out from under her long skirt. It was my turn then, and I walked over and took her hand in mine. For the first time since burning the trash all those weeks ago, I didn't have to feel guilty. Mary Lou was home and everything was going to be okay.

"I'm so glad I got to come home for Christmas," Mary Lou said.

"Yeah," I said. "Me too."

Out of habit, I woke up at 4:30 the next morning even though I didn't have to deliver the papers until 8:30 on Christmas Day. I lay in bed for a while, trying to go back to sleep, but I was too excited. Finally, I got up and went into the living room.

The tree looked beautiful. There were long strings of multi-colored lights and candle-shaped bulbs with boiling alcohol inside, candy canes and ornaments and lots and lots of tinsel. The paper garland Mary Lou and I had made was draped across the mantel. Gifts were scattered around the tree, their ribbons sparkling.

Mom walked into the room then, drinking a cup of coffee. "Morning, Tommy," she said.

"Morning, Mom," I said. "You did an amazing job."

"You like it?" She'd tied her dark hair back with a scarf. It made her look young, like a little girl.

"It's perfect," I said.

"It is, isn't it?" She sighed.

I thought back to the great time we'd had eating Thanksgiving dinner. My accordion was at Mrs. Glazov's. I'd have to get it later, maybe play a few polkas and we could all dance in the living room again. Maybe it would be just like old times.

Mom yawned.

"Did you get any sleep?" I asked.

"No," she said. "But I don't like to sleep on Christmas. It's my favorite holiday. I don't want to miss one single moment."

I knew just what she meant.

We stood there together, looking at the tree for a long time. Finally, Mom said, "Go back to sleep, Tommy. Dad won't have breakfast ready until after six."

So I did. The house smelled like sausage links and pancakes when I woke up a second time. Everyone else was already gathered in the kitchen. Pinky was bouncing in her chair at the breakfast table. "Hurry, Tommy," she said. "Mommy says no presents until we eat."

I gobbled down that food so fast, I barely tasted it. Soon as we were done, it was present time. We tore into them, bows and paper flying in the air. Maybe not as many presents as in years past, but there was a new doll for Pinky, a book for Mary Lou, a model airplane for me and a new fishing lure for Dad's collection.

When our boxes were finally opened, Dad cleared his throat. "Tommy and I have a special surprise for Mom."

My mother smiled.

"What is it, Tommy? What is it?" begged Pinky.

I pulled out Mom's package from where I'd hidden it under the couch and handed it to her. She tore the paper open.

"Is this a new dress?" She gasped, her eyes shiny and bright, her face as excited as Pinky's.

I nodded. "I thought you'd like the green. Dad saved the money and I asked Mrs. Scully to make it."

Mom fingered the fabric. "This is beautiful!" She pulled the dress out and shook it free of the paper. Then, all at once, her expression changed.

"Is this some kind of mean joke?" she barked.

I didn't know what she was talking about.

"Are you calling me fat?" she snapped.

"Now, Catherine," said my father.

"What's wrong?" I asked.

"This dress is way too small! There is no way it'll fit!" my mother screamed at me.

"B-b-but—but—" I sputtered. "We used your old blue dress as a pattern."

"That hasn't fit since before Pinky was born!" Mom screamed. "Tommy, I can't believe you did this!"

She stood up and pushed over the tree she'd worked on for so many hours. It tottered once on its stand, then slowly fell to the ground with a crash of shattering ornaments. Mom gasped at what she had done, then ran off to her bedroom.

Pinky started to cry.

My father and Mary Lou looked at each other, but I couldn't meet their eyes. For the first time, I wished Mary Lou wasn't home. At least then she wouldn't have seen how I'd ruined Christmas Day.

"Thomas," said my father quietly. "I didn't mean . . . I didn't realize that dress was too small. Holidays are hard for her and you can't take it personally."

"How am I supposed to take it?" I shrieked at him. I sounded just like my mother, and that scared me worse than anything she had done.

Mary Lou stared at the wall.

"I'm going out," I said.

No one bothered to answer.

As I walked the paper route, I kept expecting to start crying. But I didn't. Somehow, I made my way to Mrs. Scully's. I don't know what I thought I was going to do. Confront her for making the dress the wrong size?

Mrs. Scully invited me in for hot chocolate. She wore a crimson dress trimmed with white, and lipstick that matched. It made her look a bit like a candy cane. Her tree was only a plant on a table, but no one was yelling at each other. "So tell me," she said as she shoved a mug of hot chocolate into my hands, "how did your mother like the dress?"

Time froze for a moment, as I wondered what to say. I wanted to tell her the truth, wanted to blame her, wanted a shoulder to cry on, but more than that, I wanted her house to stay just the way it was, messy, happy and peaceful. "She loved it," I said.

Mrs. Scully grinned. "I'm so glad, Tommy. You're such a thoughtful boy." She hugged me tight. She smelled like peaches and petunias, and I could feel the lipstick that came off as she kissed my cheek. "I've got something for you," she said. "Come on downstairs."

I followed her into the basement, which was filled with a huge table covered with the most elaborate train set I had ever seen. It had a station and a mountain, a lake to run the train around and a forest to motor through. There were all sorts of different trains, tiny signals and people, small figures waiting to get on, to journey to who knows where.

"You must think I'm strange," she said. "To live here all alone. When my husband died, I thought about getting a smaller place, but then what would I do with the trains! Aren't they lovely?"

"Yes," I marveled. "They're magnificent."

I watched the train, running in circles around the track. I could have stood there for hours.

"You did say you were a cowboy fan, right?" Mrs. Scully started rummaging through a box in the corner.

"Yes."

She pulled out a small train. "This is just like the engine in *High Noon*. You know the one, when they're waiting for the bad guy to come into town. Grace Kelly gets on it, like she's going to leave and abandon her husband, but of course at the last minute she jumps off and she doesn't. You have seen *High Noon*, haven't you?"

"Five times," I said.

"Oh, you're a fellow fan. This'll be perfect, then." And she handed the train to me.

It was heavy in my hand. Made of painted metal, it did look just like the one in *High Noon*. If only I could get on a train like that and ride away from all my problems. "It's beautiful," I said, handing it back to her.

"No, no." She waved me off. "It's for you."

"But . . . I haven't done anything," I said. "You hardly know me."

She smiled at me. "Usually I love living by myself. But at times it gets a little lonely. And you stopped by to say hello on Christmas."

• • •

Mrs. Glazov was equally excited to see me. She opened the door almost before I was done knocking.

"Tommy," she exclaimed. "Merry Christmas."

She made me tea and served cookies. While we ate and drank, she read me every headline on the front page of the *Tribune*. I felt as proud as a mama bird that's just taught her fledgling to fly. After the reading, she announced, "Now we play." We ran through all our favorite Christmas carols, ending with "Silent Night." When we were done, I sat there quietly for a minute. This is what Christmas should be like, I thought.

"Now," she said quietly. "You go home. Things calmed down."

"What?"

"Sometimes I hear," she admitted. "Yelling. Crying. No more today. You go home."

I lugged the accordion back with me, and poked my head into the living room. Dad had finished sweeping up the glass and the tree was standing again, sparkling as if it had never been knocked over at all. Pinky was playing with her new doll.

Mom walked into the room, carrying a pie. She'd gotten dressed, combed her hair, put on lipstick. But her eyes were still red from crying. "Oh good, Tommy," she said brightly, as if nothing had happened. "You're back. And you have the accordion! Play us something. A polka maybe. I love polkas!" She pulled out a chair from the dining room and placed it in the center of the room for me.

My father nodded, and pushed back the couch.

I picked up the accordion and sat down on the chair and started to play the brightest, happiest polka I could. This was my plan. This was what I had wanted. My dad asked my mom to dance and they began to whirl across the floor, just as they had on Thanksgiving. Pinky clapped her hands. Mary Lou looked over at me and smiled.

And that's when I started to cry. Huge tears that rolled down my eyes, so I couldn't even see my parents. I wasn't sure I would be able to finish the song, but I did. Mary Lou finally noticed. "What's wrong, Tommy?"

"I'm just so happy," I lied.

Mom smiled and went off to cook Christmas dinner. Dad patted me on the shoulder. I pasted on a smile so fake, I thought my skin would crack. We never mentioned the tree again.

29

PAIN PILLS

If Christmas Day was bad, the week afterward was even worse. I guess I'd thought I'd spend the break with my sister, talking and playing games, like we always had before. But Mary Lou's bandages needed to be changed every few hours and ointments needed to be applied. Mom insisted *she* was the only one who could do it properly, since she had picked Mary Lou up from the hospital and been instructed by the nurses. More than once, I found Mom clutching a soiled bandage, tears running down her face. Every time I offered to help, she shook her head and told me to go away.

I discovered that when Mary Lou said she could walk from the bed to the bathroom, she meant if she had twenty minutes and an hour to lie down afterward. Mom went after her like a drill sergeant, yelling and screaming and cursing at her to do the stretches from the hospital or to hobble down the hall one more time. Mary Lou yelled back at first: "I'm trying!" or "Get out of my way!" Then it changed to "I can't do it," and "Leave me alone," and finally she just meekly tried to comply, tears running down her face.

Mom and Dad started arguing too, screaming behind closed doors, as if a skinny old wooden bedroom door would prevent us from hearing what they had to say. "I thought you said they were suggestions," Dad argued. "It's vacation. You don't have to force her to do them every single day."

In the living room, Mary Lou and I concentrated on our game of checkers. Pinky watched intently.

"They said it would be good for her!" Mom countered. "Don't you want what's best for your daughter?"

"Of course I do, but—"

"You don't care if she's deformed or can't walk. If she doesn't get better, no one will ever want to marry her and we'll be stuck with—"

Pinky's eyes were wide. "Is Mary Lou going to turn into a monster?" she asked.

"No," I said.

"Take her outside," said Mary Lou. "She doesn't need to hear this."

"You come too," I said.

Mary Lou shook her head. "It's too cold for me since I can't . . . move around fast enough to stay warm."

"But—"

"You take Pinky. It doesn't bother me, Tommy."

But I knew it did bother her. The next day when I got up at 4:30 to do the paper route, I heard Mary Lou crying in her room. When I opened the door to check on her, she rolled over and pretended to be asleep. I couldn't wait for school to start again so I could escape to St. Joe's. I missed Eddie, but he had gone out of town to visit relatives. I thought about playing marbles with Peter and Luke. Heck, I would even have been happy to see Little Skinny.

And if the yelling wasn't enough, Mom started rationing Mary Lou's pain pills too, stretching out the time between doses a little bit more every day, or cutting the tablets in half. "You're stronger than that," Mom told Mary Lou when she complained.

When the pain got so bad that all Mary Lou could do was lie on her bed and cry, I snuck into the bathroom and got the other half of the pill that she was supposed to have had in the first place.

Those days were so awful, I jumped out of bed at 4:30 each morning, relieved to have an excuse to get away from the house for a few hours. One morning when I returned from the route, Mom was waiting for me in the kitchen, holding the bottle of pain pills in her hand.

"Yesterday when I counted these pills, there were six. Why are there now only four?"

"Mary Lou was in pain," I explained. "She hurt so much she couldn't even sleep."

"Do you want to turn your sister into a drug addict?" Her face was red with anger, her jaw clenched.

"The doctor prescribed them!"

"I'm doing what's best for her." Mom's hair flew out of her bun as she shook the bottle of pills.

"But Dr. Stanton prescribed those sleeping pills for you."

"Tommy!"

"You don't seem to have any problem taking them!" That's when I saw she already had Dad's belt curled up in her hand.

"Don't speak to me in that tone!" she screamed.

"It doesn't matter what I say," I muttered. "You're going to hit me anyway."

And she did. And I let her. Pulled down my pants and just stood there. I hated her for punishing me this way, when I was just trying to help my sister. And even though I swore I wouldn't, I starting crying, not from the pain, but because I was so angry.

Mom yelled at me to stop, and I tried to, I really did. I wanted to be tough and stoic, but the tears kept coming.

'Course crying only made it worse, 'cause Mary Lou heard me. She hobbled into the kitchen, holding on to the door frame to keep her balance. "Stop it, Mom! Stop!" she shrieked. "I don't need the pills. I won't take them anymore."

I knew Mary Lou was trying to help, but it was mortifying to have my older sister see me, my pants around my ankles, crying like a baby. I wanted to scream at her to go away, but I couldn't get out the words.

Mom just ignored Mary Lou and kept hitting me.

Boots joined in then, barking desperately, although he stayed in the doorway at Mary Lou's feet, not daring to set foot in the kitchen.

"Catherine!" Dad boomed, appearing behind Mary Lou.

Mom paused, the belt dangling from her hand.

Thank God. Was Dad going to finally step up for me?

Mom was breathing hard, sweat on her forehead, even though it was cold in the room.

Mary Lou was weeping quietly now. "Take me back to the hospital. Please, take me back! I can't stand it here another minute!"

Dad led her out of the room. Boots stayed, watching me and whining softly.

Mom hit me once more with the belt, then dropped it on the floor. The house was still. It seemed, suddenly, too quiet with no one yelling or crying.

"I have a headache," said Mom. "I'm going back to bed." She left the room without even picking up the belt.

As I pulled up my pants, I heard the car roar to life. They were leaving now? Didn't Mary Lou need to pack? I ran to the garage to say good-bye, but they were already gone.

Boots and I sat in the garage all afternoon, waiting for my dad to return. It was cold and my backside ached. My hands felt numb, even as I buried them in Boots's warm fur.

Finally, my dad returned. "Tommy, what are you doing here?" His long gray overcoat fluttered as he slammed the car door.

"Why didn't you stop her?" I asked.

"You disobeyed your mother."

"Mary Lou should have had those pills in the first place. You know that!"

"What do you want me to do, Tommy?" Dad screamed. "What do you want me to do!"

"Nothing," I said. I went inside and lay down on my bed. Boots pressed up against my side and I cried myself to sleep.

AT THE HOSPITAL

It was the Sunday after New Year's and I was sitting in the waiting room at the hospital again, coloring with Pinky. Mom was upstairs with Mary Lou. I hadn't seen my sister since the argument about the pain pills. I wasn't sure what I would say when I did.

The stairway door opened and Little Skinny slipped out. He walked toward the waiting room, but froze when he saw Pinky and me.

"Hey, Little Skinny!" I called.

He turned and headed back toward the stairs.

I ran after him, catching up with him just as he was pushing open the door. "Little Skinny!" I said. "I wanted to talk to you."

"My name is *Sam*," he said.

I felt awful then. I'd forgotten I'd promised to call him by his name.

"And I don't want to talk to you." Little Skinny crossed his arms.

"Okay, okay," I said. "I get it."

He glared at me.

"You were so mean!" he said.

After everything that had happened over Christmas, I had almost pushed the coal stockings out of my mind. Add that to my list of things I wished I could forget. I shrugged. "It was just a joke."

"It was not a joke," he said. "It was horrible!" Little Skinny turned bright red as he got more and more worked up. "You're a different person at the store, Tommy. I don't know how you can be so cruel at school."

"Did you even look in the stocking I made?" I asked. "There was an orange and a nickel and a tin soldier."

"No," he said. "It was filled with coal."

"I only put a couple of pieces on top so Eddie wouldn't know."

"So Eddie wouldn't know what?" he asked. "That you were being nice to me? That sometimes you act like you're my friend, and then you're horrible again?"

"I—I—" I didn't know what to say. "It was Eddie's idea," I finished lamely.

"It doesn't matter whose idea it was! It was really mean."

It was mean. I knew that.

"It's not fair, Tommy," Little Skinny went on. "Just 'cause you're good-looking and clever and know how to charm people doesn't mean you get to stomp on the rest of us. You're lucky and you don't even appreciate it!"

"Oh, so you think my life is so perfect, huh?" We were practically yelling now.

"It's looking pretty good from where I sit."

"You need to get your eyes examined. My sister is half burned up!" I was screaming now. "She almost died!"

"But she didn't," Little Skinny screamed back. "And my mom's going to!"

Little Skinny and I stood in the doorway, glaring at each other. In the waiting room, Pinky colored so hard, her crayon snapped. The nurse at the reception desk stared, wide-eyed, not even pretending she wasn't listening.

The worst part was, Little Skinny had a point. Mary Lou was getting better. And his mom wasn't. "I'm sorry," I said. "I'm so sorry. About your mom and everything else."

He rubbed his eyes and we both pretended not to notice he was crying. "We're going to have to leave, you know. My dad said we're closing up the store the last week in January and going to live with his cousin in Chicago."

That was my fault too. But at least he didn't say it.

"Mom will have to stay here," Little Skinny went on. "She's been in the hospital since August."

"That's not fair," I said.

"No," he agreed. "It isn't."

"Really," I said softly. "I'm sorry."

Little Skinny said nothing. But he came back to the waiting room and sat down on the brown couch. "I'm not scared of you anymore. With Mom dying, you just don't seem that important."

I smiled and sat down next to him. "How was your Christmas?"

Little Skinny snorted.

"That good, huh?"

We both giggled a bit, though I saw a tear run down his scar.

"Yeah," I said. "Mine was about the same."

He didn't say a word. We sat in silence for a while, until Pinky said she had to go potty and Little Skinny stood up and said, "I'll take her." As they walked off, I tried to imagine what it would be like to be an only child like Little Skinny. At least I had Pinky and Susie to take care of and Mary Lou to give me advice. I had a dog to lick my face when I was sad and Mrs. Glazov to play accordion with me.

I wasn't sure I deserved it. I'd been mean to Luke and Peter on the bus, and awful to Little Skinny. I'd destroyed Mr. McKenzie's reputation, sworn I'd clear his name and then gotten caught up in my own problems. I didn't keep my word. I wasn't a nice friend.

It was a new year and I wanted to change.

31

RACING WITH LITTLE SKINNY

Every January, the nuns took us over to Prince Pond for an afternoon of skating. Prince Pond was a small pond, about the length of one block, that froze over every winter. With the money from the paper drive, the homeowners' association had constructed an open shelter at one end where you could build a fire to stay warm.

Sister Ann and the other nuns chatted on the bank, their arms tucked under their habits so that they looked like giant bowling pins waiting to be knocked over. Peter was fooling around, skating in circles and throwing snowballs at any girl who turned her back. Little Skinny sat in the shelter with Lizzie Johnson and some of the other girls from our class. Every now and then one of them would add a bit of wood to the fire.

Not that we really needed a fire. The past ten days had been unseasonably warm, making it above freezing for a good portion of each day. It was probably 35 or 36 degrees that afternoon, not cold at all for Downers Grove in the winter.

In any case, hot from all the skating, I'd left my jacket on the bank.

Eddie had just beaten Peter and Luke in a race and he threw himself down on the ice, breathing hard. "So," he called out, confident as a cowboy on a prize-winning steed, "who's going to race me next?" He leaned back on his hands like he was at the beach. Everyone stared at him. "No takers?"

Little Skinny walked slowly over from the shelter. He still had his shoes on and he slipped, almost falling, waving his arms like a bird to catch himself. "I'll race you," he said. "But I don't have any skates." He looked over at me.

It was like he was challenging me to see if I'd be nice to him at school, in front of the others. I took the dare.

"I'll loan you mine," I said. I pulled off my skates and gave them a little push so they glided across the ice to Little Skinny.

He smiled and put them on quickly, almost without looking at the laces. "Three times around the pond?" Little Skinny suggested.

Eddie nodded. "Fine with me."

They both skated over to the charcoal line we'd been using as a starting mark. There was a large ring of stones around the middle of the pond. The other boys and I had placed them there when we'd first arrived, creating a makeshift lane around the edge for racing. That way the girls could skate in the middle without getting in our way.

"Here are the rules," I said. "Stay in the lane, three times around, no funny business—no tripping, pushing, stuff like that."

They nodded.

"On your mark," I said. "Get set. Go!"

During the first lap, Eddie and Little Skinny stayed pretty even. I was surprised. Little Skinny was actually a good skater, moving smoothly across the ice. By the time the second lap was done, Little Skinny was slightly ahead.

"Come on, Eddie!" Luke called.

I wasn't sure who to root for.

Eddie skated faster, really giving it his all. But Little Skinny did too, pulling ahead a little bit more. By the final turn, it wasn't even a contest. Little Skinny was a full body length ahead. A moment later he crossed the finish line first and raised his hands in the air. "I won!"

Everyone, on the ice and in the shelter, was looking at him.

Angry, Eddie purposely crashed into the lane, sending the rocks flying. "You can skate!"

Little Skinny grinned. "Ever since I could walk," he said proudly. "I can ski too. Everyone can, where I'm from. There were lots of mountains."

"You tricked me!" Eddie said.

"What's wrong, Eddie?" Little Skinny taunted. "Did I embarrass you in front of your friends?"

"You little communist!" Eddie yelled, and took a swing at Little Skinny.

Little Skinny ducked and stumbled on the ice, but he didn't fall.

"He's not a communist," I said quietly.

"Well, his dad sure is," said Eddie. "I heard my father talking about it."

I grabbed Eddie's arm and pulled him a couple of steps away from Little Skinny. "Take it back!"

"No, I won't," he said. "And why do you care, Tommy?"

"It's not true," I argued. "You shouldn't be spreading lies about Mr. McKenzie!"

"But everybody knows he's a communist. It's why no one shops there anymore," said Eddie.

"It's not true!"

"How do you know?" asked Eddie.

My stomach hurt like I'd been punched. "Because I was the one who put the copy of the *Daily Worker* in his store."

"What?" said Eddie. "The one you found on the paper drive?"

I nodded. "Didn't you figure it out?"

"But I thought Mr. McKenzie was the communist?"

Luke and Peter stood watching us, taking in every word.

"It was just a joke," I said. "I didn't know everyone would take it so seriously!"

The nuns rang a bell then, signaling it was time to return to school. I started obediently back to the bank, but Eddie stood there in the center of the pond.

So did Little Skinny. And something had snapped in him, because his eyes were no longer sad, they were mad.

"One time," he said. "I got the best of you one time. And you had to go and ruin it!" He took a deep breath like he was going to start crying. Instead, he punched Eddie in the stomach.

I was so surprised, it took me a moment to react. By that point, Little Skinny had his full weight on top of Eddie and was pounding away. One hit after another. I could see the blood spurting out of Eddie's nose.

Eddie was yelling and I tried to pull Little Skinny off, but he threw me aside, like a bear with a dog. For the first time, I could see Mr. McKenzie's toughness in Little Skinny. He kept pounding Eddie, but maybe Eddie deserved it. For the coal. And the candy. And all the ways we'd hurt Little Skinny. Maybe I deserved to be beaten too.

The nuns were gathered around the edge of the pond, yelling. None of them had skates on and they kept slipping as they tried to venture onto the ice. Then there was a loud cracking sound, almost like thunder.

"Stop," I yelled. "Sam, stop!"

Little Skinny stopped pounding Eddie and turned to look at me. The pond rumbled again.

Eddie scrambled to his feet.

"The ice!" cried a girl from the bank.

Everyone scattered, Eddie and I reaching solid ice just in time. But Little Skinny stood still for just a moment too long. By the time he started to move, there was another *crack,* even louder this time, and the ice broke up beneath him. He fell into the water.

The pond was only three feet deep, so it wasn't like he was going to drown or anything. But when Little Skinny stood up, he just looked so cold and miserable with the water running down his face.

Peter started to laugh. I pulled out a handkerchief and handed it to Eddie. He pressed it against his nose to stop the bleeding.

Little Skinny tried to pull himself onto the solid ice, but his weight was too much and the ice kept cracking as he tried to scramble out.

The nuns screamed for someone to find a rope. Peter kept laughing. I had another idea. I ran to the shelter and grabbed the fire poker. Then I ran, sliding without my skates, back onto the ice. When I got close to the hole, I lay down on the ice and held out the poker.

"Grab it," I said.

Little Skinny did. With a huge effort, I managed to pull him onto the ice. He followed me, crawling almost all the way back to the bank before daring to stand up again.

Peter was laughing so hard, he was doubled over, clutching his stomach. I knew he expected me to join in too, play it off as a huge joke, but I just couldn't. Luke wasn't laughing, but he wasn't helping either.

The nuns came running over. "Are you all right, Samuel?" Sister Ann cried.

"Cold," he choked out. He was shivering so badly, I thought his skeleton would shake right out of his body. I grabbed my coat from the bank and handed it to him.

Sister Ann ushered Little Skinny over to the fire. But once he warmed up a bit, she started to lecture. "Samuel," she said sternly, "we saw you hitting Eddie. Fighting is strictly forbidden at St. Joe's. I'm afraid you'll—"

"No," I said suddenly. "It wasn't his fault. Eddie hit first."

Eddie looked at me, surprised and bewildered. We didn't rat each other out. We kept each other's secrets.

But I went on. "Eddie provoked him," I said. "Called his dad a communist."

Sister Ann sighed. "Even if Eddie was teasing him, that's no reason to—"

"No," I insisted. "His dad is going to lose his store because of those rumors. And it's my fault too because I was the one who started them."

Everyone was suddenly quiet and staring at me. Even Lizzie was looking at me with a little half smile on her face that made me think maybe she didn't hate my guts quite so much anymore.

Sister Ann, however, looked exhausted. "Eddie, are you hurt?" she asked.

"Yes!" He held up the bloody handkerchief.

"Do you need a doctor?"

"No," Eddie admitted.

"Good. Samuel, are you okay?"

"Cold." Little Skinny's teeth chattered and he was shivering violently.

Sister Ann nodded decisively. "Tommy, take Samuel home and get him some dry clothes. Everyone else, back to school!"

32

THE APARTMENT

The store was closed when we arrived, but Little Skinny had a key. "Dad's probably at the hospital," he said. And he didn't have to say the rest: *because Mom's not doing so well.*

The dark, empty shelves gave the store an eerie feel. Little Skinny marched right through it, heading for the stairs. I'd never seen their apartment before, but I followed him up the narrow staircase.

There was a simple living room at the top, a couch, a table and an armchair. The furniture was well-worn, but everything was neat and tidy.

"Wait here," said Little Skinny. "I'll go get some dry clothes."

While he was gone, I looked around. In one corner, there was a small table with a funny metal machine on top. It had a round drum and a handle.

"What's that?" I asked when Little Skinny returned.

"A mimeograph machine," Little Skinny said, drying his hair with a towel.

"Where'd you get it?" I asked.

"The church was throwing it away," he said. "I fixed it myself. I'm good at things like that."

"How does it work?"

Little Skinny sighed. "You put this special sheet, it's called a stencil, in the typewriter and type out what you want to say. Then you can run off as many copies as you want. My dad writes family letters every month, and I make copies of them so he can send them to all his relatives. He lets me use the extra stencils."

"For your stories?"

"Yeah."

"Going to let me read one?"

"No." But this time he said it with a smile. It was odd to think he had secrets, a whole other life, one where he wrote stories and was good at skating and could fix things.

"Ready to go?" Little Skinny asked.

"What about your wet clothes?"

"What about them?"

"Don't you need to wash them?"

He shrugged. "I'll do it when I get home."

"I'd be afraid my mom would beat me if I left wet clothes lying around," I said without thinking.

Little Skinny laughed.

But I wasn't joking. And I guess after a minute Little Skinny realized that, because as we were walking back down the stairs, he asked, "Your mom hit you a lot?"

I shrugged. "She always used to yell, but since Mary Lou has been in the hospital, she's . . . gotten worse."

When I reached the bottom of the stairs, I peeked over, expecting to see pity in Little Skinny's eyes, but he just looked surprised. As if he hadn't realized I had another life too. "You always seem so confident, Tommy. Like nothing ever bothers you."

"Ha!" I laughed, short and bitter. "Wouldn't that be nice."

"But you do stuff," said Little Skinny. "I've wanted to go out and steal a bunch of yo-yos more than once." We walked back through the dark store. "I just don't have the guts."

Was he saying he admired me? For stealing yo-yos? "Nah," I said. "Guts are overrated."

Little Skinny laughed, then looked embarrassed.

"We'd better get back to school," I said.

"Yeah," he replied.

We walked the rest of the way in silence. Then, right before we went inside, he said, "You called me Sam. Before the ice cracked." It was almost a question.

I nodded. "Isn't that your name?"

He smiled. "Yeah, it is."

That afternoon, I was a few minutes late leaving the building after school. I had to finish the math assignment I'd missed when I was with Sam. And I wanted to make sure I didn't run into Eddie. So by the time I made it outside, Mom was waiting by the car. She was leaning against the hood, her arms crossed over her chest. She looked like a mess. Her hair was uncombed, her dress wrinkled. Her eyes were wide and a bit unfocused, as if she'd taken one of Dr. Stanton's pills and then drunk a whole pot of coffee to stay awake. "You're late."

"Little Skinny, I mean Sam, fell through the ice."

"Don't lie to me." Mom sneered.

"I'm not."

Mom slapped me.

The sound seemed to echo across the school yard. Everyone turned to look at us. Sister Ann stood in the school doorway, watching. I thought I would be embarrassed, but maybe, like Sam, I'd just had enough.

I turned the other side of my face toward her. "Go ahead," I said. "Slap the other side."

She did.

Sister Ann walked up to our car then. "Is everything all right, Mrs. Wilson?" she asked, her wimple blowing in the wind.

Instantly, Mom was all smiles. "Of course, Sister Ann. Tommy was just being disrespectful."

"I see," said Sister Ann. She looked at me, but I didn't say a word, just got into the backseat with Pinky.

My sister climbed into my lap and gave me a big hug. "Mommy's in a bad mood."

"I know."

"I wet my pants this morning," she admitted. "I'm almost five! I'm not supposed to do that."

"It's not your fault." But Pinky still didn't let go.

Mom got into the driver's seat, and I was surprised when Sister Ann climbed into the front beside her. Mom said, "We're ever so grateful, Sister, that you're coming to the hospital to tutor Mary Lou."

"It's my pleasure," Sister Ann said.

I guess Father Miskel had approved of the idea. No one had bothered to tell me.

Mom drove way too fast, skidding on the ice when she turned. No one said a word all the way to the hospital. As soon as we arrived, Sister Ann and Mom went up to see Mary Lou. They were gone a long time.

When I finally got to see Mary Lou, my sister chattered on and on, about how great it felt to do her school lessons. "Sister Ann said if I worked really, really hard, I might even be able to graduate with the other eighth graders!" She grinned. "And it's all thanks to you, Tommy!"

But it didn't feel great. It felt like everything was falling apart.

I sat in the chair next to her bed and looked out the window as I listened.

"Is something wrong?" Mary Lou asked. "You're quiet today."

I just shook my head. I didn't know where to start.

33

THE COMMUNIST

Later that evening, I was in the kitchen doing the dishes. My whole body hurt from falling on the ice and I could still feel the sting on my cheeks from where Mom had slapped me, even though they weren't red anymore. I was about halfway done when Dad came in and tapped me on the shoulder. "Can I help?"

I shrugged and Dad took that as a yes. Oh, I knew he was trying to be nice, but I needed help with Mom, not with the pots and pans! Still, I washed the plates while Dad did the glasses.

"I heard Sister Ann came to tutor Mary Lou today," he said, wiping a smudge of lipstick off a water glass. "Mom said it was your idea."

I shrugged again.

"It was a good one, Tommy. We should have thought of it before."

That sounded almost like a compliment. I scrubbed a bit of dried food off a plate, kind of embarrassed.

"I also heard that Eddie got into a fight at school. Something about him picking on—"

"I didn't hit anyone!" I said.

"I know," he said. "Just making sure."

"What does that mean?"

"Nothing."

"Dad!"

"Well, you sometimes act impulsively. Like you think you really are a cowboy."

"I like cowboys." Dad said it like there was something wrong with being one. "Cowboys are brave and strong and honest."

"They're also reckless, vengeful and independent to a fault." Dad sighed. "Take your idea about 'finding the communist' and 'clearing Mr. McKenzie's name.'"

"What about it? You defended Mr. McKenzie at the card party."

"I like Mr. McKenzie just fine," Dad said, "but—"

"Then why don't you want me to help him? I feel bad that I haven't!"

"Tommy, it's not—"

"I really should keep trying. That's what a cowboy would do."

"Thomas John Wilson, this conversation is over."

"Why?"

"Because I said so."

"Oh, that's a good reason," I scoffed.

"Tommy!" Dad's face was getting redder and his hands trembled as he washed the glasses. Any second now, I thought he was going to go get the belt and whip me himself. But I just couldn't stop.

"Or maybe," I said, "you just don't like me!"

Dad froze, a glass in one hand. "Tommy, is that what you think?"

I realized I was breathing hard, my heart pumping as if I'd just finished a race.

"Yeah."

Dad looked horrified. "That's not true. I . . . I don't want you pursuing this anymore because I already know who the 'communist' is."

In the harsh glare of the kitchen, every line in my dad's face stood out. He looked as tense as Gary Cooper heading to the final shoot-out all alone. "Who?" I asked.

"Me." He whispered the word so softly, I wasn't quite sure I'd heard him.

"You?" I asked. "You're a communist?" Part of me wanted to laugh, but his face was tight and pinched and it certainly didn't look like he was joking.

"No, of course not. But the paper came from me."

"I don't understand."

He sighed. "When I was in college, I attended a meeting or two. Maybe I bought a few papers. I was curious. There was a professor I admired who invited me and . . . it doesn't matter. I never joined anything. Everything is packed up in some old boxes in the attic. Your mother took it upon herself to get rid of one of the boxes without asking me, and I guess one of the old papers got mixed up with the new ones."

I couldn't believe what my dad was telling me. All this time and he hadn't said a thing. "You could have saved Mc-Kenzie's store!"

"How?" Dad countered. "Officer Russo went around telling people it was a schoolboy prank. It didn't do any good. What would have happened to me if I had actually admitted owning that newspaper? Who would have supported you and Mom and your sisters if I had lost my job?"

I didn't answer.

"Oh, I shouldn't have told you," he said almost to himself. His hands were still shaking as he started drying the glasses. "But I couldn't let you think I didn't care!"

My thoughts were spinning. I'd always believed communists were evil, bad people. And my father had associated with them! What did that make him? And did he just say he cared about me after all?

"Tommy, you can't tell anyone about this. Look at what happened to Mr. McKenzie, and he didn't even do anything!"

"But it's not fair that Mr. McKenzie is suffering because of you."

"No, it's not," Dad agreed. "And if you hadn't put that paper in his store, this would never have happened."

I picked up one of the clean dry glasses and threw it to the floor. It shattered into a million pieces.

"Just like your mom." He shook his head. "Not a word to anyone!" Dad threw down his dish towel and stormed out of the room.

I was left in the kitchen alone. I knew I had to clean up the mess before Mom came in, but every shard of glass I picked up made me feel even worse. I *was* like my mom. I had a bad temper. I threw things when I got angry.

And worst of all, my father was the communist.

34

THE SEAMSTRESS

Sunday after church, I told Mrs. Glazov I wasn't feeling well and went to the movies. It was mid-January and I hadn't been to the Tivoli since I'd started giving her reading lessons. Usually I went with Eddie, but he still wasn't talking to me. I wanted to lose myself in a good film and forget all my problems for a little while.

The movie that day was called *Red Planet Mars*. It was about two American scientists, a husband and a wife, who started receiving radio messages from Mars. "The whole world is scared," said the wife. "Why shouldn't I be?"

She was talking about the Soviets who may—or may not—have been faking the radio messages in an attempt to cause chaos in the American economy. But I could relate. I was scared too. What if someone found out about my dad? Would someone throw a brick through our front window? Draw a hammer and sickle on our car? Would Dad lose his job at Western Electric? My dad wasn't going to take over the world or redistribute our property or even stop going to church. He wasn't a bad person. Sure, he sometimes made me mad, but I loved him. Oh, why had he gone to that stupid meeting?!

"We've lived on the edge of a volcano all our lives," the scientist in the movie continued. "One day it has to boil over."

She could have been describing my life. Sometimes, I felt like a big explosion was coming, but no one would believe me and I had no way to stop it. I left the theater more exhausted than when I had arrived.

My thoughts were still running in circles on Monday morning when I woke up. It was snowing, a heavy, wet snow that would make delivering the papers even harder, but I didn't care. It matched my mood.

I gobbled down my breakfast as Boots paced the kitchen, impatient to get outside and run. When it was time to go, I realized I'd left my snow boots outside on the back porch. Melting snow had run off the roof and now my boots were sopping wet. Great.

I ran back to my room to pull on my cowboy boots instead. There was something sharp in one of them. It was the silver sheriff's star from Mary Lou. I put it in my pocket.

Outside, it was still snowing. I placed a big tarp over the papers on the sled, but I knew some of them were still going to get wet. I hoped no one would complain.

The streets were deserted. This was a morning for curling up in bed or drinking a cup of hot chocolate and watching the snow fall from the kitchen window. The only sign of life was at Ma and Pa's house. They were up early, as usual, and Ma invited me in for some cocoa, but I said, "No, thank you." I didn't want to talk to anyone today. I felt so ashamed. As if *Son of Communist* was branded on my forehead.

Soon as Boots and I got back on the road, we spotted a rooster there, shivering, like he'd gotten out of his coop and couldn't find his way home. Great. Now I'd have to go back to tell Ma and Pa and—

By my side, Boots growled.

"No," I yelled, but it was too late.

Boots tore off after the rooster. The bird dashed down the road, crowing like it was already sunrise. I ran after them both. If Boots killed that bird, I'd have to pay Ma and Pa back. 'Course it was probably going to die anyway because of the cold. It was snowing even harder now, and my hat fell off in the wind. I stopped to pick it up and didn't even notice when a car turned the corner and headed straight for me.

At the last minute, it honked. I glanced up, and jumped out of the way. There was a loud *thump* as I fell into the snowbank on the side of the road.

The car kept going, the driver not even stopping to see if I was hurt. I'd pulled the sled over when I jumped and the papers were scattered all over the road. I was sore and bruised, but nothing hurt too badly. The papers were ruined. By the time I gathered them all up, I'd probably be late for school. I was cursing my luck when I heard a small whimper.

There was a small, hairy lump lying in the middle of the road.

Boots! The car had hit him, not the sled or me. That was the thump I'd heard. The stupid rooster was still running around in circles, like he'd had his head cut off.

"Boots," I called. "Are you okay?"

He tried to pick up his head but couldn't. Ice and snow clung to his dark fur. His tail gave the tiniest flicker of a wag.

I went closer. There was a huge red gash from one end of his belly to the other.

He whimpered again.

I was pretty sure I could see his guts hanging out.

"It's going to be okay," I said, knowing I was lying. I pulled the sled upright and threw the rest of the papers off, leaving just one layer of dry ones. Then I ran back to Boots and ever so carefully picked him up and laid him gently on the sled.

"It's okay, boy," I said again.

He didn't even try to wag his tail this time. I pulled the tarp over him and tried to figure out what to do. I couldn't go home. With all the medical bills, I knew Mom and Dad had no money for a vet. *Think, Tommy, think,* I said to myself. Boots needed stitches. I knew how to sew a button on, or hem a pant leg if it came undone, but a dog? My dog? There was no way. Boots was going to die and . . .

Then I remembered Mrs. Scully. She was a seamstress. Surely she'd be able to help.

I didn't allow myself to think about it any more, just ran to her house pulling the sled behind me as gently as possible. It had almost stopped snowing by the time I reached her place. I scooped Boots up in my arms and carried him up the porch steps. He was trembling as I banged on the door.

It seemed like forever before Mrs. Scully came out in her bathrobe. Her hair was a mess and there wasn't a drop of makeup on her face. She looked young and pretty and a little scared.

"Tommy," she cried. "What's wrong?"

"My dog" was all I could choke out.

She touched Boots gently and when she took her hand away there was blood on her fingers. "What happened?"

"He got hit by a car!" I said. "There's a big gash all down his stomach. I thought—I thought—" I started to cry great big tears that rolled down my cheeks.

Mrs. Scully only nodded. "Bring him inside and we'll see what we can do." I expected her to start crying too, but she didn't. Her eyes were hard and determined, like Grace Kelly's in *High Noon* when she decided to get off that train and start fighting back.

I followed her into the house. There was a clean towel on the kitchen table. She pointed to it. "Put him there. I'll be right back." I laid Boots down on the towel. He was still breathing. Barely.

Mrs. Scully strode back into the kitchen, her sewing basket in one hand, a bottle of pills in the other.

"Sleeping pills," she said, pressing the bottle into my hand. "Give him half of one. Too many pills will kill a dog faster than a gash in the side."

The pills spilled out all over the counter as I pulled off the lid. I grabbed a knife and cut. There was a jar of peanut butter nearby. I scooped out a spoonful and buried the pill in it.

Boots was practically unconscious anyway, but he opened his eyes when I said his name. "I got a treat for you, boy," I said, and stuck the peanut butter on his tongue.

Automatically, he swallowed it. And his eyes closed again.

"Don't you worry," said Mrs. Scully as she washed her hands. "I grew up on a farm. I've sewn up pigs and cows and . . ." She turned to look at me. "I can't make any promises, but Tommy, I swear I will do my best to save your dog."

She took a big, curved needle from her kit. My knees felt weak, and I think I wobbled on my feet.

"Get out of here," said Mrs. Scully, threading the needle.

I nodded. "I got to do the rest of the route."

"Good," she said. "Don't think about it. Just come back in the afternoon and we'll see how we're doing then."

35

THE SHERIFF'S STAR

It took me a long time to do the paper route. There was a lot of snow. I was cold and slow and I had no idea what time it was by the time I finally got back home.

Mom was waiting for me at the front door, the vein on her forehead pulsing like a red worm, the leather belt coiled in her hand. "You missed the bus!" she hissed.

"But I—"

"Now I'll have to drive you to school. I'll be late to see Mary Lou. There's a meeting with her doctors and I promised I'd be there."

"Boots got—"

"Don't give me your excuses!"

I tried to push past her, but she grabbed my arm and pulled me into the kitchen. She didn't even wait for me to pull down my pants this time, just slammed my hands down on the counter and started hitting me.

"Stop it, Mom!" I wailed. "I didn't do anything!"

I was too terrified to cry. Her blows were wild now, as

likely to hit my back or my legs as my buttocks. Panic rose in my throat. What if she didn't stop? Boots wasn't there, and neither was Mary Lou. My dad was at work and wouldn't be home for hours.

I looked back at her. Mom's face was as red as Sam's scar, as if she'd been the one burned in a fire. What was I going to do?

"Stop it, Mommy," cried a tiny voice. "Stop hurting Tommy!"

It was Pinky. She was standing by the back door, tears running down her face.

"Pinky!" I called out, not sure if I was asking for her help or warning her to stay away.

Mom hit me again and I winced.

Pinky ran over and threw her arms around my waist.

The belt flew through the air again.

Pinky gasped. A big welt rose up on her skinny little arm.

"Get out of the way, Pinky!" Mom ordered.

My little sister shook her head.

"Run!" I hollered. "Pinky, run away!"

But Pinky didn't move.

So Mom hit us again.

Time seemed to slow down. And I thought of Cardinal Mindszenty's line in *Guilty of Treason*: "One must take a stand somewhere. One must draw a line past which one will not retreat." This was my line. Mom could hit me, but I was not going to let her hit Pinky.

I whirled around and grabbed the end of the belt, yanking it out of Mom's hands. She stumbled and fell against the wall. "Leave us alone!" I screamed.

For the first time, I realized I was almost as tall as she was. I threw the belt to the floor.

"Don't you dare—" she snapped. She rose to her feet and took a swing at me, but I jumped out of the way. Mom picked up the belt and came after me.

I ran to the front door.

"Come back here!" she screamed.

I kept running. The sidewalk was slippery and I fell down in a snowbank. My left side was instantly wet and cold.

"Tommy! Tommy!" I heard Mom yelling after me.

I scrambled to my feet and ran on. Someone was crying, great big gasping sobs. It took me a minute to realize it was me. I had a stitch in my side and my knee was bleeding, but I kept running.

I slipped on the ice and fell down again. But this time I stayed there, half-frozen in the snow. A train whistle blew; a train was pulling into the station. I'd run clear across Downers Grove, all the way to the center of town. I was lying in a snowbank next to the train station.

I imagined stealing some money. Buying a train ticket and riding out of town into a new life. If I hurried, maybe I could even make the next train.

I scrambled to my feet in the icy slush. My fingers were freezing and I'd left my jacket at home, so I stuck my hands in my pants pockets to warm them up. My fingers hit something sharp. "Ow!" I said aloud, and pulled the item from my pocket.

It was the sheriff's star from Mary Lou.

I suddenly remembered how Gary Cooper had wanted to flee his problems too. At the beginning of *High Noon*, he'd gotten in his wagon and ridden away. But he'd turned around. He'd come back.

I longed to be a cowboy. Not a bully. But a cowboy who stands up for others. Who fights for the people he loves, for the town they live in.

Even if I could leave, I wouldn't leave Mary Lou. It wasn't right to let Eddie get in trouble for fighting Little Skinny. I couldn't let Pinky and Susie grow up with Mom and no one to protect them. Sam would need a friend when his mom died. And if I couldn't save Mr. McKenzie, at least I should help him pack. And Boots. The little dog had never abandoned me. Didn't he deserve the same?

"All aboard!" the conductor called.

I held the star tightly in my hand, and like Gary Cooper, I watched the train start to pull away. The caboose went by and across the tracks I could finally see what film was showing at the Tivoli.

One week only! the marquee said. *Back by popular demand. High Noon.*

36

ROUNDING UP A POSSE

As the train whistled in the distance, I walked over to the station and sat down on a bench. The star was cold in my hand as I touched each of the six points one by one. What was I going to do?

A tall, thin figure walked out from behind one of the columns at the train station. He wore an old tweed suit with a red bow tie and an overcoat that was frayed along the edges. He was clutching a cane in one hand, but not leaning on it to walk. His whiskers were gray and neatly trimmed, though his face was so gaunt, he looked like he could have used a couple of extra sausages at breakfast.

And that was what reminded me that it was actually Mr. Kopecky, otherwise known as Pa, the doctor-turned-chicken-farmer.

"Tommy?" Pa called. "Tommy Wilson? Are you all right?"

I rubbed my eyes angrily, as if that would wipe away the red. "Yes," I said. "I'm fine."

He looked pointedly at my ripped pants and the blood on

223

my knee, but he didn't comment on it. "Oh," he said. "I just missed my train. The door on the chicken coop is broken and the rooster got out this morning. Took a while to catch him."

That made me think of Boots. I wondered if he was okay. "Sorry you missed your train," I said finally.

Pa shrugged. "Not a problem. There'll be another one soon."

That was true. The commuter trains ran every half hour.

"Mind if I sit with you while I wait?" he asked.

I shrugged.

He lowered himself slowly onto the bench, laying the cane beside him. "Don't need the darn thing," he told me, "but it makes Ma feel better if I take it."

A weak smile was all I could manage.

Across the street the Tivoli's marquee flicked on and off, as if someone were testing the lights.

"Where are you going?" I asked. It wasn't like I really wanted to know. I was just making conversation.

"To Chicago. Once a month I meet up with a bunch of other old men. From Prague, Vienna, Budapest. Some of them are even psychiatrists like me."

"What's that?" I asked.

"A kind of doctor," he said. "I thought I could help people who were angry. Or sad. Or crying all the time."

"There are doctors who do that?" I asked.

Pa sighed. "Well, there are doctors who try. But in the end, I'm not sure I did much good. There were so many sad people in Europe after the war."

Dr. Stanton hadn't been able to help Mom. Was it possible

that Pa could? I remembered how Gary Cooper had gone from person to person in his town asking everyone to stand with him against the villain who was coming on the noon train. And how they'd all turned him down. But he'd asked. And asked. And kept asking. I took a deep breath. "I think my mom needs a doctor like that."

"Why, Tommy?" he asked, so softly I could barely hear him.

And I started talking about how my mom had always been moody, but how she'd had okay times too. Times when she was fun, and made jokes, and danced around the house. And how that had all started changing when Busia died and Susie was born. I kept talking as another commuter train came and left. Pa didn't move a muscle, just nodded his head.

So I went on talking, about Mary Lou getting burned and stealing the yo-yos and picking on Sam and planting the paper in Mr. McKenzie's store. I told him about Mom beating me and the medical bills we couldn't pay and even about poor Boots and the rooster. "It's all my fault." I started shivering.

Pa didn't say a word. Just stood up and took off his coat and held it out to me.

"No, that's okay," I said.

"Put it on," he said.

So I did. The jacket was still warm and smelled like a pipe. And then I thought, why not? Why not just tell him everything? "And guess where the commie paper came from?" I said quickly, before I could chicken out.

"I don't know," Pa said evenly.

"From my dad. My dad is the communist!"

"Really?" Pa asked mildly.

"Yeah," I said.

"Pfft," he said, waving a hand in the air. "Reading a paper doesn't make you a communist."

"Sure it does."

"Does stealing a yo-yo make you a thief?"

I thought about that. I didn't think I was a thief. And yet I had stolen a yo-yo. But I had realized I'd made a mistake. I kept thinking and thinking as yet another train pulled into the station. "Well," I said, embarrassed, "thanks for listening."

"Are you done?"

"Don't you have to go?" I asked.

He looked thoughtful for a moment, chewing on the white whiskers on his upper lip. "No," he said. "They are sad old men who only complain about their lives."

"But if they're your friends . . ."

"I think . . . ," Pa said slowly. "I think, here, I might actually be able to do something."

He stood up and leaned on the cane for a moment. "Don't tell Ma I actually used it!" he warned.

I zipped my lips shut.

"Come on," he said. "We've got to get you home."

Pa hailed a taxi. The car was warm and dry. But the closer we got to my house, the more I shivered. "Pinky and Susie . . ."

"Yes," Pa said. "We'll check on them now."

In no time at all, we were pulling onto my street. The front door was slightly open. Mom's car was gone. I wasn't sure if that was good or bad.

Pa paid the taxi driver and together we walked up the front steps. The coat was big on me, the edges dragging in the snow. Pa gripped my arm and I was surprised at how much braver I felt, even if he was just a wrinkled old man.

"Hello," I called out as I pushed open the door.

No one answered, but the living room was a mess. The coffee table was overturned, magazines and newspapers scattered everywhere. Dad's belt was still lying on the floor.

"Hello?" Pa called. "Anyone home?"

Mrs. Glazov hurried out of the nursery. She was wearing Mom's flowered apron. "Oh, good, Tommy. It's you."

I was surprised to see her. "What are you doing here?"

Her milky blue eyes filled with tears, and she picked at a string on the pocket of the apron. "I sorry, Tommy," she said finally.

"For what?"

"I live right next door," she said sheepishly. "I hear things. Like today. But I not know what to do. I mother, I lose my temper too. When's too much . . ." She shook her head. "I should help. I see your mother drive off, crazy-like. And still, I not act. But when I see Pinky, alone in snow, calling for you. I know I need to do something."

She put her hand on one of mine.

I blinked, my eyes blurry. "Where is Pinky? And Susie . . . ?"

"They fine," said Mrs. Glazov. "Both sleeping now."

"And Mrs. Wilson?" asked Pa.

"Gone," said Mrs. Glazov. "I not know where."

The three of us walked around the house, and it was like I was seeing it again for the first time in a long while. The dishes piled in the sink. The dust bunnies under the tables. The piles of laundry in the bedrooms. "This house is a mess," said Pa.

I felt angry. "I'm doing my best! Mom doesn't help anymore. She just lies in bed and—"

"Tommy." Mrs. Glazov laid a gentle hand on my shoulder. "It not your fault."

Pa nodded. "I'll call Ma. Have her come over and help us clean up."

While Pa dialed his wife and talked to her rapidly in a language I didn't understand, I walked around the kitchen, opening drawers. Finally, I found it. Mom's notebook of phone numbers. On the first page was listed: *Robert John Wilson, Western Electric.* I'd never called the number before.

"Yes, yes," Pa added in English. "I still have the cane!"

He hung up. "Not a word!" he said to me. "If she finds out I actually used it, I'll never be allowed to take a step without it again."

I smiled. "I found my dad's number," I said. "Do you think . . . ?"

Pa nodded. "Call him." He left to join Mrs. Glazov in the living room. I could hear them talking quietly as they picked up the papers and magazines and righted the coffee table.

The phone sat on the wall like a big black beetle. I took off Pa's coat and laid it carefully over a chair. Then I took a deep breath and pinned on Mary Lou's star.

My fingers trembled only a little as I dialed the number.

"Hello, Western Electric. How may I help you?"

It was a woman's voice. I'd expected my father. But of course there'd be a telephone operator instead. "Hi," I said. "May I speak to my dad? Please."

The woman giggled a bit. "Sure, hon. Who's your father?"

"Robert John Wilson."

"One moment."

It seemed like she was gone forever. The house was quiet. So quiet. In the nursery, Susie started to cry and Pinky called out, "Mommy!" I heard Mrs. Glazov shushing them.

"Tommy?"

It was my dad this time.

"Tommy, are you okay?" I didn't think I'd ever heard him so worried. It kind of made me feel good.

"Yeah," I said, "I'm fine."

"Then why . . . is Mary Lou . . . ?"

"No," I said. "It's Mom." I explained how she'd beat me and hit Pinky and I'd run away and how Pinky had been out in the snow alone, and how Mr. Kopecky and Mrs. Glazov had come to help, and I sounded calmer than I'd imagined I would.

"Let me call the hospital," he said. "I'm sure she's just gone there. I'll call you back in a minute."

He hung up and I stared at the dishes. There was a great big pile of them on the counter. I did my best in the evenings, but I never quite managed to get caught up. I heard the front door open, and a moment later, Mrs. Kopecky barreled into the kitchen. "Okay, Tommy," she ordered, hands on her hips. "We wash."

Without another word, she started filling the sink with sudsy hot water. I helped Ma wash the dishes and the hot water felt good on my cold hands. I was so worried and angry, I wanted to pick up a glass and smash it against the wall. But I didn't. I didn't want to be like Mom.

When the phone rang again, I jumped. It kept ringing as I quickly dried my hands on a dish towel and went to pick it up. "Hello?"

"Tommy." It was my dad. "I found your mother. She's at the hospital."

"Oh yeah," I said, remembering. "She said she had a meeting with Mary Lou's doctors."

"No," my dad said. He sounded funny. "She was . . . injured."

"What?" My breath suddenly caught in my throat and my feet felt colder than they had in the snowbank. Ma must have noticed too, because she froze, a dirty plate in the air, a bunch of soap bubbles dripping off one edge. I watched them fall onto the counter. Sometimes I hated my mom, but I didn't want her dead.

"What's going on?" I said. "Tell me!"

"Your mom did drive to the hospital to see Mary Lou. But as she was pulling into the parking lot, apparently she had an accident."

37

THE ROPE

Dad didn't know exactly what had happened, just that Mom had been admitted. Ma and Pa decided they would drive me to the hospital to meet Dad. Mrs. Glazov would stay home with my sisters. I nodded and followed Pa to the car, obedient as a lassoed calf.

We got stuck at the railroad crossing, just like on that other ride, the one I had taken with Mom and Mary Lou. Was Mom hurt bad, as bad as Mary Lou? Pa chattered on and on as he drove.

"From what you say, Tommy, I believe your mother is suffering from melancholia. A damping of spirits, brought on by a number of different factors. She probably always had an innate tendency to it, but it can be greatly exacerbated by major life events such as death, birth, injury, all of which your family has experienced in the past year.

"I studied this in Vienna, before the war. I never missed the Saturday-evening lectures by Dr. Sigmund Freud at the university. There are many techniques to be used in such a case: dream analysis, hypnosis . . ."

He continued on and on, but I found it hard to listen. If Mom died, she couldn't whip me anymore. Maybe then I could breathe in my own house. But the fact that I was even thinking that made me feel awful. I loved my mom! Didn't I? Sometimes she was nice. And what would Pinky and Susie do without her? They were still little, and little kids need their mom.

The car was old and the shocks were bad. Every time we went over a bump, I remembered Mary Lou moaning in pain. Ma had insisted on sitting in the back with me. She reached over and held my hand. I squeezed it back and held on tight, as my thoughts went round and round.

When we arrived, Dad and Dr. Stanton were sitting in the waiting room, talking in low voices. Dad was sitting stiffly, as if he'd been riding a horse all day and hadn't quite remembered he was out of the saddle. Dr. Stanton looked tired too. He ran his hand though his salt-and-pepper.

Dad stood up as we entered. "Tommy!" He ran over and gave me a hug. I wasn't sure when was the last time he'd looked that happy to see me. It made me glad, and then I felt awful. Awful to feel happy that now my mother was in the hospital too.

"Is she . . . is Mom going to be okay?" I asked.

Dad nodded. "She's got some bruises and bumps and they're going to keep her in the hospital overnight, but, yeah, she's fine. Physically, at least."

I was so relieved, my legs went rubbery and numb and I had to sit down on the couch.

"I spoke to the physician who treated her," Dr. Stanton said. "I'm not sure what to recommend once she's released. We could send her to a sanatorium, but . . ."

"A sanatorium?" Dad asked.

I wasn't exactly sure what that was, but the look on Dad's face made me think it wasn't good.

"Perhaps," Dr. Stanton said gently.

"You've been our family doctor a long time." Dad sounded defeated. "We'll do what you think best."

"If I may," interrupted Pa, "perhaps I can offer another solution. I am a doctor of psychiatry, trained with Freud, Adler and Jung before the war, even published a couple of articles about melancholia, though that's years ago now. I would be happy to try treating her at my home."

"At your home?" Dad asked.

"Yes," Ma continued. "We'd be more than happy to have Mrs. Wilson stay with us for a few weeks. It's no imposition. The rest would do her good as much as anything else."

Dad looked confused. He glanced at Dr. Stanton.

"I don't really believe in the talking cure," Dr. Stanton said. Then he shrugged. "But I guess you could try it, rather than immediately sending her away."

"I don't know," Dad said. "I just don't know what to do." He buried his face in his hands. Dr. Stanton put a hand on his back.

"It's up to you, Robert," Dr. Stanton said kindly.

Dad took a deep breath. "We'll manage all right with her at home. I'll do more and Tommy . . ."

I couldn't believe it. Dad was turning them both down. I

didn't think I had it in me to do any more. There was already the paper route and the dishes and the cleaning and taking care of Pinky and Susie, all the while tiptoeing on eggshells around Mom. "No, Dad," I interrupted. "I'm sorry. But we just can't handle Mom by ourselves anymore."

Dad sat down next to me on that ugly brown couch, the one I'd sat on so many times with Pinky, and he started to cry. It was even worse than when Mr. McKenzie had cried, because this was my father. Dads weren't supposed to cry. I wanted to run away again, but the sheriff's star was still pinned to my shirt. I had to make him understand.

"Dad," I said. "Do you remember the time the Lone Ranger was stuck in the mine, all alone, and he tried everything but couldn't find a way out? And then Tonto came and lowered a rope to him?"

"Yes," my dad choked out. "We listened to that episode together. Why?"

"Please," I said. "Let them be our Tonto. 'Cause we really, really need a rope."

He looked up at me then, the tears moistening the crevices in his cheeks like a desert canyon after a hard rain. "Okay," he said.

"So what would you like to do?" asked Dr. Stanton. "The sanatorium? Or the talking cure?"

"The talking cure, I guess," Dad said. "I'm not ready to send Catherine away."

Pa looked thrilled. I remembered how he'd never liked being a chicken farmer. He had been a doctor and now he could be one again.

The grown-ups huddled together to work out the details. I

slipped away and ran up the stairs to tell Mary Lou the news. But my sister wasn't in her bed. I glanced around and saw her halfway down the hall. She was walking! I mean, she was holding on to the railing on the side of the wall for dear life, but she was walking.

"Mary Lou!" I cried.

She turned, smiled and nearly fell.

I rushed to grab her arm.

We grinned at each other for a moment.

"Did you hear about Mom?" I asked.

Her grin disappeared. "Yeah. Are they going to send her away?"

"No," I said. "She's going to stay with Ma and Pa."

"The Kopeckys?" Mary Lou asked, surprised.

I nodded. "He's a doctor."

"Oh, I didn't know."

"Do you know where Mom's room is?"

Mary Lou nodded this time. "I was going to see her. The elevator is down the hall."

I took her hand and we walked together, taking tiny steps. But unlike at Christmas, she didn't wince in pain with each one. I felt dizzy with all that had happened that day. In the elevator, I accidentally leaned against my sister, and for a moment, it seemed like she was holding me up.

We got off the elevator and took a couple more steps. Mary Lou stopped. "Here we are," she said.

We looked at each other, and pushed the door open. Mary Lou and I, still holding hands, crept inside.

It was just like when I'd first seen Mary Lou. Mom was turned away, facing the wall, her long black hair in a tangle on the pillow. She was asleep, her breathing slow and gentle. She had one black eye and a bandage over a huge lump on her forehead. For the first time ever, I noticed her nose was shaped just like mine, with a little ski jump at the end.

I hated her. And I loved her. And at that moment, I wasn't sure which one was stronger. All I knew was that I was glad to see her breathing, her chest going up and down. Glad to see she was alive.

Mary Lou ran her fingers through Mom's matted hair. "I'll have to bring my brush," she whispered. "She brushed mine. I don't remember much about those first few weeks in the hospital, but I remember her brushing my hair."

We waited a long time, but her breathing remained slow and steady. Finally, Mary Lou and I went back to her room.

"You're walking pretty well," I said.

"Yeah." Mary Lou smiled. "I guess I am."

Dad had taken a taxi from work, so Ma and Pa drove us home. No one spoke in the car. When we got to our neighborhood, I asked them to drop me off at Mrs. Scully's. "Why?" Dad asked.

"Long story," I said. "Maybe Pa could fill you in?"

Pa nodded.

As I walked up Mrs. Scully's steps, my heart was beating like I'd been running up a hill. I knocked, soft and hesitant. Mrs. Scully didn't answer.

My stomach dropped. Boots had died during the day while I'd been at the hospital. I knew it. My body went numb all over, like I'd suddenly turned into a giant ice cube and . . .

A dog barked.

It sounded like it was coming from inside the house. I opened up the screen door and went inside.

And there, on the kitchen floor, running around like he didn't have an eight-inch gash in his tummy, was Boots. He was drinking water from a bowl, but when he saw me, he stopped and ran over to greet me. I knelt down and let him lick my face.

"That dog is a Sherman tank," said Mrs. Scully, walking into the room. "He woke up this afternoon when I was frying sausages for dinner and started begging like nothing had happened."

Boots kept licking my face and wiggling his tail. His breath smelled like sausages.

"Don't give him anything else to eat." She sighed. "He already got three pieces of sausage out of me. He needs to take it easy until he heals."

I swallowed. My mouth was dry and my hands were shaking. I'd managed to hold it together all day, with my mom and seeing Mary Lou, but now that I knew Boots was okay, I was falling apart. "Thank you."

"Oh, Tommy," said Mrs. Scully, sitting down heavily in the kitchen chair. "I'm so happy myself."

Boots sat in my arms as I walked home, his nose up in the air, sniffing away. I carried him inside. Mrs. Glazov was at the stove making dinner. "Pa told us," she said. "How is dog?"

"He's all right," I answered.

Mrs. Glazov wiped her hands on the flowered apron and came over to examine him. "Such even stitches." She nodded in approval. "I send mending to Mrs. Scully from now on."

I smiled at her. She looked different. It took me a minute to realize why. Her white hair had been combed and pulled back into a neat bun. Even her dress seemed a little less faded than normal. Like Pa, she seemed not at all put out by us needing her help. She seemed happy.

"Dinner ready!" Mrs. Glazov called. Susie gurgled in her high chair. She was seven months old now and gumming a cracker. Pinky ran into the kitchen.

"I'm not hungry," Dad said from the kitchen doorway.

"Sit," Mrs. Glazov ordered.

"Better do what she says," I said. "She can be very bossy."

So Dad sat, and when he saw Boots, he smiled. "I'm glad he's okay, Tommy," he said with a wide grin.

"Yeah," I said. "Me too."

It was a good evening. Mrs. Glazov had made a Russian noodle dish, not exactly like Busia's pierogi, but almost as tasty in a different way. Pinky chattered away happily, like she hadn't done in months. After dinner, Mrs. Glazov gave Pinky a bath and put Susie to bed. Dad and I did the dishes. When Mrs. Glazov came out of the nursery, she was smiling. "Beautiful baby," she said. "Real doll." She put her hands on her hips. "Good job on dishes. I come back and help again tomorrow."

My dad shook his head. "You've already done so much."

"Please," she said. "Make me feel useful. Let me come. I come every day if you want. No vegetables to plant in winter."

"But we don't have any money to pay you. We can't even pay the medical bills for Mary Lou."

"Tommy taught me to read," said Mrs. Glazov, without looking at me. "Tommy plays accordion with me," she continued, "and Tommy invited me to Thanksgiving. Think it's time I do something for you."

Dad looked at me as if he were seeing me for the first time.

"Tommy good boy," Mrs. Glazov said.

"Yeah," my dad agreed. "He's pretty amazing."

As I lay in bed that night, I kept hearing my dad's words again and again. And I couldn't stop smiling.

38

TRYING TO FIND THE WORDS

When Mary Lou was burned, everyone asked me about it. On the paper route, at Mass, in the classroom. But no one mentioned what had happened to my mother, even though from their looks and whispers, I knew they'd heard. I guess being burned in a fire was okay, but melancholia was something no one wanted to talk about.

When I went out for the first morning recess, I stood by the wooden horses for a moment, trying to pull myself together. It was fine. If no one wanted to talk about my mom, I wouldn't either. But I couldn't quite decide what I wanted to do. After a while, I realized Sam had walked up and was standing next to me. "Tommy, are you all right?" he asked.

"My dog got hit by a car," I said. I could see Sister Ann and the other nuns at the far end of the girls' side of the playground. One of the third graders had fallen jumping rope and was crying loudly.

"That's awful!" Sam said.

"Boots needed stitches," I said. "But I think he's going to be okay."

240

Eddie had been avoiding me all day, but he sauntered over to us now. His forehead was wrinkled, his eyes blazing with anger. "Talking to your new best friend?" he asked.

Sam blushed and looked at the ground.

"Come on, Eddie," I said quietly. "You know you're my best friend."

"Do best friends rat each other out?"

"No." He was right: friends keep each other's secrets. Maybe we weren't friends anymore after all.

"So why'd you do it, then?" He pushed me in the chest.

I just stood there and looked at him.

"Come on!" he yelled. "Tell me." He shoved me again.

"Eddie," said Sam. "The nuns are right over there." He seemed nervous, jumping from one foot to the other like he had to go to the bathroom.

"Why don't you tell him, Sam?" Eddie hissed his name like it was a bad word. "We're already in trouble. They might even expel us."

"What?" I asked.

"Yeah," said Eddie. "Because of the fight at Prince Pond last Friday. Thanks a lot, buddy." Then he slugged me in the stomach.

I wasn't expecting the blow and I fell to the ground. My belly ached, twisted in knots, and for a moment, I thought I was going to throw up. I stood up slowly, boiling mad. Ready to hit him. Ready to beat him. Just like Mom had beaten me.

But before I could take a swing at him, I saw Sam watching me, and Sam made me think of Mary Lou, and I waited to see what she would say. To see if she would tell me not to hit him. And I did hear a voice. But it wasn't Mary Lou's. It was

241

mine. It was as if I could hear myself, as if I were standing there right next to me, saying, *Tommy, don't do it!*

And suddenly, I didn't want to hit Eddie. I was sick of it all. The fighting and the lying and the pretending everything was okay when it really wasn't.

"I'm sorry," I said. Then I turned and walked away. Maybe it wouldn't do any good, but I could try to save him.

"Chicken!" Eddie yelled after me. "Commie!"

A rock flew through the air, whizzing past my leg.

I kept walking. Sister Ann was still at the far end of the playground, putting a bandage on the third grader's knee. I was pretty sure she hadn't seen Eddie hit me. When she was done, the girl went off with her friends and Sister Ann turned to look at me. "Is something wrong, Tommy?"

"May I speak to you about Eddie, Sister?"

"Ah," said Sister Ann. "I'm sorry, Tommy. I know Eddie is your best friend, but we have a very clear policy against fighting at St. Joe's."

"But—but I didn't tell you everything," I stammered. "It's true, Eddie has been picking on Sam all year, but so have I. You just didn't catch me. So if you're going to punish him, you'd better punish me too."

Sister Ann pursed her lips. It was cold and they were chapped. Her nose was red too, now looking more like a beet than a pickle. But her eyes were smart and warm.

"Please give him another chance," I said. "And Sam too. Really, he didn't do anything wrong."

Sister Ann nodded. "I will be speaking to Father Miskel this weekend. He wanted a week to think things over. He will make the final decision, but I will let him know what you have said."

"Thank you," I said. "And thank you for tutoring Mary Lou too." I turned to walk away.

"Tommy!" Sister Ann called after me. "If you need anything, please, just ask."

I knew she was trying to be nice, but part of me was kind of annoyed. Asking was usually the hardest part.

The next day on the paper route, my hands started to sweat as I approached Ma and Pa's house. I knew they had gone to the hospital the day before to pick up Mom and take her to their house. She'd only been in the hospital one night. I knew Ma and Pa had a guest room, the one for when their grandson visited, and Mom was going to sleep there. I imagined her lying on a twin bed with a blue comforter, baseballs in the corners of the room, and a whole stack of *Boys' Life* magazines in the closet.

I didn't want to see her. But I also kind of did. Maybe I was a chicken, but that morning, I didn't leave my sled, just threw their paper up onto the front porch and kept walking.

That day at school, everyone left me alone. Sister Ann didn't call on me all day, even when it was clear I wasn't paying attention. Eddie threw snowballs with Luke and Peter. Sam wasn't there. He didn't show up on Thursday or Friday, either. I wondered if he was sick. Or maybe his mother was doing worse.

On Saturday after my paper route, I decided to stop by

McKenzie's store. The front door was locked and a sign reading STORE CLOSED hung in the front window, but I rang the doorbell anyway. After a moment, Sam came out of the back room and let me in.

"Tommy," he said, "what are you doing here?"

I shrugged. "You missed a lot of school."

"We've been at the hospital with Mother." His eyes got glassy, like muddy puddles, but they didn't overflow.

"Sorry," I said.

He shook his head. "Dad's in the back. Want to help us pack? We've got three weeks before the move."

"Sure," I said.

The shelves were mainly bare, but Sam and I worked steadily, putting the leftover cans into a box. "How's your mom?" Sam asked.

This time, I could feel my eyes fill with tears. "I'm not sure. You're the only one who's asked," I whispered. "No one else will mention it."

We packed silently for a few moments.

"I wish someone would talk to me about my mom," Sam said. "What will happen to us when she dies? Who will take care of Dad and me?"

"She's been in the hospital for a while now," I said quietly. "You two have been doing okay."

"But we always thought she'd come home."

That was true. It was awful having Mary Lou gone, but everyone kept reassuring us that eventually she would come home.

"The worst part is, sometimes I wish she'd just hurry up and die. Just so this'd all be over. But I don't really mean it," Sam added quickly. "Do you think I'm awful for saying that?"

"No," I said, remembering all my thoughts about my own mother when I'd been driving to the hospital with Ma and Pa. "Not at all."

"Sometimes I wonder," Sam went on, "what will happen to *her*? Will she go to heaven? Where will she be buried? If we move into the city and she stays in the hospital here, will she be alone when she dies?"

I didn't know.

"And then sometimes, I worry about stupid things. Like, what will we do with her clothes? Her pictures, her diaries and papers. They're all in this big box. She used to write, like me . . ."

"Maybe you could ask her?" I suggested. "About the clothes at least."

"Yeah," Sam said, placing the last can in the box. "Maybe I will."

Mr. McKenzie came out of the back room, carrying a box. "Hello, Tommy," he said.

"Hello, Mr. McKenzie," I answered.

The doorbell rang then, and we all turned to see who it was.

My father, in a casual shirt with no tie, was standing outside. "Tommy told me he was thinking of stopping by," he yelled through the window. "I thought you might need some help packing up."

I'd mentioned it in passing at breakfast. I hadn't even realized Dad had been listening.

"We can always use an extra hand," said Mr. McKenzie,

unlocking the door and letting him inside. For the next two hours, we packed and loaded boxes onto an old truck. The leftover inventory was being sold to another store owner, a few towns over. "We're not getting much," said Mr. McKenzie, "but it's better than nothing."

We were almost done with the packing when Dad cleared his throat and said, "Did Tommy tell you?"

"Tell me what?" asked Mr. McKenzie.

Dad's face was ashen, but he plowed on. "It was my paper. The copy of the *Daily Worker*. In college I—"

"What?"

"In college, I attended a few meetings, but—"

Mr. McKenzie stood up, suddenly furious. "You knew where the paper came from all along?!"

"My wife threw out some old papers without asking me. Tommy just accidentally found it at the paper drive."

"Why didn't you ever say anything?!"

My dad didn't answer.

Mr. McKenzie turned bright red, and I swear I saw a vein throb on his forehead, just like Mom's. He picked up a glass jar of pickles and threw it against the wall.

Sam and I jumped as bits of glass and cucumber flew everywhere. It was like when Mom broke the vase. When I threw the drinking glass. Now Mr. McKenzie was furious too.

But Mr. McKenzie wasn't screaming or yelling. He was looking out the window, taking one deep breath and then another.

"I'm so sorry," Dad said quietly. "If I'd admitted what had happened in the beginning, if I'd told the truth—"

"You might be the one without the job now," interrupted Mr. McKenzie. "I can't blame you for doing what you thought you had to do to keep your family safe."

He sat back down on the box he was using as a chair. It was as if breaking the glass had caused the anger to explode out of him, like popping a balloon.

I stood up. "I'll clean up the broken . . ."

"I made the mess this time," Mr. McKenzie said. He smiled at me, and I was pretty sure he was remembering the jar I'd broken on my first day at the store. "I'll clean it up."

"No," said my dad. "We'll all help."

So I got the mop and the broom from the back room. Mr. McKenzie swept. Sam sopped up the pickle juice with a towel. And Dad took the dustpan with the bits of glass and dumped it into the wastebasket.

When we were done, Mr. McKenzie made us all sandwiches on his thick, crusty bread.

He pulled the two last root beers out of the cooler for Sam and me, and two beers for him and Dad. We clinked the bottles together before we drank.

"Good sandwiches," I said, my mouth full of bread. "I'm gonna miss them." What I really wanted to say was *I'm going to miss you,* but I couldn't quite get the words out.

Mr. McKenzie smiled. He'd lost weight over the past few months, which had given his face a gaunt look, sort of like my father's.

"When I was a kid," Mr. McKenzie said, "I dreamed of having my own sandwich shop."

"I'd buy your sandwiches," I said.

"Yeah, well." Mr. McKenzie shrugged. "Dreams don't always

come true, Tommy. Sometimes you try and try and it still isn't enough."

Dad looked like he wanted to say something, the skin around his eyes wrinkling like he was trying to figure out just the right words. But I guess he didn't find them, because he only took another sip of beer.

39

DOUBTS AND DISEASES

I thought about what Mr. McKenzie had said all day. When you're little, you think you can do or be anything. Then you get older and realize, no, John is better than you at baseball, and Maria's better at math.

If I was being really honest, I knew I was never going to be a cowboy. There wasn't a Wild West anymore, no outlaws to be hunted down on horseback with a lasso and a gun. It was just a dream. Just a stupid dream that was never going to come true.

The mood stuck on me like a fog I couldn't shake. That evening, I played a duet with Mrs. Glazov in our living room after Pinky and Susie were in bed. I didn't miss any notes, but the music still sounded wrong, hollow, empty, as if the accordion knew my heart wasn't in it.

Mrs. Glazov stopped suddenly in the middle of "On Top of Old Smoky." She gave me a funny look, but didn't say anything about my playing. "Tommy," she said. "I have news."

She pulled a crumpled piece of newspaper out of her pocket. "Look what I read in paper!"

It was from the *Downers Grove Reporter*. Apparently, a group of local musicians was starting a musical society.

"You not teach me to read, I never see this!" she raved. "I went to meeting last week. We planning concert. At Tivoli. Trumpet player, his cousin run the projector and he talk to boss and he say we have it cheap. Wednesday, April 21. It January 23 now. We have three months get ready!"

"What do you mean, 'we'?" I asked.

"You play too. I be music teacher again! You my star student!"

I'd never heard her talk so much. She was dreaming, just like Mr. McKenzie. It would only end in disappointment.

"No," I said. "I'm sorry, but I don't want to. Not in front of all those people."

"But, Tommy . . ."

I got up and ran to my room.

Later that night, Dad knocked on my door. I didn't answer, but he still came in.

"Mom is settled at the Kopeckys'," he said. "She's going to be there for a few weeks, resting. Kind of like a holiday."

I nodded. Not having her in the house was kind of like a holiday for me too. I felt bad thinking it, but it was true.

"And you know Mrs. Glazov is going to keep coming over, as sort of a housekeeper and a nursemaid for the little ones."

I nodded again.

"Things are going to get better, Tommy. They really will."

He smiled, but his voice was strained, like he was trying to convince himself.

"Sure," I said. But really, I thought, what was going to change?

"You seem down tonight," Dad said on his way out the door.

I shrugged.

"Don't worry about Mary Lou's bills," he said. "We'll figure something out."

But he had to force his voice just a little too hard to sound cheerful, and that gave me even more to worry about.

The next day on the paper route, I slipped and fell on a patch of ice right in front of the Kopeckys' house. The sled didn't tip over or anything, but I fell on a rock and there was a big cut on my knee, the same one I'd skinned running away from Mom.

It hurt pretty bad, but surely I could hobble down the road to the next house. I didn't want to go into Ma and Pa's to ask for a bandage because I might see my mother. I had only gone a few steps when Ma came out on her front porch. "Tommy! I saw you take that horrible spill. You get in here right now and I'll fix you up!"

"I'm fine!" I called.

Boots looked at me and whined.

"Tommy! Right now!"

There was no arguing with Ma, so I slowly made my way up the steps. It did feel good to go inside the warm house. I took off my jacket in the foyer and followed Ma into the kitchen. It was the same size as ours, but the cabinets were painted blue, the countertops were white, and there was a blue-and-white-checkered cloth on the table.

There was no sign of my mother. Bacon was frying on the griddle. A pile of pancakes waited on a platter on the counter.

I sat down at the table and Ma placed a plate of food in front of me. "Eat!" she ordered. "I'm going to go get the iodine."

I dug in. It was delicious. As I ate, I noticed a framed quote on the wall. Someone had written in fancy calligraphy: *Medicine heals doubts as well as diseases.* I liked that.

I heard footsteps outside the kitchen. What if it was my mother, coming in for breakfast? What would I say to her? The pancake stuck in my throat.

But it wasn't my mom. It was Pa, wearing a navy-blue bathrobe. "Morning, Tommy," he said, as if he saw me in his kitchen every morning.

"Is it true?" I asked.

"What?"

"That quote on the wall." I gestured to the frame. "Can you do that?"

"Ah. Medicine as healing doubts. Words of wisdom from our dear friend Karl Marx."

"Karl Marx said that?" I asked.

Pa laughed. "Do you have a problem with that?"

"Karl Marx is the father of communism!"

"He came up with the idea of communism. I'd say it didn't turn out quite like he expected."

Pa sounded almost like my father, and yet I was pretty sure he wasn't a Soviet spy either.

252

Ma came back with the bandage for my knee, and we all sat down for breakfast.

As we ate, Pa and Ma told me all about Prague. That was the capital of Czechoslovakia and it was where they had come from. There was a castle and a river. "And so many churches," said Ma, her eyes bright and shining, "that people called it the city of a hundred spires!"

"If it was so great, why did you leave?" I asked.

"We didn't want to," said Pa. "After studying in Vienna, I became a professor of medicine at Charles University. It is one of the oldest and most prestigious universities in Europe."

"He speaks Czech, Slovak, English, German and Russian," Ma said proudly. "I only learned Czech, Slovak and English."

Two more than me, I thought to myself.

Pa sighed. "We outlasted the Nazis, and when the war ended, I thought our problems were over. But in 1948, the KSC, the Communist Party of Czechoslovakia, took over. Because I spoke out against them, I was dismissed from my post at the university and forced to flee."

"It's okay," Ma said, patting his wrinkled hand like he was a tired child.

"No, it's not," Pa said. "There, I was an educated man. A leader. Here, I am a poor chicken farmer."

Pa turned to look me in the eye. "The communists didn't just take away my right to vote and express my opinions, they took away my job and my home. Yes, I have read Karl Marx, Tommy. I like some of the things he said. But I am not a communist."

This was too much to think about so early in the morning. It was time to go. My knee felt better, and I had to finish the paper route. I walked to the door, put on my coat and heard a little intake of breath, almost like a tiny gasp.

There in the hallway was my mother.

She still had a bandage on her head, but it was a smaller one now. Her black eye had faded to yellow and purple. Her long dark hair was tangled, as if she had just woken up. She wore a white long-sleeved nightgown that came down to her ankles and made her look like a ghost.

My arms and legs tingled. I felt like I needed to run. We stared at each other, not saying a word. I wanted to leave, but I couldn't seem to make my legs move.

Ma walked into the hallway. "Ah, Catherine," she said, taking Mom's arm and leading her into the kitchen. "I've got the coffee all ready. You must be hungry."

The spell was broken. I slipped out the door without saying a word.

Monday morning, Sister Ann pulled Eddie, Sam and me aside just before the afternoon recess. "Good news, Eddie," Sister Ann said. "Father Miskel has reconsidered your expulsion. Instead, you and Tommy"—she turned to look at me—"will spend the next month cleaning the boys' restroom during recess."

"What's going to happen to me?" asked Sam.

"In light of the information Tommy provided," Sister Ann said, "you are being let off with a warning. Tommy and Eddie, you two may start your punishment now." She handed us each a bucket and scrub brush.

I thought Eddie would be happy he wasn't getting expelled, but he said nothing. Once we got to the restroom, he started to scrub so hard, I was afraid he was going to rub the bristles right off his brush. He wouldn't even look at me. It was a long afternoon.

40

EACH ACCORDING TO HIS NEEDS

The last Sunday in January, Dad and I drove to the hospital. It was early evening and snowing lightly, the flakes big and almost blue in the moonlight. The windshield wipers swished back and forth. All week, I'd been haunted by memories of Mom: standing in her white nightgown in the Kopeckys' hallway; holding the belt as it flew through the air and hit Pinky; throwing the pierogi on my birthday.

"Dad?" I asked.

"Hmm?"

"Why didn't you ever do anything?"

"About what?"

"About Mom."

Dad glanced over at me. The streetlights reflected off the snow, making my dad's face glow like a jack-o'-lantern. "Don't worry, Tommy," he said. "When Mom comes home, I'm sure things will be much better."

He'd ignored my question. Again. It made me angry. "You really think everything will be fine?" I scoffed. "She'll just stay at Pa and Ma's for a few weeks and they'll fix her up, good as new!"

"Tommy, your mother is . . ." Dad stopped, unable to find the right way to describe her.

"Why didn't you ever say anything?"

"I don't know," Dad said. "I don't know."

Swish, swash, swish, swash. The wipers droned on. The snow fell, quiet and peaceful. Dad was silent so long, I didn't think he was going to answer. Then he said, "My parents spanked me. *Spare the rod, spoil the child.* I wanted to believe that was all it was."

"She knocked over the Christmas tree!"

"Women act strange when they've had a baby and—"

"Dad!"

"I know," he said, so quiet it was almost a whisper.

"We needed you to do something!"

"I'm sorry," he said. "I didn't know what to do."

I'd never heard him apologize to me before. It made me feel like he was actually listening to what I had to say. And knowing that my dad sometimes made mistakes was scary and terrifying and kind of wonderful all at the same time. *He didn't know what to do.* I understood that. I'd felt that way a million times.

"What about Mr. McKenzie and the paper?" I asked.

"Yeah," Dad said. "Honestly, I should have done something."

He looked so miserable, his eyes drooping, his shoulders slumped, that I finally asked, "Why did you go to those meetings anyway?"

"I don't know," he said. He was silent for a long time, but at last he went on. "After the First World War, many people thought communism was an idea worth talking about, one that might have prevented much of the suffering of the Great Depression. Part of the reason I got a good job in the factory at Western Electric, one that paid enough to support you and your mother and your sisters, is because the unions got ideas from Karl Marx. Ideas about working-class people gaining power and influence. It doesn't seem right to just forget about all those ideas now that I'm a manager.

"Karl Marx's original view of communism was a utopian society where everyone would share everything, and everyone would have what they needed. 'From each according to his abilities, to each according to his needs.'

"I liked the idea that if someone was in need, someone else would volunteer to help. It reminded me of why I moved to Downers Grove. I hoped a small town would be a place where we would all . . . take care of one another."

Dad shook his head.

"But when Stalin came to power in the Soviet Union, he did horrific things in the name of communism. Millions of people were executed or died from disease and starvation when they were sent to Siberia or forced-labor camps. The communists arrested people who spoke out against them, took over governments of other countries in Eastern Europe and outlawed religion. Stalin's version of communism was nothing like the utopian ideals that we discussed in the meetings I attended.

"And now McCarthy has embarked on this witch hunt, saying anyone who ever thought about a different idea, anyone who ever considered another viewpoint, is a traitor to our country."

Dad shook his head again. "No, Tommy. I'm no communist. But I do believe the great thing about the United States is that we are free to have whatever ideas we want, even the bad ones. At least—we were until McCarthy came along."

My head was spinning, all my old beliefs about right and wrong melting away like the snowflakes on the warm windshield. For the first time, I could really picture my father as a young man, like me, learning new things, meeting new people, taking risks, making mistakes.

We pulled into the hospital parking lot. "Come on, Tommy," he said. "Let's go see Mary Lou."

Dad went off to talk with the doctors, and Mary Lou and I practiced walking up and down the hallway. But it had only been five minutes when Mary Lou said, "All right, Tommy. Spill the beans."

"What?"

"I can tell something is wrong. You might as well admit it." She gripped my arm. Her fingers were cold as icicles. "Did Sister Ann say something? Am I not working hard enough? Am I not going to graduate on time? Please, Tommy, just tell me, I want to know!"

"No," I said. "It's nothing like that."

"Then what?"

I sighed. I'd never told her what I'd done to Mr. McKenzie. "It's kind of a long story."

Mary Lou snorted, most unladylike. "Well, I got plenty of time."

So we sat down in her room and I started talking. About

259

planting the paper in Mr. McKenzie's store. About him losing the business. And finally, about Dad being the communist.

When I'd finished telling her everything, even what Dad had said to me in the car, she leaned over and gave me a hug. "Oh, Tommy!"

"Aren't you going to say *I told you so*?" I asked.

She shook her head. "No. It sounds like you've suffered enough. That's a lot to deal with all by yourself."

I shrugged. "I didn't want to burden you."

"Still," she said, "I wish you had told me before."

"Told you what?" Dad asked, walking into the room.

"About your college activities, *Comrade Dad*," Mary Lou teased.

But Dad did not laugh. All the blood drained from his face as he shut Mary Lou's door. When he turned back toward us, he looked as serious as a skeleton. "Did you tell her?" Dad asked me.

"Yeah."

"Tommy!"

"It's just Mary Lou!" I didn't see what the big deal was.

"I told you not to tell anyone!"

"I'm not going to tell, Dad!" Mary Lou sounded offended.

"The more people who know, the greater the chance of it coming out. The greater the chance of something awful happening."

"But you told Mr. McKenzie," I pointed out.

"We owed him. And it was probably a mistake."

"Dad, we know how to keep a secret," Mary Lou said softly.

"I hope you do," he said angrily, "because this isn't a game. If anyone gets a whiff of a rumor that I might be a communist, I could lose my job at the plant. And then who would . . . who would . . ."

Dad stopped talking and sat down on the edge of the bed. He covered his face with his hands and I was afraid he was going to start crying again, like he had when Mom had been hurt. I knew what he was going to say. If he got fired, who would earn money for the family? Who would pay the hospital bills?

Mary Lou was as white as the hospital sheets on her bed.

"I'm sorry, Dad."

Dad took a deep breath and stood up. There might have been tears in his eyes, but I didn't want to look too closely. "Come on, Tommy. We need to go."

I jumped up.

"And both of you, not a word!"

"We promise," Mary Lou and I said at the same time.

Dad and I walked a few paces down the hall in silence, when one of the nurses stopped me. "Hey, it's the famous accordion player," she said, and patted me on the shoulder. "You were great!"

"I'm not that good." I blushed.

"Yeah, you were." She added, "I'd pay money to hear you play." She winked at me and walked on.

We were almost out the door when a man in a suit ran up to us. "Mr. Wilson," he said, "may I speak to you for a moment?"

They went into a little office and left me outside, but I

could hear snippets through the closed door. *Payment late. Again.* Dad apologizing, his voice low and gravelly. *Trying to be understanding, but . . .*

I stepped away, not wanting to listen any more. In the car, I thought about the man in the suit and the nurse, and about what dad had said about people helping one another. My thoughts slowly packed together like a snowball. Mrs. Glazov was planning a concert. She wanted me to be in it. What if we made it a concert to raise money for Mary Lou's medical bills?

It had started to snow again and that reminded me of something else. "Hey, Dad," I said. "Remember that movie we saw at the Tivoli last year? The Christmas one with Jimmy Stewart."

"Yeah," Dad said. "*It's a Wonderful Life.*"

"That's it," I said. "I liked the end. When the town just gives him all the money to replace the bank deposit he lost."

"Yeah, me too," Dad said absently.

Surely it wouldn't be asking for charity if we offered people a concert in return. And what was so bad about accepting charity anyway?

Maybe I could make Dad's vision of Downers Grove come true after all.

41

THE RIGHT WORDS

That evening after dinner, while my dad was putting Pinky to bed, I talked to Mrs. Glazov about my idea to raise money for Mary Lou. "Wonderful!" she exclaimed. "Concert to support local burned girl—everyone will come!"

I grinned.

"And you must play too," Mrs. Glazov said. "Brother of Mary Lou—you will be star!"

I wasn't sure I liked the idea of sitting on the stage at the Tivoli with everyone looking at me. But Mrs. Glazov was smiling at me with a wide, toothy grin I'd never seen before. Surely anything that made her that happy couldn't be bad.

I nodded.

The next morning, I couldn't wait to tell the Kopeckys about my idea. I hadn't talked to Dad yet, I wanted to be sure it would work out first so I could surprise him, but I was pretty sure Ma and Pa would love the idea. In fact, I was so excited about telling them that I decided to risk the possibility that I might see Mom. I knocked, softly in case Ma and Pa were still sleeping, and of course it was my mother who opened the door.

Mom looked better. It had been about a week since I'd seen her. The bruises on her face had faded, and the cut on her forehead was now only a faint scar. There was gray in her hair that had never been there before, but it made her look kinder and less on edge. Even her eyes were not as tired.

"T-T-Tommy," she sputtered. She seemed surprised to see me. "A couple of chickens escaped again. Pa and Ma are out back trying to catch them."

"Oh."

"You look well, Tommy."

It was a little odd to hear that from my mom, as if I were an acquaintance she barely knew, not her only son. But even if they weren't exactly the right words, at least she was trying. "Thanks," I said. "How's it going with Pa?"

Mom shrugged, just like I did when I didn't really want to answer a question. "All right, I guess. I just sit on a couch and he asks me questions about my childhood or my dreams."

"Oh," I said again. "Is it helping?"

"The verdict's still out," Mom said with a little half smile.

I smiled too, wanting to be happy she was acting normal again, when all I could really think was, how long is this going to last?

Pa walked up to the doorway then, his tall, thin frame slicing through the tension. "We found the chickens so you can—oh, Tommy!"

Mom and I both stared at the floor, like we were guilty kids who'd been caught with our hands in the cookie jar.

"Would you like to come in for some eggs?" Pa asked.

I shook my head. "No, thanks, I'm already late. But I could come by sometime next week and put a new door on the chicken coop."

Pa nodded. "That'd be great."

I turned and ran back to the sled. It wasn't until I was already three houses down that I realized I'd forgotten to tell them about the concert.

Mrs. Glazov was frowning when I got home from the paper route. "I realize problem." She sighed as she handed me my lunch. "No money to advertise. No money for flyers. Without advertise, no one will come."

Flyers. "Like you make on a mimeograph machine?"

"Yes."

I knew who had one of those. "Don't worry," I said as I rushed out the door to catch the bus. "Leave that to me."

Sam wasn't at school that day, so I didn't get a chance to speak to him. I told myself he was just sick, had the flu or a bad cold, but he had missed a few days of school the week before as well. To miss again so soon . . . I was afraid I knew what that meant.

After school, I stopped by Mr. McKenzie's again. I told myself I was only going to ask about the mimeograph machine, but really I was worried about Sam. When I got to the shop, Sam and his father were just coming out. Mr. McKenzie looked at me, his eyes as hollow as an empty bird's nest in a cactus. He opened his mouth like he was going to say something, then just shook his head and got into the car. My breath caught in my throat, a hard sharp pain, as if I'd been hit in the stomach.

Sam stood beside me for a moment. His face was blank and so tense that even the skin on the smooth cheek was pulled tight. His eyes were tinged with red. "She died, Tommy," he said. "Early this morning."

I put my hand on his shoulder. He was trembling, just like Boots when he'd gotten the huge gash on his belly and I'd carried him up the steps into Mrs. Scully's house. I felt awful for him.

"But I talked to her. Before she died. She said Dad and I could take care of each other. She didn't care where she was buried. And she told us 'wedding ring.'"

"What does that mean?"

Sam shrugged. "I don't know. I asked Dad, but he said Mother didn't have one. She lost it years ago." He started to cry. When he continued, he sounded defiant, almost angry. "But she said it, right? Three times. Just before she died. It must be important!"

"Yeah," I said. "It must." I wanted to say something else, wanted to find the right words to make him feel better.

Mr. McKenzie honked the car's horn.

"I have to go," Sam said. "My dad's cousin in Chicago is going to pay for the funeral. We have to go talk to him."

I nodded.

"She wasn't alone. That means something, right?"

"Yeah. It does."

Sam smiled weakly and got into the car. I watched them drive away. Even though I'd only met Sam's mom that one time, I felt like crying too. It could have been me in that car. If Mary Lou had been burned just a little bit more, or if Mom had been driving just a little bit faster, it might have been me. And I suddenly felt less angry about all the people who had said nothing to me about my mother. Sometimes the right words were hidden away, like a legendary lost treasure, nearly impossible to find.

42

THE WEDDING RING

The viewing for Sam's mom was held Friday, February 5, at the Toon Funeral Home on Main Street, just a block from the school, from four to six in the evening. Just as I was planning to walk there, Dad showed up on our front porch, wearing his dark gray overcoat.

"You're home early," I said.

Dad looked me over. "Going to Mrs. McKenzie's viewing?"

I nodded. I'd put on my best pair of pants and a fresh white shirt. I didn't have a suit, so my navy school blazer and tie would have to do.

"Can I come?" he asked.

"Sure," I said.

We walked slowly into town together. Dad didn't know Mr. McKenzie well. I didn't think he'd ever met his wife. I guess he figured he owed it to him because of all the trouble we'd caused him. Or maybe Dad liked the idea of people in a small town sticking together. Or maybe Dad was just there for me. In any case, I was glad to have him along.

When we arrived at the funeral home, Dad went off to speak to Mr. McKenzie. He was talking to someone I thought must have been the cousin from Chicago, since they both had the same burly build and bushy eyebrows. I wandered off to look for Sam.

At the far end of the main room was another door, and inside that door was the room with the coffin. No one else was there. I'd never seen a real dead body, and I couldn't decide if I was excited or terrified as I walked over to the coffin and peeked inside.

Sam's mother was lying on her back, her eyes closed. People often said dead people had gone to sleep, but she didn't look like that. She looked like she'd been dipped in wax and had on too much makeup. Her thin gray hair was curled and arranged on a silk pillow. There was a white lily in her hands. She was so incredibly, impossibly still.

Someone sniffed and I jumped.

Sam was sitting on the floor behind the door. He was wearing a plain black suit that was a little bit too big, probably borrowed from someone at the church.

"Thanks for coming," he said, glancing up at me. His eyes were red and watery, as if he'd been squinting into the sunset for way too long.

"Sam, I'm so sorry," I said.

"Me too."

"I'll leave you alone," I said.

"No," he said. "Stay. Please. Just . . . you don't have to say anything."

So I went over and sat next to Sam on the floor. We sat

there for a long time, watching the mourners wander in and out to pay their last respects. Most never even noticed we were there.

My legs had both fallen asleep from sitting in the same position for so long, when I heard my father asking people, "Have you seen Tommy?"

I turned to Sam. "I'd better go."

"Thanks," he said.

"What are friends for?"

"Is that what we are?" he asked. "Friends?"

"Yeah," I said slowly. "I think we are."

Sam wasn't at school all the next week, so I didn't get a chance to mention the concert idea to him until Saturday, February 13, just a couple of days before they were planning to move. The door was unlocked when I arrived, so I let myself into the empty store. It was sad, seeing all the empty shelves. "Sam, Sam!" I cried. "Are you here?"

"I'm upstairs," he called.

I ran up the stairs two at a time. "Sam, I have a favor to ask you." I didn't wait for him to answer. "I need to use your mimeograph machine."

"It's right over there," he said. He was sitting on the floor, a box in front of him and piles of papers spread out all around.

The machine was squatting on its table. Just like always.

"But Dad's selling it," Sam said.

"Why?" I asked.

"Tommy, we need the money," Mr. McKenzie said, walking into the room.

"But I need to make some flyers!" I quickly told them

about my plan for the concert for Mary Lou. "We need to advertise. And I'm the paperboy. I can just put the flyers in all the papers."

"That's a great idea," Mr. McKenzie said. "But a lady is coming to buy the machine today."

"Oh," I said, disappointed.

"How am I going to make copies of my stories?" Sam asked crossly.

"Sam!" Mr. McKenzie sighed, like they'd had this conversation before. "We need the money. My cousin already paid for the funeral. I can't ask him for anything else."

"*Mom* thought my stories were important."

"I do too," Mr. McKenzie insisted. "It's just that . . ."

This was beginning to sound like a conversation at my house before my mom had gone to stay with Ma and Pa. The arguing made my palms sweat, and I tried desperately to think of something, anything else to say.

"So, what are all these papers?" I asked, gesturing to the files spread out on the floor.

"Nothing," said Mr. McKenzie. "Files. Old clippings. Diaries. Medical records. Bills. Maybe a letter or two."

"It's Mom's stuff," Sam said fiercely. "She said I could have it. And she told us to find her 'wedding ring.'"

"Sam, your mother was delirious. She lost her wedding ring years ago."

"Well, that's what she said, Dad!"

"You're welcome to look," Mr. McKenzie said. "But we can't take that huge box with us to Chicago. Pick out what you want and get rid of the rest." His voice cracked as he added, "I can't bear to look through it."

Mr. McKenzie hurried down the stairs and into the empty store.

"Scoot over," I said to Sam, sitting next to him on the floor. "I'll help you look."

"Thanks," Sam said.

We started looking through the papers slowly, one after another. If Mary Lou had died, what would I have wanted to do? Get rid of her stuff or keep it all? I wasn't sure. I shook the thought off. "A wedding ring," I said to Sam. "Gold, I guess?"

Sam shrugged. "I'm hoping Mom hid it. If we find it, maybe we could sell it and . . ."

He didn't finish the sentence. He didn't have to. Some extra money would save them now. I realized they needed a concert too. But who would come if it was for a man who was rumored to be a communist? I flipped through the papers. Bill, letter, newspaper clipping, greeting card. Medical report, bill, bill, envelope. A sealed envelope.

The bell rang. I heard Mr. McKenzie open the door.

On the front of the sealed envelope, in neat cursive letters, were the words *Wedding Ring*.

"Come on in," Mr. McKenzie said, his voice carrying up to the second floor. "The mimeograph machine is upstairs. In perfect working order. My son maintained it himself."

"Sam," I said. I handed him the envelope.

He clutched it, barely daring to breathe as he ran his fingers over it. "But there's nothing in here," he wailed softly. "There's no ring."

"Open it," I said.

Mr. McKenzie and the buyer started walking up the stairs.

272

Sam ran one finger under the edge. His nail was torn and jagged, as if he'd been biting it. The envelope opened and one piece of paper fell out.

"Nothing," I said. It was so disappointing, I wanted to cry.

Sam picked up the paper and scanned it. "I don't understand," he said, just as his father walked back into the room. "What's a 'term life policy'?"

"What?" asked Mr. McKenzie. "Let me see that." He rushed over to Sam and grabbed the letter.

"Is this the machine?" the woman asked. She wore a red pillbox hat and matching gloves. We all ignored her.

Mr. McKenzie took the letter, holding it like a hurt bird in his hands. He read it quickly, took a deep breath and read it again. "Oh, my goodness," he said. "She lied to me. All those years, she lied to me!"

Tears began to leak out his eyes. I couldn't quite figure out why it was good that she had lied, but he was smiling.

"Who?" asked Sam. "What?"

I held my breath.

"Your mother. That crazy mother of yours. She was the one who saved me from the camps all those years ago. She's the one who found a doctor who would treat you when your face was burned. And now she's saved us again."

"How?" asked Sam.

"When we first arrived in the United States, practically the first man we ran into was a life insurance agent. He wanted to sell us a policy. Your mother was all for it, but I told her no, we didn't have any money. She wanted to sell her wedding ring. I told her to keep it." He laughed, short and sweet, not bitter at all. "A month later, she told me she

273

had lost the ring. I yelled and yelled. We had a huge row."
He laughed again.

"She had life insurance?" I asked.

Mr. McKenzie nodded. "Apparently so. Not a lot. But enough to keep us going for another few months, maybe even make a few changes to the store. But she left it all to you, Sam."

"Is it," Sam asked, "is it enough for a sandwich shop?"

Mr. McKenzie smiled, the grin traveling across his face, the idea lighting up his eyes like a match. "A sandwich shop?" he repeated. "Yeah, I think it is."

"We could add you to the concert flyer," I said. "'Refreshments provided by McKenzie's Sandwich Shop. Opening soon.'"

"That's a great idea." Sam turned to his dad. "What do you think?"

"It's up to you," said Mr. McKenzie. But for the first time in months, maybe since I'd planted that paper, Mr. McKenzie looked hopeful.

"We're staying here," Sam said decisively.

"Is this mimeograph machine for sale or not?" the woman asked, the red hat bobbing on her head.

"No," we all said loudly. Then we laughed.

"No," Sam repeated. "I'm afraid it's not."

43

ANOTHER WORD FOR HELP

Mrs. Glazov loved the idea of having Mr. McKenzie provide refreshments, but the newly formed Downers Grove Musical Society was harder to sell on the plan. She invited them all over to her house on a cold evening in late February and served them tea. I was invited too.

"McKenzie's?" the trumpet player said, turning his lips upside down in a scowl. "Isn't he the communist?"

"Nah, he's not a communist," the flute player said. "But he is a Gypsy."

"Communist or Gypsy," said a bald man with a big belly, who played the guitar, "I don't like either of them."

"You know Mr. Sullivan?" added the trumpet player. "He said he caught him red-handed with a commie newspaper in his store!"

"Wait a minute!" I said. I knew the communist rumors would be a problem, but maybe . . . "Did I say the new store was going to be called McKenzie's?" I laughed. "It's going to be called Sam's Sandwich Shop."

"Who's Sam?" asked the flute player.

"Isn't that McKenzie's kid?" said the bald man. "The fat kid with the burned face?"

"Yes, yes," Mrs. Glazov said. "We help him."

Everyone was quiet for a moment. Then the bald man shook his head. "I don't know."

"If one burned kid will bring people out," the flute player pointed out, "two might be even better."

The trumpet player looked thoughtful. "Ezekiel 18:20," he said finally. "'The son shall not bear the guilt of the father.'"

They all turned to look at the guitar player.

"All right," he said finally. "No need to start quoting the Bible at me. My wife already got on my case for missing Mass last week!"

Everyone laughed.

So it was decided: the first concert would be to raise money for the medical bills of one Mary Lou Wilson, and the refreshments would be provided by Sam's Sandwich Shop.

Mr. McKenzie had no problem with changing the name of the shop. "It's a great idea," he said. "I should have thought of it myself."

Sam was thrilled to have the shop named after him, and we got right to work designing the flyers. Sam wrote out the date, time and place, neat as a typewriter, then drew a little picture beneath the words.

"Is that a boy playing the accordion?" I asked when he was done.

"Yep," said Sam.

It even kind of looked like me. We printed off a few sample

copies and I ran home, eager to show them to my dad. He was going to be so excited. I'd asked Mrs. Glazov not to say anything to him yet. I wanted it to be a surprise. I wanted to swoop in and save the day like a cowboy in the movies.

That Sunday, February 21, we visited Mary Lou at the hospital. Once Dad went off to talk to the doctors, I showed Mary Lou our flyer and told her about the concert. She was delighted. "Oh my goodness, Tommy!" she squealed. "A concert in my honor!" She was sitting in the rocking chair beside her bed, rocking back and forth.

"You're gonna come, right?"

"Of course! If I have to walk all the way myself."

We giggled.

"You don't mind taking charity?" I asked.

Mary Lou picked at one of the bandages on her legs, unrolling it and then rolling it up again. "What's so bad about accepting charity? I've been in the hospital a long time now. Five months. I've had to have help with everything—getting dressed, combing my hair, learning to walk again, even going to the bathroom! It bothered me for a long time."

It would have bothered me too.

"You know, Tommy," Mary Lou went on, "before I got burned, I believed if I just tried hard enough, nothing bad would ever happen."

"That's not true, is it?"

"No," she said. "It's not. Sometimes we all need a hand. *Charity* is just another word for *help*."

I liked that.

The rocking chair squeaked as Mary Lou glided back and forth. "Make sure you bring some extra flyers for the nurses," she said finally. "I think they're all going to want to come too."

Driving home seemed like the perfect time to tell Dad about my plan. But unlike Mary Lou, he was anything but thrilled.

"No, Tommy," he said when I finished telling him about our plans. "I don't like that idea at all."

I was irritated. If Mary Lou didn't mind, how could he object? We needed the money! I started explaining my idea again, but I didn't get very far before Dad interrupted: "No, I won't have everyone knowing that I can't support my own family."

"But . . ."

"Tommy, this is not your problem."

"But Mrs. Glazov and her friends have been rehearsing for weeks now."

"Well, they can have a concert," said Dad, "but it doesn't need to be for us."

"I thought you believed in people helping each other," I said.

"I do, but . . ."

"Then what happened to 'From each according to his abilities, to each according to his needs.'"

"That's different," Dad said.

"How? I can play the accordion to entertain people. We need money. Seems like a fair trade to me."

Dad was quiet a long time. "We have already accepted so much. Mrs. Glazov's help. Ma and Pa's. And I . . ."

"Wasn't that your dream, though, Dad? To live in a place where people help each other?"

"Yeah," Dad said quietly. "I guess it was."

"It's not only your dream. It's Mrs. Glazov wanting to be a music teacher again. She might get a bunch of new students from the concert. And Mr. McKenzie has a chance to start his sandwich shop. It's a way for people to find out about that too!"

"And we need the money," Dad added.

"Yeah."

I waited. It was a dark night, our headlights shining on the lonely road.

"It's like that movie," I said. "*It's a Wonderful Life*. Bedford Falls helped Jimmy Stewart. Let our town help us now."

"Okay," Dad said finally. "I'm proud of you, Tommy. It still makes me a little uncomfortable, but . . ."

"You're uncomfortable?" I teased. "I'm the one who has to be up there in front of everyone playing the accordion!"

Dad laughed. "Well then, you'd better get practicing."

44

TALKING TO EDDIE

For the rest of February and the first half of March, Mrs. Glazov and I practiced the accordion every night after dinner. Dad did the dishes while Pinky and Susie played on the floor and listened. Dad knew how to give Susie a bottle now. And Mrs. Glazov's cooking seemed to agree with him, because his face started to fill out, the crevices looking not quite as deep.

We'd settled into a nice routine at home. No yelling. No moods. One day, as I was doing the paper route, I realized home was no longer the wild saloon, where I *had* to stop if I wanted a drink. No, now it was more like a peaceful watering hole, where I could pull my hat down over my eyes and take a rest.

But if things were going okay at home for once, school was another matter. Recess was now my least favorite time of day. Eddie wouldn't speak to me while we cleaned the bathrooms, and worse, he spent his lunch hour harassing Sam, tripping him or stealing his jacket. I didn't know what to do. I liked

Sam, but I liked Eddie too, at least the old Eddie who used to do things with me.

One day, I was standing by the horses watching Eddie and Peter chasing Sam around the street, trying to figure out what to say to get them to stop, when Luke came up to me. That was kind of odd. He and Peter usually did everything together. "Hi, Tommy," he said.

"Hi," I said. "Why aren't you with Peter?"

"He and Eddie are teasing Sam." Luke shrugged. "It makes me feel kind of bad."

"Yeah," I agreed. "Me too."

"Come on, Tommy," Luke scoffed. "We saw what you did to Sam with those stockings before Christmas. And everyone heard what you said on the bus."

I'd forgotten about that. "I'm sorry," I said. "I shouldn't have said that about your arm."

Luke shrugged. "I know it's the only thing that's protected me from your teasing in the past. No one wants to mention it. They don't want to have the bad luck to get polio too."

"I really do feel bad about how I treated Sam," I admitted. "I guess I wanted to be a cowboy, big and strong and tough."

"I'd like to be a cowboy too," Luke said. "But there aren't any cowboys with polio."

"FDR had polio," I said.

"Yeah, yeah," Luke admitted. "Being president is pretty cool. But not as cool as Gary Cooper. Sometimes I'd just like to . . ."

"Scream?" I suggested.

"Yeah," Luke agreed. "Or hit someone. But, well . . ." He gestured to his arm.

We both laughed. It felt good to actually talk about those open secrets that everyone knew.

"Maybe I should go tell Eddie to knock it off," I said.

"Yeah," Luke agreed. "Maybe you should."

I didn't get up the nerve to talk to Eddie until that afternoon when we were scrubbing the bathroom. Usually Eddie did one side and I did the other, but that day I walked over to his section. "Eddie, I—"

"I don't want to talk to you."

"Come on, Eddie. You can't give me the silent treatment forever."

He threw down his brush. "Why?" he screamed. "Why did you turn on me?"

Eddie sounded like me when I'd thrown that glass. He sounded like my mom. I didn't like it. "I didn't turn on you," I said.

"Sure feels like it! I always kept your secrets. How many times did I get punished and you didn't, only because I kept my mouth shut?"

It had been a lot of times. "I'm sorry." It seemed like I was always apologizing now.

He crossed his arms and leaned against the wall. "Anything else you wanted to say?"

"Actually, yeah." I took a deep breath. "I think you should stop teasing Sam."

"Why?" he asked. "It's fun. You had fun picking on him too."

It had been kind of fun. "I know," I admitted. "But . . ." How could I explain it in a way Eddie would understand?

"It's like Luke. Would you ever tease Luke about his arm?"

"No!" protested Eddie.

"Why not? You don't like him much. Don't you think he's kind of stuck up?"

"Yeah, but it just wouldn't be right," said Eddie. "He didn't ask to get polio."

"Do you think Sam asked for that bomb?" I said. "Or to be born in Nazi Germany? How is Sam's face any different from Luke's arm?"

He didn't answer.

"It's not different," I said. "Except you didn't grow up with him."

Eddie was silent for a long time.

"It was all in fun," said Eddie. "Not my fault if he can't take a joke."

"But you wouldn't play that kind of a joke on Luke," I pointed out again.

Eddie looked thoughtful. "No," he said quietly, "we all play kick ball with him."

"Exactly," I said.

"You're the one who started calling him Little Skinny! Why are you so high-and-mighty now?"

I shrugged. "He's not a bad guy."

"He's a communist!"

"No—I told you. That was my fault. I planted the paper there."

"Yeah, but it had to come from somewhere. It was probably them."

I shook my head again. "No, I know where it came from."

"Yeah, right."

283

Eddie picked up his brush and started scrubbing again.

"I really do."

"Then why don't you tell me?"

I shook my head. "I promised to keep it a secret."

"Well," Eddie snapped. "I'm not the one who's bad at keeping secrets."

"I didn't mean it like that."

"No," Eddie said, "you just meant that you don't trust me. Even though I haven't given *you* any reason not to!"

I felt as mixed up as a lost calf in the middle of a cattle drive. He was right. And I didn't want to lose Eddie as a friend. There was only one way to show him that I still trusted him.

"All right," I said finally. "I'll tell you."

Eddie put down his scrub brush and put his hands on his hips.

I glanced around to make sure no one else was in the bathroom with us, even though I knew full well that it was deserted. Pa hadn't thought it was a big deal. Maybe Eddie wouldn't either.

"Well?"

I took a deep breath, trying to pretend my heart wasn't going thump, thump, thump. "The paper was from my dad."

Eddie rolled his eyes. "Ha-ha. Very funny." He picked up the scrub brush and returned to work.

"No, really," I said. "He attended a couple of meetings in college and . . ."

Eddie sat back on his heels and stared at me. His hair stuck out like bits of hay and his eyes were wide. "You're serious?"

I nodded, my words caught in my throat.

"Your dad is a communist?"

"No, not a communist. He just read about it a little."

"But you said he attended a couple of meetings?"

"Yeah, but—"

"That makes him a communist."

This was a mistake. Dad had warned me that I was impulsive. I'd wanted to win Eddie back over to my side, to let him know I trusted him, to let him know he really *was* still my friend. But now that I'd told him, I'd made our family vulnerable. What if he started a rumor about us, the way I had about Mr. McKenzie? "Eddie! You've known my dad your whole life."

"Yeah, and I've known you too. I didn't think you would betray me either."

"Communism is just an idea," I said, and I realized I sounded like Dad. "A bad idea but . . . haven't you ever had a bad idea?"

"Yeah," said Eddie. "Being friends with you."

I snorted and laughed. A big nervous laugh. "Yeah, that was a pretty bad idea."

Eddie frowned harder.

"Look, Sam is helping me organize a concert for Mary Lou."

"For Mary Lou?" he asked.

Maybe that was the way to win him over. Of course he wanted to help *her*.

"Yeah. I'm getting up at four o'clock on Sunday morning to put flyers about the concert in the paper," I said.

"Four o'clock in the morning?" asked Eddie.

"Yeah," I said.

"That's awful early," he said.

"It's when I'm getting up," I repeated. "You want to help, come to my house then."

I picked up my brush and started scrubbing, desperately trying to rub away the thought that I'd made another mistake by telling Eddie about my dad. "Seriously," I said. "You know we were awful to Sam."

"Yeah," Eddie agreed. "I guess we were."

We cleaned the floor in silence for a while. "Really?" Eddie asked suddenly. "Your dad's the communist?"

"Eddie!" I exclaimed. "You can't tell anyone."

"Yeah, yeah."

"I mean it! Look what happened to Mr. McKenzie."

"I know." He scrubbed harder, putting all his concentration onto one little spot of dirty floor. "I know how to keep a secret." And something about the way he said it, something about the way his eyes flashed dark as midnight for just a moment, made me wonder what secrets Eddie was keeping from me.

"Not anyone," I repeated.

"I don't rat out my friends," he said. "Unlike some people I know."

"Guess I deserved that," I said.

"Sure did." He turned and grinned at me.

I grinned back. I told myself Eddie would keep my secret. But I wasn't completely sure.

45

THE FLYERS

The third Saturday in March, after my paper route, I stopped by Sam's to pick up the flyers. There were lots of changes to the store already. (The insurance money had been enough to pay the back rent and then some.) The shelves had been ripped out and a black-and-white tile floor was being put in. Mr. McKenzie was busy showing a workman where to put the soda counter. "Sam's upstairs," he called to me. "Go on up!"

Sam was in the living room, with piles of paper surrounding him. His hands were covered with purple ink and the whole room smelled like chemicals. "Don't touch anything!" he said. "I've got everything ready to go." Methodically, he stacked the flyers and placed them in a large blue bag. He handed the bag to me.

"Thanks," I said.

"Tommy?"

I looked at him.

"Do you need help delivering the flyers?"

"Nah," I said. "I asked Eddie to help."

"Why didn't you ask me?"

"You already did the printing," I said. "You don't want to get up at four a.m."

"And Eddie doesn't like me," he said.

"Yeah," I added. "That too."

He snorted. "Of course, I didn't like you either, at first."

"The feeling was mutual."

And we both smiled.

Sunday morning, my alarm went off at four o'clock. I pulled on my clothes and cowboy boots and grabbed Sam's bag.

It was only thirty minutes earlier than normal, but the darkness felt thick and heavy. As I sat on my front porch, folding and placing a flyer in each newspaper, my heart felt heavy too. Eddie hadn't shown up. No one ever told you that doing the right thing would be so hard. Or feel so lonely. Even Boots was still inside, asleep on my pillow. He needed his rest and I didn't have the heart to wake him. Mechanically, I kept folding.

"Tommy?"

I whirled around. Standing in the shadows was Sam.

"What are you doing here?"

"Helping, of course," he said.

"Thanks." I shoved a pile of flyers at him. Unfortunately, it had rained the night before. Spring was coming soon, which was nice, except that the papers fell right into a puddle.

"Don't worry," Sam said. "I brought extras."

"Really," I said. "You didn't need to come."

"Yeah, well." He shrugged. "To you, I'm sure it doesn't feel like much. But to me, sneaking out of the house in the early morning feels like an exciting adventure!" Sam grinned, and for the first time since his mom had died a month and a half before, the smile reached all the way to his eyes.

"Ah," I said, remembering his words from the day he'd fallen in the lake. "You always wanted to steal some yo-yos."

"Don't do it," Eddie called out. He was approaching from the other direction. "It leads to getting up at four a.m."

He'd come after all. Maybe we really were friends again. "Good to see you," I said.

"Yeah, well . . . ," Eddie mumbled.

"Hello, Eddie," said Sam.

Eddie looked at him, directly at his scar. Sam stood still without flinching.

"Hello . . . Sam," he said.

Sam smiled. We all sat down and started folding and stuffing. We didn't really talk—it was too early and I didn't want to wake my family, but it was still nice. Almost like a party. I used to think being a cowboy meant dividing the world up into good guys and bad guys. Eddie and I were a posse, the rest of them were Indians. But maybe that wasn't really how it worked. Maybe sometimes the cowboys and Indians could be friends.

"Give me some more," Eddie said.

Sam passed them over, like a peace pipe, and before I knew it, we were done. I was ready to go at my normal time. "Well, um, thanks," I said.

They both nodded and went home. And I got on my bike to ride off into the sunrise.

That afternoon, I stopped by home to pick up some of Dad's tools and then went over to Ma and Pa's to fix their chicken-coop door. I was nervous about maybe seeing Mom again, but cowboys always keep their promises. I snuck around back without even letting anyone know I was there and started working.

It felt good to concentrate on something I knew I could fix. Felt good to pry out the broken door and frame up a new one. I was almost done when I heard footsteps behind me. I caught a whiff of perfume. I'd bought Mom a bottle of perfume last year on her birthday, right before Busia had died. She'd burst into tears when she'd opened it. Apparently, she'd wanted the yellow bottle and I'd gotten the green one.

"You've done a great job," Mom said.

I shrugged.

"We got your flyer," she went on.

I shrugged again.

"At first I was upset," she admitted. "I don't accept charity! I don't want everyone to know we're having money troubles."

I still didn't say anything. I wasn't doing the concert for *her*.

She took a deep breath. "But then I remembered what Pa is always telling me. I don't have to do everything alone. I don't have to give in to the dark moods when they come. I can wait until they pass. Or if they don't pass, I'm supposed to ask for help. I will ask for help."

I concentrated intently on pounding the nail straight into the door frame. "Mary Lou said *charity* is just another word for *help*."

"I think she's right," said Mom. "Tommy—"

"You don't have to say anything else," I said, cutting her off. We weren't arguing. She'd been nice. I didn't want to push our luck.

"I don't know if I can change," Mom went on. "But I want to try."

She walked back into the house. I'd never even turned to look at her. But as I packed the tools away, I noticed I was crying.

46

THE CONCERT

The first week in April, Dad gave me one of his old suits to wear to the concert. It was a little too big. "Not bad," he said. "But let's walk over and ask Mrs. Scully to make it fit just right." So after dinner, Dad and I walked Boots over to Mrs. Scully's house.

"Tommy," Dad said, "Mom is going to come home next week, after your performance."

I didn't answer. She'd been gone for almost two months now. And the truth was, even though she seemed better, I wasn't sure I wanted her to come home.

"It makes me a little nervous," Dad admitted, reading my mind. "It's been kind of nice without her, hasn't it? Calm and peaceful."

I nodded. I hadn't realized Dad felt that way too.

"But when Mom's not angry or upset," Dad continued, "well, she's fun. She's energetic and lively and makes me laugh. And at times, she can be so thoughtful. Remember when she baked those pies for all the nurses at the hospital?"

Yeah, I remembered.

Dad took a deep breath. "I want to give her another chance. People can change."

I wasn't sure about that. But I guessed I hoped they could.

"And," Dad went on, "if things don't change . . . well, I don't want to send her away. But if I have to, I will."

Even if I didn't feel quite ready to have her home, I didn't really want her gone either. And if Dad was willing to send her away, willing to actually *do* something for us, I guess that was proof that people could change. My dad had. And I had stopped being mean to Sam. I supposed that it was possible my mom could change too.

"Okay," I said. "We'll give it a try."

Dad threw an arm around my shoulders. And I hoped that was his way of saying, *This time, Tommy, I won't let you down.*

Mrs. Scully was thrilled to see us. "How's my favorite sewing project?" she cooed to Boots, who jumped up and licked her face, then sniffed around her kitchen, looking for sausages. His cut was healing well. The scar was still pink and raised, but I'd carefully snipped and pulled out the bits of thread a few days before and it hadn't bled a bit.

After she petted Boots, Mrs. Scully made me go into the living room and put on Dad's suit and stand on this big square box while she measured and tucked and pinned. "I'll take the shoulders in and have those cuffs sewn up in no time," she said.

"One more thing," Dad said, clearing his throat. He pulled a green bundle out of a bag. "The dress you made for Catherine turned out to be a little too small. Could you take it out a bit?"

"Of course," Mrs. Scully said, turning to me. "Tommy, why didn't you tell me?!"

I blushed and shrugged.

Mrs. Scully had the suit alterations done by the next evening. And when she brought it over to our house, it fit perfectly. Before she left, Mrs. Scully turned her attention to Mrs. Glazov, who was just finishing the dishes.

"And you, Mrs. Glazov," she said, "what are you going to wear?"

"Me?" Mrs. Glazov blushed. "Just one of my old dresses."

"Nonsense," said Mrs. Scully. And she made Mrs. Glazov hold out her arms as she measured and made notes on a small pad of paper.

"But I have no money for new dress!" Mrs. Glazov protested.

"This is a concert to raise money for Mary Lou." Mrs. Scully sniffed. "Now, I don't have a lot of cash, but I do have an extra bolt of cloth in the basement. Please. Let me make sure you are well dressed."

So Mrs. Glazov got a new dress as well, a black gown fit for an opera star. When Mrs. Scully brought it back the next week for a fitting, Mrs. Glazov wept as she put it on.

April sped by and pretty soon it was the twenty-first, the morning of the concert. Pa stopped me on the paper route. "Ma and I have something for you." He handed me a small thin box and I carefully removed the top.

It was shiny black satin bow tie with bits of silver thread running through it.

"Thought you could wear it for the concert," he said.

"Thanks," I said. "It's much nicer than my old school tie."

Pa smiled. "The chickens haven't escaped once since you fixed their coop."

"Good."

"You'd better go," he said. "It's a busy day."

"Yeah." I turned to leave, then stopped. "Do you really think Mom is ready to come home?"

"Well, Tommy," he said slowly, "I will continue to see your mother once a week. But I've taught her to take a deep breath when she's upset. And to listen more. And I've asked her to accept help when it's offered. I can't offer you any guarantees, but I do think she's changed. I think it's worth a try."

That evening, Mrs. Glazov and I were dressed to the nines. My suit was ironed and I'd polished my accordion until all the keys shone. Mrs. Glazov's long black dress swooshed as she walked, and her hair was pulled back in an elegant bun and held in place with bobby pins. Mrs. Scully had even put some lipstick on her. She no longer looked faded and gray at all.

"Ready to go?" Dad asked.

I nodded, too nervous to speak.

Pinky ran into the room then, clutching something small in her hand. "Tommy, Tommy, you can't forget this!"

It was the silver sheriff's star from Mary Lou. I stood still as Dad pinned it to my lapel.

"Come on, cowboy," said Mrs. Glazov. "Time to break leg."

We all piled into the car. There was still a big dent in the front bumper from where Mom had plowed into the other

295

car in the hospital parking lot, but our car ran fine. Luckily. There wasn't any money to fix it.

When we got out in front of the Tivoli, the first thing I noticed was the marquee. It read: *First Ever Concert of the Downers Grove Musical Society*.

I turned to look at Mrs. Glazov. "Pretty neat."

"Yes." She grinned. "Last year, I spent all time in house. All alone. Now I part of music society!" She laughed. "Very glad you came to sell me magazine."

"Me too." I offered her my arm. She took it and we started to walk inside.

"Hey, Tommy!"

We turned and saw Eddie hurrying down the street. His blond hair stood up even messier than normal. "Dad didn't want me to come," he mumbled. "Said the Musical Society is just a bunch of communists. Mom wanted to see the concert, but they had a big fight and . . . I snuck out the back."

Mrs. Glazov leaned over and gave Eddie a big hug. "We glad you're here." She picked up her accordion. "Tommy, I see you inside."

As she walked off, Eddie pulled out a handkerchief and blew his nose. His eyes were a little red and I wondered if he'd been crying.

"Thanks, buddy, for coming," I said.

Eddie stood up straighter. "What did you think? I'd miss seeing you make a fool of yourself?"

"Ha-ha," I said. "Thanks for your support."

He punched me in the arm.

"Watch it!" I cried. "That's my bellows arm."

We grinned at each other.

Mrs. Scully and a group of women in suits and fancy hats arrived next, talking a mile a minute. I figured they must be her League of Women Voters friends and I was pretty sure one of them was the lady who had wanted to buy Sam's mimeograph machine. "Did you see Edward R. Murrow on *See It Now* last month?" she was saying.

"Oh yes," replied the next. She lowered her voice to a gravelly growl. "'We must not confuse dissent with disloyalty. We must remember always that accusation is not proof. . . . We will not walk in fear, one of another!'"

Mrs. Scully laughed. "You sound just like him!"

The lady blushed. "Well, he sure put Senator McCarthy in his place."

They all breezed into the lobby then, and I followed them inside. Mr. McKenzie had set up a huge buffet and was dressed in his usual suit and white apron.

"The sandwiches look delicious," said one of the ladies.

"Sam's Sandwich Shop is opening next week," said Mr. McKenzie. "There's an order form for your next party right here." He handed them a mimeographed sheet.

Sam had borrowed an usher's hat and one of the red coats with gold braid as well. He looked delighted as he showed person after person to his or her seat. It was a dollar to enter. Refreshments were a quarter.

I stood in the wings, waiting for my turn to go on. My hands were sweating so much, I kept drying them on my shirt. First, the trumpet player played a tune, then the old lady who always played the organ at church, and then the milkman, who was actually quite good on the clarinet. The guitar player and the flutist did a duet, and finally, one of the local piano teacher's students pounded out "When the Saints Go Marching In." Then it was our turn.

I followed Mrs. Glazov onto the stage. The lights were bright and shining and at first I couldn't see a thing. She was talking into the microphone, but I couldn't understand a word. Suddenly, I was afraid that she was speaking Russian, and that this was some weird communist trap after all. But everyone laughed at what she said, and then she came over to me and said, "A von, a two, a von, two, tree," and we started playing "On Top of Old Smoky."

And as soon as we started playing, I began to relax. My fingers knew what to do. By the time our first song was over, I was much calmer. Everyone clapped as Mrs. Glazov walked back over to the microphone.

"And now," she said, "our very own Tommy Wilson will play 'The Ballad of High Noon.'"

She looked over at me and nodded. I took a deep breath and started to play.

The first few notes sounded small and weak. This was the theme song from *High Noon,* and it made me feel brave, if a little sad, every time I heard it. Mom liked it too. I pulled the bellows deeper and stronger, and the notes filled the theater like only an accordion can. Out of the corner of my eye, I could see Mrs. Glazov beaming at me from the wings of the stage. Mrs. Scully sat in one corner of the auditorium, the league ladies surrounding her. Pa and Ma were in another, swaying gently in time to the music. Sam and Mr. McKenzie and Eddie and the choirboys were down front. Officer Russo sat next to them. Sister Ann and some of the other nuns were in the middle. Even the friends Mom had insulted, the Starrs and the Colvins, were there, as well as most of the girls from my class, including Lizzie Johnson. I couldn't believe how many people had shown up.

And my family. Dad and Pinky were in the very first row. Next to them was my mother. She was wearing the green dress we'd given her for Christmas. It fit perfectly now and I couldn't even see where Mrs. Scully had made her adjustments. Next to Mom was Mary Lou. One of the nurses had offered to drive her. In fact, there were a whole bunch of nurses from the hospital, and even a couple of doctors too, all sitting in the row behind my parents.

Mary Lou smiled at me, pointed to the pin on my lapel and winked. And then I didn't have to think about playing anymore. My fingers just flew over the keys. As I started into the very last verse, I noticed my father mouthing the words to the song.

"Do not forsake me, oh my darlin'
Although you're grieving, don't think of leaving
Now that I need you by my side."

I finished the song with a flourish. There was a second of silence in the theater. And for a horrible moment, I thought they hadn't liked it, that I'd somehow messed up without knowing it.

Then there was applause.

47

AFTER THE MUSIC

After the concert, I stood in the lobby, looking back in at the theater. Not quite believing that I'd done it. That I'd managed to play and perform and *do a good job* in front of all those people. I felt a tap on my shoulder.

It was Mary Lou. She was standing. Leaning on a cane, sure, but standing. A nurse waited patiently a few feet away.

"You did a great job," Mary Lou said, smiling.

"It wasn't just me," I said. "Lots of people—"

"No, Tommy," Mary Lou said. "It was mainly you."

My ears itched and my cheeks felt hot.

"You're blushing," Mary Lou teased.

"No, I'm not."

"Anyway," Mary Lou said, "I just saw Sister Ann and she said I should be able to finish the eighth grade with my class after all and go on to high school next year." She said "high school" like it was the World Series.

"That's great."

"'Course, I need to get out of the hospital first. The doctors said maybe in another month."

"A month's not too long," I said.

"No," Mary Lou said, "it's not."

The nurse came up and gently touched her arm.

"We have to leave soon. I'm going to go say bye to Mom and Dad. See you soon!"

I gave her a big hug and watched her hobble off with the nurse standing right beside her.

Lizzie Johnson came up to me next, her red hair pulled back in one big French braid, though little curls kept escaping. I wanted to tuck them behind her ear.

"Hi, Tommy," she said. "I didn't know you could play the accordion!"

"Yeah, well, I learned."

We both stared at our shoes, as if there was something really interesting on the carpet.

"Hey, Lizzie," I said finally.

"Yes?" She looked up at me eagerly.

"I shouldn't have said your freckles looked like a lizard," I said. "I actually like them."

"Really?"

"Yeah. I mean, Mary Lou has freckles too."

"Oh." Lizzie looked disappointed.

Perhaps telling a girl she looked like your sister was not the right thing to say. "Do you like ice cream?" I asked, desperate to change the subject.

"Who doesn't like ice cream?"

"Yeah, well, they're gonna have some at Sam's shop." Then I added quickly, before I could chicken out, "We should get a float there sometime."

She smiled. "That'd be nice."

"Really?"

"Yeah."

And before I could say anything else, she walked away.

Sister Ann came over to me then, with two other nuns from school. "Tommy," she said. "You've done a wonderful thing. Over a hundred people showed up. Many gave more than one dollar." She gestured to the basket she was holding. "I'm going to take all this money over to your father."

I smiled. "Thank you."

"And I was thinking," Sister Ann said, "maybe we should have another concert next year. Make it a tradition." As they walked off, I heard her say, "Did you know, Sister Rose, that in my youth I used to play the oboe?"

Sister Rose laughed. "No, Sister Ann. I did not."

I looked for something to eat then, but the buffet Mr. McKenzie had carefully laid out had been picked over till there was nearly nothing left. Ma pointed at it as she walked off. "I do have to admit," she said, "those watercress sandwiches were really good. Almost as good as mine."

"Better," said Pa.

She whacked him with her purse, and they both laughed.

"Like your bow tie," Pa said, and winked at me.

"Thanks," I said, and smiled as they walked out.

After they left, Mr. McKenzie came up to me. "Look at this, Tommy!" He held up a bunch of papers. "Did you see how many order forms I got?"

"How many?" I asked.

"I don't know," he said excitedly. "I haven't had a chance to count them. All the league ladies ordered something. And you know that man from the hospital? Well, they're having some sort of a picnic this summer and they wanted to know if I could provide all the sandwiches. For a hundred people. And—"

"Is it . . . is it going to work?" I asked.

"I don't know, Tommy. We have minds to change. Some people will probably always think I'm a communist. But you know what?"

"What?"

Mr. McKenzie grinned, his dark eyes flashing. "It feels awfully good to have a chance to try out my dream." He picked me up in a big bear hug, lifting me off the ground.

"Hey!"

He put me back down and laughed. "Got to go count my forms!"

Mom came over to me next. The green dress made her eyes shine. Despite the new gray in her hair, she looked younger than she had before. Susie was sleeping in her arms.

"Hi, Tommy," Mom said shyly.

"Hi," I said.

"The concert was wonderful."

"Thanks."

We stood there in an awkward silence.

"I'm sorry," she said.

"For what?"

"For everything." Her voice trembled a little. "Pa suggested that maybe the next time you get in trouble, I let Dad give you your punishment. I think that's a good idea."

"Yeah," I said. "Me too."

Now *both* my parents had apologized to me. It felt weird. Not bad, but kind of strange. Maybe talking with Pa really had done her some good. And suddenly, like a flash flood in a dry canyon, all the reasons I loved my mom came roaring back. The pies she baked. How she danced to polka music in the kitchen. Even her toughness, because without that, how would she have found the strength to smother the flames and save Mary Lou?

"Does it help?" she asked. "Saying I'm sorry?"

"Yes," I said, and smiled. "It does."

Susie woke up and started to cry, and as Mom walked off to feed her, Sam came up to me. "You ever played before an audience before?"

I shook my head.

"How was it?" he asked.

"Terrifying," I admitted. "But then, once I got started, I guess it was kind of okay."

"You did a good job," he said, and handed me some rolled-up papers.

"What's this?" I asked.

"One of my stories," he said. "I figured, if you can play in front of all those people, I can let you read one of my stories."

I glanced at the front page: *The Adventures of Cowboy Sam.* "Thanks."

Sam gave me a shy smile. "I'm going to leave now before I change my mind."

I laughed as he ran off.

Everyone was just about gone by then. The lobby was almost empty. Sam had given his hat and jacket back to one of the real ushers, who was sweeping up and getting ready for the next day's show.

The only person I didn't get to say good-bye to was Eddie. Through the big glass doors, I saw him on the sidewalk in front of the Tivoli, arguing with his father. His dad pointed at us, then angrily shoved him into the car. I waved, but I don't think he saw me.

Finally, it was just Dad and me, looking at an old ad for *High Noon.*

"You know," Dad said softly when I walked up to him, "I was wrong before when I said cowboys were reckless, vengeful and independent to a fault. It wasn't the shoot-out that made Gary Cooper a great man. It was that he cared for others. He faced his problems. He didn't walk away. He solved them. A good cowboy is a leader who looks after his herd and his posse. No one goes missing. Kind of like you."

And for the first time in ages, for the first time since before Mary Lou had gotten burned, I knew who I was. I was Tommy John Wilson. A paper cowboy.

48

FISHING AT NOON

Everyone was on their best behavior on the way home. Dad drove the car and Mom sat in the front with him, Pinky leaning against her, Susie snuggled in Mom's lap. Mrs. Glazov and I rode in the back, our accordions between us. Mom's suitcase of belongings from Ma and Pa's was in the trunk.

For a few days, everything was okay. But when I came back from my paper route the last Saturday in April, Dad and Mom were already arguing again. "I don't understand why we still need her," Mom said. "I'm home!"

"What is your objection to Mrs. Glazov?" Dad snapped.

"I don't like having a stranger in the house."

"She's not a stranger," Dad continued. "Not anymore!"

Mom glanced around the kitchen. "The glasses aren't in the right cabinet," she said. "And there's grease on the stove."

"Catherine," Dad said, his voice gravelly, and I could hear the anger in his voice. He'd never really stood up to Mom before. I was kind of impressed.

"What?" she said.

"We're not even paying her! You can't criticize—"

Mrs. Glazov cleared her throat. She was standing at the back door. "I here to make breakfast," she announced. She pushed her way in between my parents and stood with her hands on her hips, looking at both of them.

Mom was going to drive her off, like she had with the women at the dinner party. She wasn't really going to accept help. And without Mrs. Glazov, Mom would get overwhelmed again and everything she had learned from Pa would go out the window and . . .

But Mrs. Glazov didn't storm off in a huff. Instead she took my mother's hand. "What you saying?" she scolded my father. "Of course she need to tell me where things go. A woman's kitchen is very important. We particular. Right?" She looked at my mom.

Mom was breathing heavily, the vein on her forehead popping in and out. She took two deep breaths and sighed. "Yes. Yes, you're right. We're particular."

"So," Mrs. Glazov said. "What else I do wrong?"

Mom laughed.

"No, tell me! Want to know."

Mom shook her head.

"Then I tell you," Mrs. Glazov said sternly. "You need new teapot."

"What's wrong with this one?" Mom asked.

"Makes terrible tea. I show you how!" Mrs. Glazov took the flowered apron off the hook by the back door and started to put it on.

Mom's eyes narrowed. I knew exactly what she was thinking. *That's my apron. How dare she!*

Mrs. Glazov must have seen Mom's expression too, because she paused and put the apron around my mom's neck instead. "This is yours," she said, as formally as if it were a crown.

Mom's face softened and she smiled as she tied the sash behind her back. They made a funny picture, the short woman and the tall one, sizing each other up, like they were cowboys in a showdown. Finally, Mom went to a cabinet in the corner and rummaged for a bit. She pulled out another apron, this one frilly and pink with white polka dots instead of flowers.

"You can have this one," Mom said.

Mrs. Glazov took it from her like a sacrament. "Thank you."

I could hardly believe it. The things Pa had told Mom, about taking a deep breath, thinking before you speak and, most of all, accepting help, had actually worked! In the doorway, Dad was smiling too. He shook his head in amazement.

Mom and Mrs. Glazov started working together, the flowers and the polka dots moving around the room like they'd always been there together. I went out to the garage and found an extra hook in the box of nails and screws. By the time I'd installed a hook for Mrs. Glazov's apron by the back door, next to Mom's, the pancakes were ready.

They tasted delicious.

A week or so after the concert, Dad, Mr. Sullivan, Eddie and I went fishing again. It was late April and the sky was blue. The clouds were white and round, like puffs of smoke from a train. All morning we pulled the fish in, one after another, and put them in a large bucket.

"Don't have room for many more," I said as I threw in another yellow perch.

The sun was high in the sky and it must have been close to noon. Way off in the distance, I could hear the whistle of a train. The birds were chirping and it was a beautiful day, but Mr. Sullivan wouldn't stop complaining.

"Can you believe it?" Mr. Sullivan moaned. "Old McKenzie renamed his store and now, just because he called it Sam's, he expects everyone to forget that he's a commie!"

"He's not a communist," Dad said.

"Yeah, that's what you say." Mr. Sullivan took another drink from the thermos he'd brought with him. From the smell, I was pretty sure it wasn't coffee, like my dad had brought. "And that old Russian lady? One little concert and my wife is nagging me to let her give my son music lessons!"

My dad coughed. "Well, Doug, Tommy has learned a lot from her. And the concert was for Mary Lou. To help pay for her medical bills." He sounded annoyed, maybe even a little embarrassed.

"Yeah, I heard that," Mr. Sullivan said. "Why are you taking charity from a commie anyway?"

"She's not a commie," I said.

Both dads ignored me.

"Didn't see you offering me any help," Dad said crossly.

"I lost my job," Mr. Sullivan said.

"Sorry about that," Dad said, "but maybe if you'd quit drinking you'd—"

"You saying it was my fault?" Mr. Sullivan demanded.

My palms were sweating so much, I could barely hold my pole. Next to me, Eddie was trying to put a worm on his hook, but his fingers were trembling so that the bait kept slipping out of them.

"No," Dad said calmly. "No, Doug, of course I'm not saying that."

Mr. Sullivan fumed quietly.

"Come on, let's just fish," Dad added.

We each cast our lines in a few times, but nothing bit. The tension was so high, I bet the fish could feel it.

"You're an old friend," Mr. Sullivan said, "but, Robert, I don't understand why you continue associating with Mr. McKenzie. And doesn't it make you nervous living next to that Russian?"

"Dad!" Eddie cried, exasperated. "Stop going on about the commies!"

"There's one here in town!"

"So what?" Eddie said.

"The commie could be gathering intelligence to feed to the Soviets," Mr. Sullivan said.

"What could the Soviets possibly want to know about Downers Grove?" Dad asked. "How many people showed up at the Tivoli on Friday night?"

"Yeah," Eddie added. "Think the Russians care how many fish you caught?"

Mr. Sullivan reached over and slapped Eddie on the cheek. Just like Mom had done to me that day at school. It felt odd, like watching myself in a movie. I knew how angry and scared and embarrassed Eddie must feel. Heck, I could practically feel the sting from the slap on my own face.

"You be respectful, boy," Mr. Sullivan growled. "Now that they are shutting McCarthy down, we'll have to root them out ourselves."

Eddie rolled his eyes. "There's nothing to 'root out,' Dad! We already know where the paper came from."

Eddie! I wanted to scream. *You promised not to tell!*

"What?" Mr. Sullivan's eyes blazed like Mom's when she was angry.

"I mean . . ." Eddie turned white as the belly of a fish.

"Where'd it come from?" Mr. Sullivan demanded.

"It was just an old newspaper," my dad said quietly, looking at me. I could feel his disapproval like a weight. He knew I'd told. After I'd promised not to. I'd broken my word. "It doesn't matter where it came from," Dad said.

"It does to me!" Mr. Sullivan stood up, grabbed Eddie by the shoulders and shook him hard. "Tell me!"

"Doug," Dad said, "let the boy go."

"Tell me!" Mr. Sullivan shook Eddie harder, causing him to drop his pole. Eddie looked at the sky and the ground and the lake, everywhere but at his dad. I was pretty sure he was crying. I bet it hurt being shaken like that. It had hurt when Mom had hit me. And no one had done a thing to stop her.

"Me," I said, standing up. "I put the paper in the store."

Mr. Sullivan let go of Eddie. "You're the commie?" he asked. His strong arms suddenly seemed scary, like a gorilla's. He took a step toward me. I backed away, but the dock was narrow. There wasn't much room.

Dad stood up and stepped between the two of us. "Tommy put the paper in the store," he said. "But it came from me."

"You?" Mr. Sullivan barked. "You're the commie?! My best friend?"

"I'm not a communist," Dad said slowly. "I just read a newspaper."

"Oh yeah, college boy? Just a newspaper, huh?" Mr. Sullivan said sarcastically. "While you were at your cushy factory job, I was fighting in Korea! At the Chosin Reservoir it was thirty below. With no good boots, all my toes froze clean off."

"I'm sorry, Doug," my dad said. "Let's just calm down and—"

"It's why I can't walk straight now. Because of commies like you!"

He lunged at my dad, but my dad ducked out of the way and Mr. Sullivan fell to the ground. "Think you're better than me, don't you?" he said, climbing to his feet.

"No." Dad put down his fishing pole and stood up to his full six feet.

"I know you're laughing at me behind my back." Mr. Sullivan walked over to the bag he'd brought and rummaged through it. He pulled out a handgun and pointed it at my dad's face.

"Dad!" Eddie sounded terrified.

My father's face was covered with a thin layer of sweat.

I started shaking.

Dad picked up the knife we used to gut the fish. "Put the gun down."

"No." Mr. Sullivan was unsteady on his feet, but his grip on the gun was firm.

They were going to fight. But this wasn't a movie, and if

someone got hurt, they wouldn't just jump up again when the director yelled "cut." There had to be a better way. But I couldn't think. It was like when Mary Lou had caught fire and I hadn't moved. Mom had had to come smother the flames, even though I'd been closer. No matter what, I couldn't let that happen again.

Suddenly, I remembered how Mrs. Glazov had handled the situation with Mom in the kitchen. She'd *agreed* with her. I could do that. I was a good talker. I just needed Eddie to follow my lead.

"Yeah." I walked over to Mr. Sullivan. "I know why you're so angry."

"Tommy?" Dad gave me a confused look.

I ignored him. My heart was galloping like a horse. If this didn't work, I didn't know what else to do. I glanced at Eddie. He had to remember. How we stole the yo-yos. One person distracts and charms. The other takes something. I mouthed, *Yo-yos,* and I could see his eyes clear. He nodded, not so anyone else could see, but I knew he'd understood.

"You know, I had the same reaction," I said to Mr. Sullivan. "My own father! A communist. It was so embarrassing." My voice sounded calm, but my legs were trembling.

"Yeah?" said Mr. Sullivan uncertainly. I could smell the whiskey on his breath.

He still had the gun pointed at my dad, but it was a bit lower now.

"I mean, he attended meetings. He should at least lose his job or something!"

"Yeah," Mr. Sullivan agreed. "Look at me. I lost *my* job!"

"It's not fair," I agreed.

I glanced at Eddie. He nodded.

My dad looked confused and hurt. I winked at him, but I wasn't sure he understood.

"He's got to pay," Mr. Sullivan said.

"Definitely," I agreed.

Mr. Sullivan raised his gun again. He was really going to do it. He was really going to shoot my father.

This was it. We had to act now. I caught Eddie's eye and whispered, "Hi-Yo, Silver."

Eddie and I both jumped onto his father, knocking him to the ground. The gun went off, but the bullet went wild, into the marshy grass.

"What the—?" Mr. Sullivan roared.

Dad put his knee into Mr. Sullivan's back, holding him down as he flailed and cursed. The gun was lying on the dock, a few inches away. I picked it up and, like I was throwing a baseball bat, hurled it into the pond. It floated for a moment, then sank with a few bubbles into the murky water.

Dad looked at Eddie and me like we were heroes, not just two scared boys with lots of practice stealing things. "Stop it, Doug," Dad growled, as tough as any cowboy. "You're drunk. You lost your job because of the drinking. It had nothing to do with me."

Mr. Sullivan stopped struggling.

"I'm going to let you go now," Dad said. "Don't try anything funny."

Mr. Sullivan stood up slowly. He had dirt on his legs and belly. There was even a big smudge on his cheek, kind of like Sam's scar.

Dad's face was angry, and somehow he still had the knife

in his hand. For a moment, I was afraid he was going to stab Mr. Sullivan. I touched Dad's wrist, and slowly he placed the knife on the ground.

Then Dad picked up our canteen of water, pulled out his handkerchief, and handed both to Mr. Sullivan. "Get cleaned up," he ordered. "We're going home."

Slowly we packed our stuff. Mr. Sullivan got in the back of the car, and as soon as it started moving, he fell asleep, snoring softly. Eddie and I sat in the front. I was in the middle, watching my dad drive.

"I'm sorry, Dad," I said. "You told me not to tell anyone. I just—"

Dad cut me off. "No need, Tommy. It was bound to come out at some point. And you and Eddie showed a lot more sense than I did. I was going to try to fight him with a knife."

I thought about that on the way home. The firefight at the end of *High Noon* had ended with four dead people. Bad people. But still. Four dead people. We had ended without a single one.

When we reached Eddie's house, Mrs. Sullivan helped Dad drag her husband into the house. Once he was settled, she came back out. "I don't know what to do," she said. "If he doesn't go back to work, we'll lose the house."

"Then maybe it's time to ask for help," Dad said.

"But who do I ask?" she wailed.

My dad took her hand gently. "Anyone. Maybe the church. Sister Ann. A cousin. Or maybe the people right next door. Downers Grove is a small town, Deborah. You ask, and they will help."

And I realized that was the difference between our town and Gary Cooper's in the movie. When he had gone from person to person asking for volunteer deputies to help him stand up to the criminals, everyone had refused to get involved. Refused to help when he needed it.

But our town had helped us. The people of Downers Grove had given my parents money for Mary Lou's medical bills. And taken my mother in when she needed a break. And sewn up my dog. And helped us make Thanksgiving dinner. And I'd helped Mr. McKenzie and Sam and now Eddie too. I'd fixed Ma and Pa's chicken coop, made friends with Mrs. Scully and shown everyone that Mrs. Glazov was a wonderful musician. We were a town, a posse, and together, nothing could stop us.

"See you on Monday at school, Eddie?" I asked.

He nodded, but he didn't look me in the eye. "Yeah."

I started to get back in the car.

"Hey, Tommy!"

I turned to look at him. Tufts of his blond hair stood on end, parts dyed brown with mud.

"Thanks, ke-mo sah-bee." He finally met my gaze.

"Hey," I said. "What are friends for?"

49

THE CEMETERY

The first week in May, Sam came up with the idea of letting the students at St. Joseph's place orders for sandwiches. This was a big hit, both with the kids (because the sandwiches were delicious) and the parents (because they didn't have to make lunches). So every morning, along with the bottles of milk from the milkman, came sandwiches from Sam's shop.

One day during lunch recess when I'd just finished my sandwich, I made my way over to the big elm tree. "Hey, Sam!" I called out, sitting down next to him.

"What?" He gave me a look. He'd played marbles with us once or twice now, but still spent many lunchtimes by himself.

"You're the one!"

"Tommy, I don't like it when you—"

"Just go on," I said kindly. "Ask it, one more time."

"The one what?" He sighed. But for the first time, there was a hint of a smile on his face as he said it.

"The best darn writer in the whole class." I slammed his

story down on the ground, like a cowboy throwing down a royal flush in a movie.

"You shouldn't say *darn*," said Peter, who'd followed me over. Luke and Eddie were close behind.

"Shut up, Peter," I said.

"Is it really good?" asked Luke, picking up a corner of the story.

"Better than *Kid Colt Outlaw*," I said.

"Can I read Sam's story?" Eddie asked.

"I had it first," said Luke.

Sam and I looked at each other and grinned.

"Simmer down, boys." I leaned over and put my arm around Sam. "He's got plenty more where that came from. But it'll cost you. A nickel a story!"

"Tommy," Sam protested. "They can read them for free."

"Sam," I said, elbowing him, "I'm trying to make you some money."

"I'd rather have the friends," he said. "A penny a story," he announced loudly.

Luke nodded. "Sounds fair to me." The boys dug into their pockets looking for change. I pulled out a penny.

"Keep it," said Sam. "You read for free."

I'd always thought it would feel embarrassing to be nice to Sam at school. But it wasn't. It felt really good. "Come on, Sam," I said.

"What?"

"We're going to play kick ball."

"Nah," he said. "I don't know how. Probably wouldn't be good at it anyway."

"I'll teach you."

"I'm writing another story."

"Sam."

"What?"

"Come on. You can finish the story tomorrow."

I grabbed his arm and pulled him up. Sam was on my team. Eddie rolled the ball to him, nice and gentle. Kick ball is pretty easy, and when Sam kicked the ball and made it to first base, everybody cheered.

After school, we all decided to go down to Sam's Sandwich Shop for root beer floats. Well, all of us except for Eddie. He kind of lurked behind.

"Come on, Eddie," I said. "What's wrong?"

"My dad's not drinking so much anymore, but he still hasn't found a job," he admitted. "I don't have any money."

Sam dug the pennies he'd collected for his story out of his pocket and pressed them into Eddie's hand. "You do now."

Eddie looked at the pennies in his hand, little copper circles on his palm. He closed his hand around them, the coins clanging together, and put them back into Sam's hand. "I can't take them. I've been so mean."

"It's a peace offering," Sam said.

"That's what I said about the stocking," Eddie said.

"Well, unlike you," I quipped, "Sam keeps his word."

Sam and Eddie both laughed.

"All right," Eddie said. "Give me back the coins."

At the sandwich shop, the five of us squeezed into a booth meant for four. When we placed our orders, Mr. McKenzie promised to give us all extra ice cream in our floats. It was only the second week the shop was open, but I guessed it was doing pretty well. There were only a couple of empty seats at the counter.

The door opened and Lizzie Johnson walked in. She was wearing a red-and-white ruffled dress that made her look like a peppermint. I jumped up and walked over to her. "Lizzie!"

"Tommy!" Her smile was wide and her blue eyes sparkled.

"Want to get that root beer float?" I asked.

"Sure."

We sat down at the counter together.

"Tommy!" Eddie called. "Don't you two want to come sit with us?"

"We're fine here," I said, and Lizzie blushed.

In the booth, I could see my friends laughing and I knew they'd tease me about Lizzie tomorrow. But I'd teased them enough in the past. Surely I could take a little good-natured ribbing myself.

The next day after school, I drove with Mom to the hospital to pay the last of Mary Lou's medical bills. She was coming home in a few days and was so busy practicing walking up and down the halls, I barely got a chance to say hello. Pinky and I ran around the courtyard we'd played in that very first day. The leaves were small and green now, the first flower buds just starting to form. Susie was home with Mrs. Glazov.

Mom took a deep breath as we left the hospital, tall and elegant as a swan as we walked to our car. "Tommy, I want to say thank you."

"For what?"

"For doing the paper route. I thought we'd have to give it

320

up when Mary Lou got burned. We needed the money, but I told Dad I wasn't sure you could do it. You really rose to the occasion. I'm grateful."

It felt nice but kind of odd to have Mom paying me a compliment. I thought of all the people I'd met on the paper route: Mrs. Glazov, and Pa and Ma, and Mrs. Scully and even Mr. McKenzie. "I'm grateful too."

On the way home, Mom hummed softly in the car. Pinky fell asleep as we drove. It was the first time I'd felt okay in the car with my mom since that horrible drive to the hospital. I was almost dozing off myself, when Mom turned away from our regular route.

I was instantly as alert as a horse that's spotted a rattlesnake. "Where are we going?" I asked, struggling to keep my voice from shaking.

Mom didn't answer.

Had she gotten another speeding ticket? Panic rose in my throat. But I wasn't the same kid I'd been then. I could handle this.

Mom didn't turn in to the courthouse. She kept driving until she reached the cemetery. Then she turned off the ignition and sat still. It was the cemetery where Busia was buried. I'd only been there once before, for the funeral.

Mom was curled up in the front seat, like a hurt bird in its nest. "I didn't go that day," she said.

I remembered. It had been hot and Mom had been hugely pregnant with Susie. And she'd been hysterical.

"I didn't go to my own mother's funeral," she said, her voice flat.

"She would have understood, Mom."

Mom snorted. I wasn't quite sure if she was sad or angry, but when she climbed out of the car, I followed her. Pinky slept on in the backseat.

It was only a few steps to Busia's grave. The headstone was dark marble. It looked nice. "I should have brought flowers," said Mom.

"Next time," I said.

"I've never been here before," Mom admitted. "Pa suggested I should come."

"Don't feel bad, Mom," I said. "You had a new baby. Mary Lou got hurt and—"

"It wasn't that Mary Lou was hurt," Mom said, "it was that Busia was my mother and sometimes I hated her."

And Mom began to cry. All the times she'd cried over the past year, all the tears and weeping and yelling, this was the first time I really understood why.

I reached out and took her hand.

Mom cried harder.

But I held on. Mr. McKenzie had cried when he thought he'd lost his store. I'd sat with Sam when he'd lost his mom. Sometimes there were words to make things better. And sometimes there weren't. Sometimes, the best you could do was just stand there and hold someone's hand.

When she was done, Mom looked more like herself than she had in a long, long time. "Come on, Tommy," she said quietly. "Let's go home."

50

MARY LOU'S WELCOME-HOME DINNER

It was early May, the day before Mother's Day, and Mary Lou was finally coming home. She'd been in the hospital almost eight months. Mom and Dad had gone to pick her up. While I was waiting, I ran my hands over the white picket fence around our front yard. The top edge went up and down in little waves. One summer when we were painting it, I had asked my father about it. "Wouldn't it have been easier to make all the slats the same length?"

"Easier, yes," Dad had said. "But life isn't like that. There are good times and bad. Ups and downs." He painted quietly for a moment, and then added, almost to himself, "Sometimes I need that reminder." I hadn't understood what he'd meant at the time, but I kind of did now.

"Tommy!" Pinky ran out the front door, stumbling on the three steps. She was five now, and looked more like a little girl than a baby. "Mrs. Glazov's making chicken and potato dumplings for dinner."

Mary Lou was going to love them. I sat down next to my little sister on the front stoop.

"Mary Lou will braid my hair?" she asked.

"She will," I said.

"And play dolls?"

"I bet she will if you ask her."

Pinky sighed. "She sounds nice."

"Don't you remember her?" I asked. "She was home at Christmas."

"'Course I do," Pinky said. "But sometimes I forget." I realized that Pinky hadn't been allowed to see Mary Lou in the hospital at all. The visit at Christmas had been awful, and except for the concert, she hadn't seen Mary Lou for five months. That was a long time for a little kid. And Susie was almost one now, but she wouldn't remember Mary Lou at all.

"Well, you'll like her," I said, giving Pinky a hug. "I'm sure about that."

Two more cars drove past, and then another, and then the next car turned into our driveway. Mary Lou was waving a mile a minute from the backseat. We ran to the car and pulled the door open.

Mary Lou smiled up at me. She'd gotten her hair cut since I'd last seen her, a couple of days before. Her brown hair was short and curly now, and it made her look more grown-up. "Give me a hand, Tommy?"

"Sure, sis." I took her fingers in mine and carefully pulled her out of the car. She put a hand on my shoulder for a moment to get her balance. "I'm fine now," she said, and I backed off.

Mary Lou moved slowly, taking small, careful strides. "Three steps," she said, looking at the front porch. "They made me practice at the hospital."

My father stood on one side and I was on the other. We gripped Mary Lou's arms, prepared to lift her, but she shook us away. "No," she said. "I can do this."

She wore a new pleated skirt, like the one she'd worn the day of the burning, but this one was longer and covered more of her legs. Still, I could see her ankles. They looked a bit swollen, her calves puffy from some bandages under her stockings, but if I hadn't known about the burns, I'm not sure I would have noticed.

Mary Lou gripped the railing and held it tight. She slowly lifted her leg up onto the step. She winced a little, but pulled her body up after it. We all held our breath as we watched her, like seeing a tightrope walker wobble on the wire high above the circus ring. Two more steps and she was walking through our front door. Mom and Pinky actually clapped.

"Mary Lou?" Mrs. Glazov called, coming out from the kitchen. She was wearing her pink polka-dot apron. "That you?"

"Yes."

Mrs. Glazov leaned over and hugged her.

"You're right, Tommy." Mary Lou laughed. "She's very friendly."

Mrs. Glazov blushed. "Dinner be ready in a few minutes. You go unpack."

"But I could help—"

"Ah," Dad said, "never argue with Mrs. Glazov."

Mom followed Mrs. Glazov into the kitchen. Mary Lou and I walked down the hall and into her room. "It looks exactly the same," she said.

I laid the suitcase on the bed for her, and she directed as I put her few things away. When we were done, I stared at the empty suitcase. Mrs. Glazov still hadn't called us for dinner.

"I'll put it back in the attic," I said.

"Thanks."

I went into the hall and pulled down the little ladder. Careful to step only on the rafters, I found a spot for the suitcase. I was about to climb back down when I spotted Dad's old cardboard box, labeled *College Days*. Jumping from one rafter to the next, I made my way over to the box.

It contained a notebook filled with my dad's handwriting. A book or two, dusty with age. And another copy of the *Daily Worker*. I held it for a moment. Strange that one little newspaper could cause so many changes.

"Dinner's ready," I heard Mom call.

"Coming!" I yelled.

And that's when I accidentally stepped off the rafter.

White plaster dust filled the room as I fell through the ceiling. I grabbed a board, my legs dangling in midair, the other half of me still in the attic.

"Psia krew i cholera!"

I looked down through the big hole I'd made. My legs were hanging directly over the dining room table. The food was sprinkled with a fine layer of plaster dust. Mom was already sitting at the table too, and her black hair was now as white as Mrs. Glazov's.

Mary Lou and Pinky and my father sat in their places, slightly less dusty, and gaped up at me.

"What are you doing?" my mother wailed. "Dinner is ruined!"

326

I pulled myself up and looked down. Mom's face was red, the little vein starting to pop out. I could see her mouth open as she prepared to yell, could practically hear the words *Go get your father's belt.*

But before she could say a word, Mrs. Glazov walked in carrying the noodles and began to laugh. Really laugh. It was a laugh I'd never heard from her before.

Mom just stared at her.

Mary Lou joined in, laughing like she hadn't since before she'd been burned. "It's so funny," she choked out. "Tommy stepped right through the ceiling and . . ." She collapsed into giggles again.

Baby Susie began to laugh in her high chair. A little tiny baby-hiccup laugh. My father joined in then, and his wasn't a little laugh, no sir, it was a big belly laugh, like I was one of the Three Stooges and I'd just stepped on a banana peel.

Pinky shook her head and little white flakes fell out of her hair. "It's snowing in the house!" she marveled, and that only made Dad and Mary Lou and Susie and Mrs. Glazov laugh harder.

"What is wrong with you?" scolded my mom. But even she sounded less angry.

"Sorry," I called down from the attic. "I was putting Mary Lou's suitcase away and took a wrong step."

Dad laughed harder. "And you used to complain he never helps out."

Even Mom cracked a smile at that. She took a deep breath. "Well, what are we going to do about this dinner? It's ruined. And I'm hungry."

Dad wiped tears from his eyes as he tried to stop laughing. Mrs. Glazov picked the chicken up from the table and dumped it into the trash.

"That was a whole chicken!"

"Oh, Mrs. Wilson," Mrs. Glazov said. "No one was going to eat it."

And that started us all laughing again, even Mom.

"Come on down, Tommy!" Dad called. "We'll fix the hole tomorrow. Tonight, let's go get sandwiches from Mr. McKenzie."

Mom sighed and went to the bathroom to brush the worst of the plaster out of her hair.

"I go home," said Mrs. Glazov quickly. "Tea and bread fine for me."

"No," said Dad, putting an arm around her. "You're family too now."

"Yeah," I said.

Mrs. Glazov smiled and brushed a tear from her eye. "Miracle," she said. "Like I got to know my grandchildren after all."

I was so glad she felt that way. I did too.

Mom came out of the bathroom then, her hair brushed clean and hanging loose around her face. "All right, everyone," she said with a smile. "Let's go eat."

51

BURNING THE TRASH, PART 2

I wish I could say things were perfect then, but of course they weren't. When she got stressed, Mom still yelled. But she went to see Pa every week. And Mrs. Glazov would come right over if Mom got too loud, even if she was in the middle of a music lesson, and so there were no more beatings.

I'd like to say that Sam and Eddie and the choirboys all got along perfectly. But that would be a lie. "You're like the center of a wheel," Sam told me one day at the shop, over an ice cream sundae. "When you're there, Tommy, it all holds together. But when you're not around, we fall apart. I'm back to being Little Skinny."

"No," I said. "You're Sam now. Even when I'm not there."

"No, I'm not," he said.

"Cowboy Sam," I said, pulling out the silver star and handing it to him.

"This was your present from Mary Lou," he said.

"Yeah," I said. "But I don't need it anymore."

Sam smiled and put it on. "Thanks." And I swear he sat a little taller. I could almost see the ten-gallon hat on his head.

• • •

Monday, May 17, was Mary Lou's first day going back to school. I woke up before my alarm. The glow-in-the-dark clock read 4:28 a.m.

I liked the dark and quiet now; it was my own special time, to think about the day and the kind of person I wanted to be. Eating breakfast alone was peaceful, Boots begging at my feet. The fur had grown back in over his belly, although if you looked closely, you'd notice that the hairs over his scar grew in the opposite direction from all the others.

The red bike in the garage was oiled and shiny now, the holes in the tires patched. I loaded up the basket and pushed off, sailing smoothly into the weakening darkness. My balance was perfect.

Pa was sitting on his front porch, watching the sunrise. "The community picnic is next week," he told me as I rode up. This was a new event the homeowners' association had started at my dad's request. We were going to meet at the Prince Pond shelter and cook out. Everyone was invited. "You're coming, right?"

"Yes, sir."

"Ma's beside herself with excitement." He grinned.

I waved at him as I rode off.

"Bring that accordion!" he called after me.

Mr. McKenzie was just turning the lights on in the sandwich and ice cream shop. He always got started early. It took a long time to bake the bread for all those sandwiches. The lights were still off in Sam's room. I'd see him at school.

Mrs. Scully was standing on the porch, waiting for me. "Tommy," she yelled as I pulled up on my bike. "I got a new train. Come by this afternoon to take a look?"

"Gladly!" I said.

She threw Boots a piece of sausage and we headed home. My legs didn't even hurt anymore. They just felt strong. By the predawn light, I could see that Mrs. Glazov's garden was already half planted. I had plenty of time to change my clothes, do my chores and catch the bus to school with Mary Lou.

My sister was standing in the hallway, looking at herself in the mirror, when I walked in. For the first time since *that day,* Mary Lou was wearing her school uniform again: navy-blue wool pleated skirt, white blouse, matching sweater thrown across her shoulders, thick white knee socks and penny loafers so new, there wasn't a scuff on them. There were only a few weeks left before graduation, but she was determined to go back.

"How do I look?" she asked. "Can you see them?"

I knew she meant the scars. There was just a hint of red on her left wrist, and an odd twisting of the flesh on her neck, barely visible under her collar. "No," I said.

And it was true. Because I really didn't see them. Not even the horrible ones across her legs before she pulled her knee socks on. Because all I saw was my sister.

After breakfast, I watched Dad lug the box that said *College Days* to the fire pit. As soon as I was done with my oatmeal, I went out to stand beside him. "You don't need a newspaper to remember an idea," I said.

"No," he agreed, and smiled.

Mom walked out then, carrying some more brown paper. She put it on the ground, and I started to ball it up, placing it around Dad's box.

"Don't light it yet," Mom said suddenly, and hurried back to the house. She returned a moment later, clutching something small and round in her hand. "Tommy," Mom said quietly, "I have one more thing for you to burn." She placed the item into my palm.

It was Dad's belt. The one Mom always used for the beatings. I looked up at her. Her face was quiet and still, her eyes calm.

"That's my best belt," said Dad.

"You've got others," Mom said.

Dad nodded and Mom smiled at me. My hands shook a bit as I placed the coiled belt carefully on top of the trash and the box. "Can I light it this time?"

Dad hesitated a moment, then handed me the matches.

I leaned over and cupped my hands. The match sprang to life and I tossed it into the pile.

The paper balls caught fire at once and flared brightly, like flowers in the desert bursting into bloom after a thunderstorm. The belt twisted like a snake as it burned. The box glowed red, a blazing treasure chest, until it collapsed in on itself, and I couldn't make out any shapes in the orange-yellow blaze.

My dad took my mom's hand as they stood together and watched the flames. I felt a hand on my shoulder and turned to see Mary Lou, standing behind me.

"What are you doing out here?" I asked.

"I had to come see," she said. "Can't be afraid forever."

I took my sister's hand in my own and we watched the fire burn. When it was only coals, we turned and went to catch the bus for school.

AUTHOR'S NOTE

I love to base my stories on real events. My first book, *The Best Bad Luck I Ever Had,* was loosely based on my maternal grandfather's memoirs. My second, *The Lions of Little Rock,* was inspired by my mother's childhood in Arkansas. So for my third book, I decided to focus on a period from my father's life.

My dad, otherwise known as Tommy to those who knew him at the time, grew up in Downers Grove, Illinois, a small town just outside of Chicago. In some ways, it was an idyllic 1950s childhood, with a loyal dog named Boots, a paper route full of friendly customers, double features at the local movie theater, lots of friends at a beloved school, and even a local pond to skate on in the winter.

But in other ways, Tommy's life was full of challenges. His mother, a loving and caring woman, struggled with mood swings that, although undiagnosed at the time, would most certainly be seen as a form of mental illness today. In addition, his sister, Mary Lou, was indeed severely burned in a fire, much as described in this story. In my previous books, the main characters came from stable, supportive households. I wondered what it would be like to write about a character for whom that was not the case.

A few additional aspects of my father's story intrigued me. One was that my dad, when talking to me about his childhood, admitted that he had been something of a bully. He had felt much regret about it over the years. His admission reminded me of a chapter in the amazing book *NurtureShock* by Po Bronson and Ashley Merryman. In a nutshell, that book describes how many bullies aren't the stereotypical "big hulking shadows" in the corner, but popular, well-adjusted kids who know exactly how far they can push things without getting caught.

This was true of my father. He was a popular, well-liked boy at school. When he asked his childhood friends if they remembered him bullying others at school, they denied he had ever behaved that way. But *he* remembered it. And I was fascinated by the idea that bullying also harms the bully. So much focus is on the victims, and rightly so, but I believe if we really want to understand bullying, we have to look at the bullies too, without creating the belief that they are all horrible, irredeemable people.

The second aspect of my father's childhood that intrigued me was the time period. The early 1950s were consumed with fears of communism, and in many ways, the Cold War spilled over into my own childhood. As a child of the 1980s, communists were our bogeymen, the villains in the popular movies. As a child, I was terrified of a nuclear war. If there was one thing I knew, it was that communists were evil.

And then in 1989 the Berlin Wall came down, and in 1991

the Soviet Union fell apart, and in 1992 I went to work as an au pair in Vienna, Austria. While I was living in Europe, I studied German at the local university. My class was filled with people from the old Soviet republics, Hungary, Poland, Czechoslovakia, Yugoslavia—real live former communists!

Of course, what I discovered was that they were just normal men and women like me, with varying viewpoints and opinions. It's been almost twenty years since I was in that class with the "former communists." To this day, I think of them often, especially when dealing with people whose opinions or beliefs seem so foreign to me that I am tempted to dismiss them as simply being wrong. Because of that class in Austria, I always try to take a minute to understand a new point of view, even if I don't agree with it.

Finally, talking to my father about his childhood reinforced my belief in the importance of community. The old woman who lives next door might need some company. The annoying boy on the playground might be longing for a friend. Even when a parent is sick or a child injured, it's not always easy to see the need or what to do about it. But when people do step in and help, when they take a chance and engage with their neighbors, amazing things can happen. My father greatly benefited from the close-knit community in 1950s Downers Grove. My hope for my readers is that they, much like Tommy in *The Paper Cowboy,* will never stop striving to find ways to create a supportive community in their own lives.

Mary Lou before the fire

Tommy's birthday

Mary Lou, Susie and Boots

Prince Pond in the 1950s

ACKNOWLEDGMENTS

So many people helped me with *The Paper Cowboy*!

My research started with a wonderful trip my father and I took to Downers Grove. From that visit, I'd like to thank Mary Mengel from Dream Interiors for showing us priceless historical photos of the town, Raymond J. Jilek for graciously guiding us around his property and allowing us to look at the house where my dad grew up, and Ed Briner, an old friend of my father's, who helped arrange a tour of St. Joseph Catholic Church and School. At St. Joseph's, Rita Stasi, the principal, and Father Jerome Kish, the pastor, were welcoming and generous with their time. In addition, the Downers Grove Public Library, Anderson's Bookshop, the Aurora Public Library, and the Downers Grove Historical Society all provided invaluable information and assistance.

A number of my father's childhood school friends generously answered questions about growing up in 1950s Downers Grove. Special thanks to Maralee Kopis, Mary Beth Doyle, Marlene Handscheigel, Jack Foley, Phil Verveer, Marianne

Patty, Mary Ellen Heelan, Rita Mathern, Judy Everson, and Larry Cerny.

I'd also like to thank some of the first readers of this manuscript. Jessie Auten and Debbie Gaydos, I greatly value both your opinions and your friendships. Cassie Beutelscheis, thanks for being an early teen reader and sharing your thoughts. My writing group—who suffered through about twenty-five different openings to this book—what would I do without you? Patty Pearson, Justine Moore, Kathi Morrison-Taylor, Mary Olson, Lela Faulkenberry, Olivia Burley, Linda Cortes, and Heather Quartetti all provided feedback and encouragement.

My dear agent, Kathy Green, not only offered professional advice but was always willing to talk about non-book issues as well. My fabulous editor, Stacey Barney, provided me with insight into my own work, pushed me to make the story even more than I thought it could be, and was always understanding when I needed extra time to do so! Thanks, ladies, to both of you.

I'd also like to thank Irene Vandervoort for working so hard to design just the right cover, Chandra Wohleber for being an amazing copy editor, Marikka Tamura for designing the interior, and everyone else at Putnam for making the process of publishing a book go so smoothly.

This book was written during a difficult time in my life. My "whine night" friends really helped me through it. So I just want to include a shout-out to Polly Papp, Diane Cramer, Maria Brandao, Allison MacMahon, and all my other old and new friends, who provided a listening ear when I needed one.

In addition, I want to thank all my family members who made this book possible. Of course, I'd like to thank my immediate family for their invaluable support, including my father, "Tommy," for his inspiring stories; my mother, Marlene, for hours of babysitting; and my sister, Erika, for her unwavering friendship. I'd also like to acknowledge my grandparents Robert and Florence, who died before I could know them well, my late aunt Mary Lou, my aunt Susan ("baby Susie"), my late uncle Bob, and my uncle Bill. You are all intimately bound in the backstory of this book.

Finally, I want to thank my children, Charlotte and Kara, for being my greatest cheerleaders. And a special thanks to my ex-husband, Adam Levine, for being a great co-parent and a good friend.

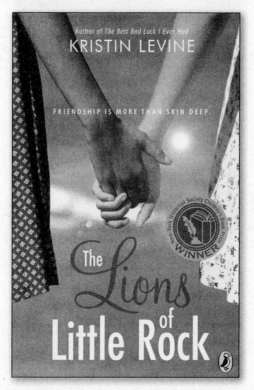

1

THE HIGH DIVE

I talk a lot. Just not out loud where anyone can hear. At least I used to be that way. I'm no chatterbox now, but if you stop me on the street and ask me directions to the zoo, I'll answer you. Probably. If you're nice, I might even tell you a couple of different ways to get there. I guess I've learned it's not enough to just think things. You have to say them too. Because all the words in the world won't do much good if they're just rattling around in your head.

But I'm getting ahead of myself. To understand me, and how I've changed, I need to go back to 1958.

It was a beautiful day in September and I was standing on top of a diving board. The blue sky was reflected in the water below, the white board felt scratchy under my feet, and the smell of hot dogs wafted up from the snack stand. It was a perfect summer day—the kind you see in the movies—and I was positive I was going to throw up.

You see, it wasn't just any high dive. Oh, no. It was the super-huge, five-meter-high platform diving board, the tallest at Fair Park Swimming Pool, probably the highest in all of Little Rock. It might have even been the highest in all of Arkansas. Which wouldn't have been a problem if I hadn't been afraid of heights. But I was.

1

Sally McDaniels had told me she was going to jump off and asked if I wanted to come too. Everyone over the age of ten had already jumped off the board a dozen times that summer. Except for me, and I was practically thirteen. It was easier to nod than say no, so there I was.

Sally was waiting behind me on the ladder. Blond and blue-eyed, she wore a pink suit the exact color of her toenails. Sally wasn't really pretty, but no one ever noticed because she acted like she was. "Are you all right?" she asked.

No, of course I wasn't all right. I mean, I wasn't sick or anything, but I was standing perfectly still, frozen as a Popsicle, counting prime numbers in my head. A prime number is a number that can only be divided by itself and one. There are twenty-five of them under a hundred, and reciting them sure does help me when I'm nervous.

"Go ahead and jump," said Sally.

I didn't move. A plane flew across the clouds . . . 2, 3, 5, 7, 11 . . . I wished I were a stork and could fly away. Or a flamingo. Or a penguin. Except I didn't think they flew.

"Marlee," Sally said. "There's a bunch of people behind us."

I hated holding them up, so I took a step toward the edge of the platform . . . 13, 17, 19, 23 . . . but then I got dizzy and fell to my knees.

"Come on," cried the boy on the ladder behind Sally. "Hurry up and jump."

I shook my head and clutched the board . . . 29, 31, 37, 41. It didn't work. I wasn't ever letting go.

Sally laughed. "She said she was really going to do it this time."

I squeezed my eyes tighter and kept counting . . . 43, 47, 53 . . .

2

"Isn't that Judy Nisbett's little sister?" someone said.

It must have only have been a minute or two, but I got all the way to 97 before I felt Judy's hand on my shoulder. "Marlee," she said quietly, "come on down. I already bought a Coke and a PayDay. We can share them on the way home."

I nodded but didn't move.

"Open your eyes," Judy commanded.

I did. Not that I always do what my sister says, but—well, I guess I usually do. In any case, when I saw my sister's clear brown eyes looking at me, I felt much better. She was sixteen and going into the eleventh grade. I could talk to my sister. She was smart and calm and reasonable.

"Do you want me to hold your hand on the way down the ladder?" Judy asked.

I nodded again. It was embarrassing, but I didn't think I could do it on my own. Once I felt her palm on mine, it only took a minute for us to make our way down together.

"What a baby!" said the boy who had been behind me as he brushed past us to climb up again. Sally laughed, and I knew they were right. I was a baby.

"Come on," said Judy. She picked up her book and her bag from the lounge chair where she'd been reading.

"See you at school tomorrow," said her friend Margaret.

"See you," Judy replied, waving good-bye.

Judy hadn't even gotten her hair wet. She'd recently cut it into a short bob and wore it pulled back with a ribbon. My hair was the same brown color as my sister's, but it was long and wavy, and sometimes I still wore it in braids. Sally said I looked like Heidi, but I didn't care. I liked Heidi. She had that nice grandpa and her friend with all those goats.

Goats are okay, but what I really love are wild animals, like

3

the ones you find at the zoo. The Little Rock Zoo was right across the street from the swimming pool. In the gate and down the hill, I knew the lions were pacing in their cages. At night, Judy and I listened to them roar, but during the day they were quiet like me. Judy and I sat on the wall by the zoo entrance as we shared a candy bar and a Coke.

"Sorry," I said. I'd ruined our last day at the pool before school started again.

Judy sighed. "Why are you even friends with Sally McDaniels?"

I shrugged. Sally and I have been friends ever since we were five and she pushed me off the slide at the park.

"She likes to boss you around," Judy said.

That was true. But she was also familiar. I like familiar.

"You need to find a friend you have something in common with," said Judy. "Someone who likes to do the same things you do. That's what . . ."

I stopped listening. I knew all her advice by heart. I needed to find someone who was honest and friendly and nice. I knew all the ways I was supposed to meet this imaginary friend too. *Just say hello. Ask someone a question. Give a compliment.* Maybe it would work, if I could ever figure out the right words.

I know it sounds odd, but I much prefer numbers to words. In math, you always get the same answer, no matter how you do the problem. But with words, *blue* can be a thousand different shades! *Two* is always *two*. I like that.

Judy finally finished lecturing, and I said, "It's easier to put up with Sally. Sometimes she's really nice."

"Yeah," Judy said. "Sometimes."

2

COFFEE, TEA OR SODA

That evening after dinner, we all sat down in the living room to watch TV. By "we" I mean my family: Mother, Daddy, Judy and me. I have an older brother too, David, but he'd just moved out the week before to start college. My sister and brother and Daddy are the only ones I feel really comfortable talking to, so I missed David something terrible. In fact, when Mother made a fresh batch of iced tea for dinner, I almost started crying.

You see, to me, people are like things you drink. Some are like a pot of black coffee, no cream, no sugar. They make me so nervous I start to tremble. Others calm me down enough that I can sort through the words in my head and find something to say.

My brother, David, is a glass of sweet iced tea on a hot summer day, when you've put your feet up in a hammock and haven't got a care in the world. Judy is an ice-cold Coca-Cola from the fridge. Sally is cough syrup; she tastes bad, but my mother insists she's good for me. Daddy's a glass of milk, usually cold and delicious, but every once in a while, he goes sour. If I have to ask one of my parents a question, I'll pick him, because Mother is hot black tea, so strong, she's almost coffee.

Mother and I don't exactly see eye to eye, or even elbow to elbow. She's always trying to get me to do stuff: *invite that girl over, volunteer at church, read to that poor blind lady down the street.* I know she loves me, but sometimes I think she wishes I were more like Judy. Mother and Judy like to read fashion magazines and go shopping. They get their hair done once a week and read long, romantic novels like *Gone With the Wind*. Despite our differences, Judy and I get along, but Mother expects me to be thrilled when she brings me home a new skirt or a sweater set, when what I'd really like is a new slide rule.

Ever since the Soviets sent up that Sputnik satellite last year, I've been studying really hard. Maybe someday I'll study mathematics at college and become a rocket scientist. Only thing is, when our teacher told us last year that our country needs more of us to study math, I think she meant more boys. I watched all those talks on TV about the satellite really closely, and I didn't see any experts who were women.

That evening we were watching our brand-new 1958 RCA 21-inch mahogany television console. It was so large, we had to move an armchair into the garage to make space for it in the living room. With rabbit ears on top, it got three whole channels.

Governor Faubus was on television, giving some sort of talk about Southern pride and communists and, okay, I tried to pay attention, but it didn't really make much sense. I was more worried about who my teachers would be this year. Teachers are definitely coffee. When they call on me in class, it makes me so nervous, I can't say a thing. Even when I know the answer. So there's always a rough patch at the beginning of the year when I'm breaking them in.

People sometimes think I'm stupid because I'm so quiet. But I'm not stupid, I'm scared. Scared my voice will get all squeaky and people will laugh. Worried I'll look dumb if I say the wrong thing. Concerned about being a show-off if I get the

6

answer right. Convinced that if I start talking, people will notice me, and I won't like the attention.

"Turn off the TV, Marlee," Daddy said suddenly.

I jumped up to do as he asked. I could tell by his tone that something was wrong.

"I can't believe the governor would rather close the schools than have you go with a couple of Negroes," Daddy said to Judy.

"That's not what he said," Mother snapped. "It's about states' rights, preserving our way of life and respecting Southern traditions. Not to mention maintaining the peace."

"There you have it, girls." Daddy's voice was pleasant, but there was a bite to it.

Judy frowned. "But what will I do all day?"

"You can get a head start on the fall cleaning," said Mother. "Maybe wash the windows?"

Judy made a face.

"Or you can help Betty Jean with the laundry. It's up to you. I'll bring home a reading list and a math book to keep you busy after that."

Betty Jean was our new maid. We'd never had one before, but with Mother going back to work, we needed someone to do the laundry and the cooking. Daddy's been an English teacher at Forest Heights Junior High for a long time, but Mother's first day of teaching home economics at Hall High School was supposed to be tomorrow.

"Do you have to go to work?" Judy asked.

"Yes," said Mother. "Hall is closed to the students, but I signed a contract, so I have to go."

"What about Marlee? Does she have school?" Judy asked.

That was just what I wanted to know.

"Yes," said Daddy. "Only the high schools are closed. No one is trying to send Negroes to the junior highs."

"Not yet," said Mother.

Daddy ignored her.

We kissed our parents good night and went back to our room. "Lucky you," I said to Judy as I walked into the bathroom to brush my teeth. I was starting at West Side Junior High, and I wasn't too excited about it.

"Yeah," Judy whispered. "Lucky me."

As I brushed my teeth, I wondered how I'd feel if a colored girl were sent to my school. Sally said you'd get lice if you sat too close to one of them, but Sally also said if you lit a candle in a bathroom and turned around three times, you'd see a ghost in the mirror. I'd tried it once when I was seven, and there was no ghost, just a lot of melted wax on the countertop. I didn't believe much of what Sally said after that.

There had been a colored girl in one of Judy's classes last year at Central High School, the best high school in all of Arkansas. For the first time, nine Negroes had enrolled: Minnijean Brown, Elizabeth Eckford, Ernest Green, Thelma Mothershed, Melba Pattillo, Terrence Roberts, Gloria Ray, Jefferson Thomas and Carlotta Walls. That was a mouthful, so people just started calling them the Little Rock Nine.

The integration had gone so badly that President Eisenhower sent in soldiers to help keep the peace. I remembered Daddy talking about being polite to the Negroes and Mother biting her lip. I'd been so busy watching both of them, I'd never thought to ask Judy how she'd felt about it. All I knew for sure was that she hadn't gotten lice.

When Judy walked into the bathroom, I opened my mouth

8

to ask. But my mouth was full of toothpaste and by the time I'd rinsed and spit, her mouth was full of toothpaste. And then it was time to go to bed.

Judy fell asleep quickly, but I kept tossing and turning. Usually the lions' roaring lulled me to sleep, but they were silent tonight, as quiet as the halls of Central would be tomorrow. Finally I got up and went into the kitchen for a glass of milk. Mother and Daddy were talking in the living room.

"Almost sounds like you're an integrationist," I heard Mother say.

"I don't think it's such a big deal if Judy's at school with a few—"

"You want our girls associating with Negroes?" asked Mother.

"A few colored students wouldn't—"

"Race mixing. That's what it'll lead to," said Mother.

I stood in front of the open fridge in my nightgown, clutching the bottle of milk, and shivered. Race mixing was a scary thing—at least people always talked about it like it was polio or something. The thing was, the races didn't really mix in Little Rock, not in the bathrooms of department stores, nor in the water of the swimming pools. In fact, I don't think we'd ever had a colored person in our house until Betty Jean showed up ironing last week.

"There wouldn't have even been any trouble last year if the governor hadn't—"

"Richard, watch what you're saying!"

"I'm not saying anything I don't mean."

"Do you want people to call us communists?" Mother asked.

The milk bottle slipped from my hand and crashed to the floor. So much for eavesdropping. My parents ran into the kitchen.

"Oh, Marlee!" Mother grabbed a towel and began to mop things up. "Now there'll be no milk for breakfast."

"Sorry," I whispered.

Mother just kept wiping up the mess.

My father poured me a glass of water and walked me back to my room. "We weren't arguing," he said when we got to my door.

I nodded. But when he leaned over to kiss me good night, his eye twitched like it always did when he was lying.

3

QUEEN ELIZABETH

The next morning Judy woke up early to eat breakfast with me, even though she didn't have to. She's such a good sister. I made two bowls of oatmeal and put one down in front of her.

"Promise me something," Judy said.

"What?" I asked.

"Promise to say at least one complete sentence today."

"Yes, ma'am," I said. Sometimes Judy was as bad as Mother.

"I mean it," said Judy. "At least five words. Together. In a row. *Yes* and *no* don't count."

"I promise."

"That's only two," said Judy.

"To talk a lot," I added. "That makes six."

Judy laughed. I grinned and finished my oatmeal.

"Marlee!" My father poked his head into the kitchen. "You ready?"

Last year, Daddy had started driving me to school. The first time was the day after one of the colored girls from Central had been surrounded by a mob at the bus stop. In the picture in the paper, the white people were yelling at her, and yet she'd held her head up high. I couldn't understand why half of Little Rock was screaming over a few colored kids. Surely they weren't all stupid enough to believe Sally.

It happened again a few months later. Daddy had invited a colored pastor to come talk to his Bible study group at church. He said the meeting had gone well, but the next day, he'd found a note tucked in with the morning paper. He didn't let any of us read the note, not even Mother, but he drove me to school every day after that.

Daddy and I didn't talk in the car, but it was a comfortable silence. The closer we got to school, the more nervous I became, so I started counting prime numbers in my head again. I'd reached 67 by the time Daddy dropped me off at the front entrance to West Side Junior High. It was a large building, but of course I'd visited when Judy had been a student, so it only took me a minute to find my seventh-grade homeroom and sit down.

I knew pretty much everyone there. Sally was two rows over, talking with Nora. Unlike Sally's strong cough syrup, Nora was a weak fruit punch. She had horn-rimmed glasses and was convinced they made her ugly, even though she had a long neck and the straightest, smoothest hair I'd ever seen.

In the back was a new girl. She had short dark hair, just like Judy's, tied back with a ribbon. She had neatly trimmed fingernails (which reminded me to stop chewing on my pinkie) and a lovely tan too, like she'd been at the pool all summer, though I hadn't seen her there once.

Sally got up and walked over to her desk. Nora went too. "Hi, new girl," Sally said in her bright, clear voice. "What's your name?"

The new girl looked up and smiled. A wide, honest, open smile. I knew she thought Sally was being sincere, but I would've bet you all the money in my piggy bank that she wasn't.

12

"Elizabeth," said the new girl. "What's yours?"

"Sally," said Sally. "It's nice to meet you, Bethie."

"Oh, it's not Bethie," said the girl.

"Lizzie?" guessed Sally.

"No, Elizabeth," said the girl. "Like the Queen."

Sally looked at her blankly.

"The Queen of England."

"Did you hear that, Nora? Her name is Elizabeth, like the Queen of England." Sally burst out laughing.

I couldn't bring myself to look at the new girl. I was sure she felt awful. I started counting prime numbers again: 2, 3, 5, 7, 11 . . .

But the new girl started laughing too. "Yeah, like the Queen of England. But you can just call me 'Your Highness.'"

Nora tittered.

"Your Highness?" repeated Sally.

"That's right," said Elizabeth. "Unless you prefer 'O royal one.'"

Nora had to gulp down a giggle. I couldn't quite tell if she was amused or nervous. No one spoke this way to Sally.

The new girl suddenly grinned and slapped Sally on the shoulder. "I'm just kidding, of course. Liz is fine."

Sally gave a little smile. Before she could say anything else, Miss Taylor, our homeroom teacher, walked in, and Sally and Nora sat down.

Miss Taylor was one of those teachers you just can't imagine anywhere but school. She'd been teaching forever and always pulled her blond hair back into a bun. As she handed out our schedules, I noticed her sweater had a couple of dropped stitches on the back, as if she'd made it herself. I had Miss Taylor again for history in the afternoon. She frowned a lot

13

as she talked, and I couldn't decide if she was plain old coffee or something worse, like the vinegar pooled at the bottom of a jar of pickles. Though I'm not sure why anyone would drink that.

After homeroom came English, then science, and right before lunch I had math. Since math is my favorite subject, sometimes I talk in class, but only if the answer's a number. Like 43. Or 3,458. Or 36.72. But if the answer is "eight apples," all you'll get out of me is "eight." You'll have to provide the apples yourself.

My math teacher this year was Mr. Harding. It was his first year at West Side, and he was young, almost as young as my older brother. Mr. Harding got to work right away, writing problems on the chalkboard. By the end of the period, chalk dust had turned his hair (and his suit) prematurely gray. He called on everyone in the class at least once, even the girls. Even me. (I answered. It was 345.) My old math teacher had asked the boys to answer three times as often as the girls. I knew because once, last year, I had gotten really bored, and I'd kept track of who she'd called on for a whole week. I decided Mr. Harding was a chocolate malt shake, and I liked him a lot.

Pretty soon it was lunchtime. Mother always packed me a lunch, because I didn't like to tell the lunch ladies what I wanted. I sat down at an empty table and wondered if Sally would sit with me like she had in elementary school. If she didn't, I'd just sit alone. There are worse things in life than sitting alone. Like leprosy. Or losing a limb. Or maybe getting your period in the middle of gym when you're wearing white shorts and the teacher is a man and you left all your sanitary napkins at home. Not that that's ever happened to me.

I was just biting into my pimento cheese sandwich when I

heard someone clear her throat. It was the new girl—Elizabeth or Liz or whatever she wanted to be called.

"It's Marlee, right?" she asked.

I nodded, wondering how she'd already figured out my name.

"Mind if I sit here?"

Truth was, I did mind. But if I shook my head, it would mean I didn't, and Liz would sit down. If I nodded, she might think that was a positive response and sit down anyway. I couldn't say no because that would be rude, and so I looked up at her, hoping she'd understand and go away. In that moment, with her hair pulled back and her clear brown eyes, she looked just like Judy.

"Please sit down."

Liz sat.

It took me a second to realize I had spoken. To a stranger. Mother would be thrilled. Judy would say this was real progress. Even if it had only been a reflex since she looked so much like my sister. I cursed myself for only using three words. Now I'd have to work another two in sometime this afternoon.

"Thanks so much." Liz smiled. "I hate eating lunch alone."

I hate eating lunch alone too, and I knew that was the polite thing to say. But I didn't say it.

"Don't worry," Liz continued, taking a bite of her sandwich. "You don't have to actually talk to me. Just sitting here is enough."

I snorted and looked up to see her grinning at me. A sense of humor was on Judy's list of what makes a good friend. But what was Liz's drink? Was she really as wholesome as whole milk? Or was she like a shot of whiskey given to you by your older cousin? I couldn't place her, and it made me nervous.

15

Sally and Nora finally arrived at the table. "That's my seat," Sally said, pointing at Liz's chair. Nora hovered behind her.

"Oh, is it?" said Liz mildly.

Sally stood there for a moment before she realized Liz wasn't going to move. "But you can sit in it," Sally said suddenly, like she was being really nice.

"Why, thank you," said Liz.

"Marlee doesn't talk," said Sally, pointing at me. "That's why I have to sit next to her. We've known each other a long time."

"She doesn't?" said Liz. "But she just invited me to sit down."

"She did?" Sally asked, and looked at me.

I was about to nod when I realized if I said something, I could bring my word count for the day up to five. So I kind of squinted at Liz until she went blurry and I could pretend she was Judy, and I took a deep breath and counted 13, 17, 19, 23 and said, "I did."

Liz nodded and smiled. Her teeth were straight and very white. Oral hygiene is very important. I never skip brushing my teeth myself.

"Why didn't we see you at the pool this summer?" asked Sally, tossing her blond hair. She always did that when she wanted someone to stop what they were doing and pay attention to her.

"You're Sally, right?" said Liz.

Sally looked pleased that Liz had already learned her name. "Well, my family just moved here . . ."

And with that, Queen Elizabeth started her reign.